THE CLIFF
HOUSE

Cover and internal design by New Found Books Australia Pty Ltd

New Found Books Australia Pty Ltd
www.newfoundbooks.au

ISBNs as follows:
Paperback — 9781923172388
ebook — 9781923172500
Hardback — 9781923172623

Distributed by New Found Books Australia Distribution and Lightning Source Global

A catalogue record for this work is available from the National Library of Australia

More great New Found Books titles can be found at:

www.newfoundbooks.au/our-titles/

We acknowledge the traditional owners of the land and pay respects to the Elders, past, present and future.

THE CLIFF
HOUSE

MICHAEL CRANNOC

For Karen, my best friend.
Always the one who believed.

I'd like to acknowledge New Found Books Australia Publishing, for having faith in a new author.

Thankyou to my close circle of test readers. You rock!

Lastly, thanks to the Queensland Writers Centre, a wonderful source of local expertise and support.

CHAPTER 1

The tide was out. Sebastian ran, lengthening his strides, enjoying the feeling of wind on his face, the smell of salt and the sea-spray that rose off the distant waves as they crashed. The long dusk shadows of the land cast the town in a deep purple silhouette, hiding the steeple of the church of St Anthony and the pillars of the town hall in a salt-mist murk. The sea was also darkening, the white caps slowly melting from view as the sun began to dip.

The mud flat soon gave way to sand and running became more difficult. He shortened the strides, feeling sweat trickling down his back and the familiar ache that sometimes afflicted his right leg just above the knee. As he approached the town limits, shadowy figures strolled between the beachfront and the shopping strip, some in pairs, holding hands, others walking dogs.

Collapsing onto the park bench, he sucked in ragged breaths, waiting for his heartbeat to normalise. With trembling hands, he pushed sweaty hair from his eyes. Sitting up, he stretched his leg out before him, slowly massaging the ache over his knee, and watched the moon crest distant black waves.

Hearing footsteps, he observed two police officers approaching. Although the first true shadows of night had not quite arrived, one of the officers switched on a flashlight, directing the beam onto Seb's face.

'Do I know you?' said a male officer.

'Probably not,' Seb said, holding up a hand to shield his eyes.

'Put your hand down, sir.' The cop was peering at Sebastian

through wire-rimmed glasses. There was something in his voice that made Sebastian wary. Surely, they had not found him already. He had only been absent without leave for a few days. No one would be looking for him yet.

Seb squinted. 'I was just...'

'What's your name?' interrupted a female officer.

'Seb... Straeker.'

'Are you from the Cove?' said the male officer, face lost in the beam of the flashlight. He was being scrutinised. Seb had the sense that they were looking for someone.

'No, I'm from down south.' Seb glanced past the beam of light and could just make out the name on the badge – *Officer Guyatt*.

'Are you visiting someone?' Guyatt's voice was clipped.

'No – not exactly.'

Guyatt paused for a long moment. The silence was deep enough that Seb could hear the cop breathing. Finally, Guyatt said, 'People around here don't normally run. Not unless they're running from something... I see people running, and well – I think – what in God's name is that asshole running for? I can see from your fancy running gear that you must be from the city.'

At last, Guyatt lowered his flashlight, leaving Sebastian blinking. It took several seconds for his eyes to adjust to the darkness.

'Yeah... officers, I should get going home. I have to fix some dinner.'

'Wife waiting for you?' The female officer's voice held no threat. Meeting his eyes directly, she looked him up and down.

In his late thirties, of average height, Seb was lean and rangy. Not exactly reclining across the park bench, he nevertheless projected steady calm.

With an easy smile, Seb returned her direct stare, taking in her athletic frame and dark hair, tied back in a typical female cop kind of way. Although she was not his usual type, there was something about her that he liked.

'I live alone.'

She continued, 'Have friends in town?'

'No.'

'A loner, huh?'

Seb shrugged and leaned back, then stretched out both legs. 'I'm just minding my own business.'

'On vacation?' she guessed, ignoring his remark.

'Not exactly.' He looked sideways at her, trying to guess what the hell these two cops wanted with him.

'So, what are you doing here?' Although she asked this with a smile, he could tell that she was genuinely interested.

Seb wanted to explain that he was here to find his sister, Angel. But he didn't know exactly what to say about the situation. Could he say she was running with a gang and he hadn't heard from her in months? He was about to make something up when Guyatt once more interrupted. 'You have any ID?'

Seb glanced away from the female cop, back to Guyatt, into eyes that were empty, lost in the reflection of misted glasses. 'No... it's at home.' Seb glanced at them each in turn, trying to keep his growing annoyance from showing on his face.

Guyatt gazed at him without expression for a long moment, then having made some decision, abruptly walked away, playing his flashlight across the darkened park, as if he were searching for someone else to question. Sebastian followed Guyatt's progress, watching as the torch beam swept in wide arcs as the cop slowly patrolled away into the parkland between park benches and trees.

The female cop stared after Guyatt for a few moments, then sighed loudly before deciding to wander after him. Seb heard her say, 'He likes to catch kids necking. I think it turns him on.' He sensed that she smiled. 'I'm... Officer Benson,' she said, as if he should remember her name. Moving away, her torch switched on and she called back, 'You should get going, Mr Straeker. The night gets cold along the coast up here, and all that sweat could give you a chill.'

3

Seb's car was parked in the nearby lot. Sliding into the Camaro, he drove a little faster than the limit through the streets above the Cove. Past dimly lit shop fronts, under flickering streetlights, then onto the ocean road, the town lights abruptly disappeared from his rear-vision mirror.

Switching back and forth between the headlands, he climbed further into the hills, and a darkening forest. Occasionally he was rewarded with a view of the moon-dappled ocean. Shifting into the top gears, feeling the car leap, he stretched the motor to the red line, replaying the encounter with the cops in his head, wondering who they were really looking for.

It was eighties night for the local radio station, and they were pumping out some of his favourite music of the era. By the time he swung the Camaro off the road, INXS, Madonna and David Bowie had all made an appearance. The dirt driveway climbed steeply off the road, amongst shadowy trunks and leaves that hissed in the stiff night wind. So obscured was the view back toward the road that only headlights would be visible should anyone approach.

As David Bowie's *The Man Who Stole the World* ended, a husky voice announced, *This is Charlie J, and you're listening to Bay Radio.* Her voice was low and cool, like a breeze blowing through palm trees. Pocketing his keys, he approached the darkened house, lit by a single porch light at the head of the stairs. Sitting in the glow of the light, looking pleased to see him, was Ripley.

She padded into the kitchen behind him, making low snuffling noises. Stamping a paw on her food bowl, setting it spinning in a circle, Ripley jumped back as if it had come to life.

'Steady, girl, I'll get something for you.'

She snuffed.

Seb opened a tin, his nose wrinkling as he spooned half the can into the dog's bowl. 'How can you eat this stuff, girl?'

From the tip of Ripley's tongue, resinous drool dripped onto the floor.

'I guess you missed me, huh?'

Patting her head as she chomped and sucked her food, he said, 'Hope you like it here, girl.'

In the bathroom, he peeled out of his running gear, then reached past a vinyl shower curtain and turned the faucet. A yelp escaped him as he climbed into the cold spray where he had expected heat.

'God dammit,' he growled, almost falling out of the shower, his hand failing to find purchase on the plastic curtain. Ripley stuck her head in to see what the commotion was. 'Get outta here!'

Afterwards, back in the living room, Seb threw open the window to allow fresh air to wash in off the bay. He discovered Charlie J once more on the airwaves, now playing moody tunes of lost love. Foreigner's *Waiting for a Girl Like You* and Roxy Music's *More Than This* had made it onto Charlie J's evening playlist, and although he enjoyed her selection, it left him feeling empty.

He must have dozed, for when he woke, the air felt chill.

Charlie J's sibilant voice cut in, and she was both sultry and sad. *It's a minute to midnight, and the world is dark outside, folks. If you're listening in, give me a call and tell me what you'd like to hear. This is the graveyard shift and you're listening to Charlie J on Bay FM.* As her voice trailed away, and the next track kicked in – *So Far Away* by Dire Straits – Seb stood and followed Ripley to the window. Something outside had attracted the dog's attention.

Ripley gave a low growl and padded out onto the porch, her nose twitching at the air. Seb followed her outside, his bare feet making no sound. He left the porch light off to allow his eyes to adjust to the moonlight. Mist was beginning to creep onto the coast, gathering along the shore, and pooling in the valleys between the surrounding hills.

'What is it, girl?' He lay a hand reassuringly on her head and gave a rub behind her ear. His other hand snaked around into the small of his back, curling around the handle of the 9mm Beretta tucked behind his belt. Ripley licked at his fingers and went very still.

Seb left the porch and walked down the driveway, going from tree to tree, stepping carefully. There was a car parked down the road, half hidden under the shadows of a tall pine. Someone was leaning against it, silent, a grey insubstantial silhouette against the deeper shadows.

Then a match was struck, the sudden bloom of light illuminating Guyatt's face as he lit a cigarette. From the tilt of his head, Seb guessed that he was gazing up at the bungalow. After a few minutes, the cop dropped the cigarette on the ground, climbed in the cruiser, swung it around, then sped away.

Where the vehicle had been parked, Seb found five cigarette butts in a neat pile on the gravel verge. Standing where Guyatt had been, he looked back up at the house, shrouded in trees, and noted that the cop couldn't really see anything, even if he wanted to.

CHAPTER 2

Seb rose the next morning to the feeling of a wet tongue, flicking into his ear. 'Get off... *crazy bitch*,' he growled, shoving Ripley away.

Claws clipping on the hardwood floor, the dog retreated to the kitchen to lie beside her food bowl where she would wait patiently.

In the shower, cold water brought him fully awake – a habit learned in a hot, foreign land. Then brushing his teeth, he stared at his reflection, wondering how his hair had grown out so quickly since he had walked off base. He took a minute to style his hair, which had not been long enough for over five years to actually even bother with a comb. Lifting the razor, he immediately dropped it back on the sink. Without shaving cream, he'd just cut himself, and so he decided to embrace a three-day grunge.

On the porch steps, cradling a black coffee, he examined Angel's note. The creases in the paper had worn almost through. Smudged ink, the writing hastily scrawled, he again read her last words to him.

Sebastian,

I've really screwed up... these people – this gang – DAGON'S RIDERS, do some fucked-up shit.

I want out, but they're always watching me. If you were here, you could come and get me... But if you never hear from me again, you know I at least tried to get away.

Angel.

Ripley leant against him affectionately, and he scratched her ears. 'I've got to find her, girl.' She gazed at him, and then licked his hand, and whined. 'I should have done this years ago.'

Not the kind of person to ever ask for help, Angel must be in real danger. But her note had failed to mention where she was. It was the one detail he needed. If she'd written the note and carried it around with her for a while, not knowing where she was going next, then it made sense. The postage mark was therefore all he had to go on, and it indicated that the letter had been posted in Crabtree Cove.

Seb left the house, watching as Ripley settled in at the front window, her gaze sorrowful. 'You stay!'

She barked once and then disappeared somewhere into the house, lost from view.

Thirty minutes later, he drove into town, pulling into a parking bay halfway up the hill. Depositing change into the meter, he locked the car and followed the smell of coffee to a nearby diner. The sign over the door, in faded gold letters, said, *Lucille's*.

He slid onto a cracked, vinyl seat in a window booth with a good view of the street.

An older lady, presumably the owner, Lucille, was perched behind the counter, pretending to do a crossword. Her eyes occasionally flicked up to observe three teen girls employed to wait the tables.

Over a radio playing rock'n'roll, Seb could hear the conversation of two men cooking on a griddle somewhere behind the counter. The pop and hiss of bacon frying, combined with the aromas of fresh coffee and pancakes, made him wish they would just hurry up and take his order.

Two waitresses were checking him out, giggling with embarrassment or perhaps just trying to get his attention. A new guy in a small town sometimes doubled the population of eligible bachelors. Too old for foolish games, Seb turned his attention to the foot traffic just outside the window.

The owner called, 'Grace, Lola – how is that coffee going?' Her question had the girls hurrying to snatch up coffee pots and fill some cups, all the while smiling and making small talk.

Lucille crooked her head forward and called to Seb, 'Sorry about that.'

Ignoring the comment, Seb turned back to the road, unaware that his cup was being refilled. When he looked back, the young waitress – *Grace*, according to her name tag – finally took his order.

On the edge of the table was a small stack of dusty brochures, which looked like they were published in the middle of the last century. Flipping through it, he saw photos of high, rugged cliffs above crashing waves. Far from welcoming, he thought the images depicted a wild and lonely place. The brochure went on to encourage tourists to *hike in the hinterland or fish along the coast*. It promised *pristine forest, scenic streams and lakes*, with *hidden nature trails across rugged hills*. There were phone numbers for weekend cabins for those wanting to *get away from it all*.

As there was a simple map in the brochure, he stuffed it inside his jacket, then settled back to wait for his breakfast. The Cove had very few roads into town and the interstate freeway was more than a dozen miles inland. Although the Cove didn't qualify as lonely, Seb felt the town was isolated.

As his meal arrived, the owner continued, 'Can I ask – are you in town long?'

'Maybe... I'm on kind of a working vacation,' lied Seb, swallowing a mouthful of bacon.

But this only made her more interested. 'Oh? What is it that you do?'

'Ma'am, I'm just here for breakfast.' He belatedly added a smile to soften his brisk response.

Lucille's smile froze and she gave a polite nod. Seb finished his plate, slurped down the last of his coffee, then left a modest tip on the table before stepping outside.

Angel had to be here somewhere. He just needed a good, hard look around. Perhaps he could find out where these Dagon's Riders boys liked to hang.

Downhill, there were blocks of red brick shop fronts, many with second-storey apartments. Beyond them lay the beach, already explored during his evening run the previous day. In the middle of the harbour, surrounded by warehouses, fishing boats were tied to an old wooden jetty in a deep-water dock.

Up the hill, the tree-lined road held a certain charm, and it was all that he needed to explore in that direction. At a brisk pace, he strode past homes with views of the Cove, that probably dated to the civil war era. Once they might have been loved, but now many were falling into disrepair, half hidden amongst overgrown trees and tall weeds. The salt-laden air had peeled paint, leaving greying boards. As the foot traffic was light, Seb found himself examining every face that he passed.

A cathedral-scale church loomed, casting long shadows across the streets, dwarfing the buildings around it. From within large grey stones, an arched stained-glass window shimmered in reds and greens, depicting *David entering the lion's den*. Toward the rear of the church, a spire reached high into the air, providing an *eagle's nest* view over the town. Seb walked along the sidewalk; there was an arched doorway close to the curb, and near the entrance, a statue of the Madonna. Her once smooth white stone face was now pitted and mottled green with lichen. Black mould shrouded her eyes, and it seemed to Seb that her sightless gaze held all the warmth of a medusa.

Stopping, he glanced within. Beyond the glow of candles, at the far end of the hall, he spied the back of a priest. Moving on a few steps, a noticeboard showed three mass times, and the name of the priest – *Father John O'Malley*.

Continuing up the hill, he passed side-streets, a pizza-place, closed now, with a sign that said it would open at five o'clock. Further along, he found a laundromat, then a small theatre, playing some older movies – classics, like Hitchcock's *North by North-West*.

There was an old garage, with a single gas bowser out front.

A guy in faded overalls was sitting on a chair, eyes closed as he absorbed some rays.

'Good morning.' Seb nodded toward the mechanic, who seemed reluctant to open his eyes. Seb approached and pulled a photo of Angel from his wallet. 'Have you seen this woman?'

The guy gently took the photo in sausage-thick, grease-blackened fingers, lifted the image close to his eyes and with a furrowed brow, grunted, 'Why?'

'I'm looking for her. She's my sister.'

The mechanic glanced up and slowly shook his head. 'No one looks like her around here. A woman like that... I'd remember her.'

Seb nodded and replaced the photo. Then, with a sigh, he decided to retreat back down the hill to his car.

Arriving at the Camaro, he found Deputy Benson leaning casually against the hood, her arms folded.

Under the windscreen wiper, there was a ticket. Shaking his head, he snatched it off the glass. Lucille was looking out the diner's window, just the barest hint of a smile touching her smug lips. Seb pictured her swallowing the ticket, her face going beat red as she tried to breathe and chew at the same time. In the end, he smiled and waved back at her.

'Anything you want to say to me?' asked Benson.

'You could have just asked me to dinner. No need for parking tickets.'

'Where I'm from, it's up to the boys to ask the girls out.'

He looked her up and down, in the same way she had given him the *once over* the previous evening. Her hair was tied back and he wondered what she might look like in more relaxed circumstances. 'I tell you what, Officer...'

'Benson,' she supplied, pointing to the name badge just above the swell of her tight uniformed shirt. 'I think you remember me.'

'Tell you what, if you could see yourself clear to withdrawing this ticket, I would be more than happy to ask you out.'

Her smile faded a little. 'Are you looking to bribe an officer of the law?'

'Look…' Seb began, holding up a hand.

'It's okay, I'll let you off with a warning this time.' She snatched the ticket from his fingers and tore it up in front of him. 'But from now on, make sure you keep the meter full. Officer Guyatt looks for any excuse to hassle *out-of-towners*.'

'Speaking of *your colleague* – Guyatt.'

'Yeah?'

'I think he was watching my place last night.'

'Huh?'

'Yeah, I saw him. Tell him that the next time he comes around, he should just knock and I'll give him a beer.'

Benson stared, not knowing how to respond.

He continued, grinning, 'I don't know what he thinks I'm doing out there. He sure is one suspicious son-of-a-gun.'

Confused by what Seb was telling her, Benson abruptly turned and walked away down the street, nodding to a few people who greeted her by name. Just once, she glanced back at him, over her shoulder, her expression thoughtful.

Seb stepped into his car. He drove away, coasting up the hill. When he passed near St Anthony's, he glanced out the window. Father O'Malley had come to stand outside the entrance, and for a moment their gazes locked. The priest neither smiled nor waved, but instead just stared after Seb with haunted eyes that Seb found unsettling.

CHAPTER 3

J az Freeman drove into town in a dark hatchback rental, stopping
   at the only diner she had seen – a place called *Lucille's*.

Positioned behind the counter, Lucille glanced at Jaz before
her eyes returned to something she was reading. A girl appeared
straight away, taking her order. They only had one type of salad – a
'garden salad', which Jaz suspected would be heavy on the lettuce
and not much else.

Jaz was pushing forty-five but could have passed for thirty-five,
with a slender, athletic build. Dressed casually, with a light denim
jacket just large enough to conceal a shoulder holster, she took
comfort from the feel of the snub-nosed .38 nestled against her side.

She heard a text message arrive, then levered herself up from
the booth to pull her phone from her tight jeans. It was from her
boss, Harvey.

Jaz, I know you were due some leave, but where are you?

Damn right, she was due leave. Close to burnt out, she hadn't
taken a vacation for over two years. Stuck in a basement office,
really just a converted lunchroom close to a records section, she
had been working cold case homicides for five years.

The salad arrived on a large plate and although she hadn't asked
for it, there was a slice of bread on the side, as if to say to her that
no one should have to eat a salad alone.

What the FBI didn't know was that she had come to Crabtree
Cove to follow a lead, or more accurately, a *hunch*, or if she was
being really honest – *a long shot*. Over the course of the last few
years, she had seen many cases cross her crowded desk, some so

cold they dated back to the sixties and seventies, when forensic science in the law enforcement space was rudimentary. After a few years working cold cases, she started to see a pattern emerge. But to admit there was a pattern was to expend precious, stretched resources, on what could end up as a nothing at all. So, Jaz was on a working vacation, the type that could help scratch a couple of her itches. She would get some much-needed rest, and at the same time, she could also follow a hunch or two.

She finished the salad. But before she left, she picked up the phone and sent a reply to her boss – *I'm in Crabtree Cove. I'll be back in a few days!* She inserted a smiley face emoji.

Immediately he sent back his own smiling face emoji and a '?'.

As much as she wanted to send back *Mind your own fucking business*, she instead texted, *Gone fishing.*

Jaz wondered if her boss knew what she was doing here. The guy was younger than her, and a real *go-getter.* He was a bit of a control freak too, and just smart enough to be a pain in her ass. She slipped the phone into her pocket, leaving the cash on the table with the tip.

The street sloped away downhill toward the harbour and it drew her eyes. Up the street, however, she had seen a 'for rent' sign outside a large block of flats that were built into the side of the hill, each with a small balcony facing in the direction of the harbour. It was an old place, surrounded by large trees that grew at either side, branches reaching up, partly obscuring it. Jaz thought that there was something charming about the building.

The front entrance was only a half-dozen steps off the pavement where French doors opened to a foyer that smelt musty. A steep set of stairs led up to the higher floors, and to the right, she could see a deserted common room with tables and chairs.

On a door that said 'Enquiries', she knocked for a few moments before an old guy appeared, his white singlet clinging to a bony chest. His eyes widened before he closed the door. A few moments later, the door opened again, the old guy now dressed in a garish Hawaiian shirt.

'Sorry, I was just... watching TV.'

'That's okay. I was hoping that room is still free.' She had to speak over the TV in the background.

His eyes brightened. 'Oh yeah, that's right... we have rooms to let.'

'Well, sir, I only need the one.'

He nodded, taking down a key from a board. 'I have a room on the top floor with a view.'

Jaz nodded, then allowed the old man to enter the corridor.

'I expect you will want to see the room before you decide.'

'Well, actually, sir...'

'Call me Clem,' he interjected.

'Yes, sir, Clem, I am only here for a few days. I'm sure that what you have will do me just fine.'

Clem started up the stairs, each step creaking underfoot. 'It's ten dollars a night,' he announced over his shoulder, and then paused on the first landing. 'I hope that's alright.'

'I was expecting to pay more than that,' admitted Jaz, smiling.

'You haven't seen the room yet,' he said, turning and continuing to the next floor. 'I haven't changed my rates in twenty years.'

'I can tell.'

They climbed to the top floor, past low-volume TVs and muffled voices emanating from other rooms.

The apartment was what some might call *retro*, and others would call shabby. There was a kitchenette and small bathroom, an ancient television complete with rabbit-ear antenna, and a low coffee table. To the left was a doorway leading to a double bedroom. Clem opened the door to the balcony with a screech, the frosted glass door reluctantly sliding in its tracks. The balcony was small, with a pair of chairs to take in the views of the harbour. Jaz stepped out and breathed deeply, feeling a salt-laden breeze caress her. Making a show of enjoying the view, she smiled at Clem, who returned a yellow-toothed grin.

'I'll take it,' she said and handed over a hundred dollars. 'This can go toward my bill.'

Clem tucked the cash into his top pocket, hidden amongst the bright hibiscus flowers on his shirt. 'I wish we could offer breakfast, Miss...'

It was then that Jaz realised that she hadn't introduced herself. 'Freeman, Jaz Freeman.'

'That's a nice name,' said Clem, handing her the key before retreating from the room.

Jaz surveyed the town from the vantage of the balcony. It seemed quiet, with orderly buildings huddled along narrow streets. The harbour looked like a good place to stroll when she needed a break from the investigation. Looking down at her car on the street below, she sighed, realising she had to cart her gear up to her room.

Ten minutes later, opening the notebook computer, she pulled up the latest files she had been working on. A map covered the screen with markers placed around twenty small towns, each showing a date and the face of a victim. They were in a perfect arc around Crabtree Cove. The dates ranged widely across a decade.

It was time to test her ideas, to challenge the pattern only she had seen. Her theory was underpinned by the concept that all of these victims had crossed paths with the outlaw bikie gang known as Dagon's Riders. It was a theory which had been dismissed by her colleagues.

Glancing down at the screen, the faces of the thirty-four victims stared back at her, familiar faces that now haunted her when she closed her eyes to sleep. Only five of these people's bodies had been found. Of the thirty-four, twelve were considered 'missing', rather than the victims of homicides. Town officials didn't like to admit they had a killer or killers at large, and so would rather believe, in the absence of a body, that the person had simply left town without telling anyone.

When Jaz viewed the smiling faces – so familiar to her now, their images captured in high school yearbooks, family portraits, later as selfies on cell phones – she tried to banish the crime scene photos – of the same people, but with unfocused eyes, pale, sometimes bloated bodies, or unnatural stiffening limbs.

She glanced up, feeling that the town below had lost its charm as the lights began to wink into existence around the bay, accentuating hidden shadows and lurking stillness.

Could a gang of bikers be serial killers? Extortion, prostitution, drug running, even smuggling – all could be expected from organised gangs. But random kidnappings... possible homicides? Gangs were committed to making cash, to gaining prestige and building reputation. If they *were* involved, what were they doing with the bodies? This had been the sticking point, the contention between Jaz and her FBI brothers and sisters – the idea that a biker gang was capable of crimes that seemingly had the hallmarks of serial killing. And if she suspected their involvement in these thirty-four cases, how many more did she not know about?

The last victim on Jaz's list was a young woman, remains found burnt in a fire pit near a campsite, deep in a forest. On this occasion, the link was a dozen motorcycle tracks found around the site.

Of the five known victims, where remains were found, not one had useful information that would lead to a killer or killers. Not one of the bodies was able to show anything other than the person's identity, and then, only after DNA matches to living relatives, or through dental records.

Closing the notebook computer, she stowed the slim device under the sofa lounge, satisfied it was well hidden. Sliding the balcony door shut against the suddenly chill breeze, she decided to leave the flat and find some dinner.

About to exit, she paused, put the snub-nosed .38 back in the holster and flipped on her denim jacket. Jaz felt nothing strange about the town, but she was not about to be caught unaware.

Closing the door, she locked it firmly behind her, her stomach growling in protest at having only eaten a measly salad for lunch.

CHAPTER 4

The *Pizza Joint* was what it was unimaginatively called. Jaz found it a couple of blocks down and one block over from where she was staying. All she had to do was follow the aroma, conjuring images of garlic, roast peppers and pepperoni. She entered through a shabby exterior, finding a charming warmth within. A bell tinkled as the door eased shut.

She paused in the foyer, near a takeaway counter, and glanced around. Pockets of people sat at tables, talking animatedly. On the far side of the restaurant, swinging doors led to the kitchen. There were booths nearest to the street, and in one, away from everyone else, sat a guy watching the world outside.

As Jaz walked in and took a seat in her own booth, she could see him in the reflection of the window, deep in thought, his eyes bleak. Although she was used to vacationing alone, she never remained alone for long. Quick to make friends and easily bored, she would draw people around her into conversations.

Look up, she thought. *Look up at me, dammit. You won't see anyone finer than me tonight.* But Seb never looked up at Jaz, not until she leant into his line of sight, gave a bright smile, and said, 'Hey!'

Seb was thinking about Angel. He was mulling over all the things he should have said to his kid-sister after their folks had died in the car wreck all those years ago. He was contemplating the ways in which he might have stopped her downward spiral, into the drugs and the bad company that led her into that life. He was wondering what she might have been doing in Crabtree Cove, which seemed like the last place you might find an outlaw motorcycle gang.

18

Then a woman a booth over was talking to him and he wondered why.

'Hey, I'm Jaz.'

'Sorry, are you talking to me?' asked Seb.

'Is that okay? I didn't think it was against the law. You look like you could do with some company. I know I sure could.'

'I'm Seb.'

He gave a half-smile, which wasn't much, but Jaz thought it kind of nice. He'd been thinking about something, lost to the world before she'd dragged him back.

Seb thought Jaz attractive. He was drawn into her large, rich chocolate eyes, which gave her an overall feline appearance. *Exotic*, he would call her look, at least for a predominantly white town like the Cove.

'I'm on vacation,' she announced with a smile.

Seb nodded. 'That must be nice.' He wasn't sure he wanted a conversation. He needed space to think.

But then she spoke again, and he realised that she wasn't ready to leave him to his thoughts. 'You on vacation?'

Seb shook his head. 'Not exactly.'

'Not exactly,' she repeated. 'What does that mean?' Her smile stayed in place.

Grace, the same waitress he'd seen at *Lucille's*, appeared and served Seb first, and then reluctantly turned to Jaz and took her order. Grace smiled at Seb in a way that was a little obvious, adjusted her cleavage, then walked away, hips swaying. Seb tried to avert his eyes.

When the waitress departed, Jaz gave a silvery laugh. 'I think she likes you.'

'She's *way* too young for me,' said Seb, glancing up at her.

'I'd check her driver's license first, if you know what I mean,' agreed Jaz. Then she added, 'Maybe she thinks you're her ticket outta town.'

19

The ghost of a smile escaped him. 'The Cove is okay. In another life... maybe I could live in a place like this.'

'Wow, a real smile,' she said. 'I wondered if you could.'

Grace returned, this time carrying a jug of water in each hand. She stepped up first to Seb's booth, setting the jug down carefully, bending forward and allowing Seb a good look at her T-shirt, which sat directly under his eye-line for a long moment. Then, turning, she almost banged the other jug down before Jaz, the water spilling slightly onto the table.

Seb grinned at Jaz, and she realised Seb *was* handsome. What she had first seen in the reflected glass, in those blue eyes, initially mistaken for bleakness, was in fact *intensity*. As she gazed at him, she wondered what *his story* was.

They sat for a while in silence, which for Jaz felt awkward. She waited for Seb to pick up the conversation, but he continued to look out the window, retreating into his own thoughts.

'So, Seb... *are* you new in town?' pressed Jaz, trying to draw him out.

His vacant eyes slowly came back into focus, and when they settled on Jaz, she could feel that intensity again.

Jaz asked, 'What were you just thinking about?'

'Someone... something... private. I'm sorry if you think that's rude of me to say.' He offered an apologetic smile, adding, 'I don't know you.'

'Isn't that what we are doing now? Getting acquainted?' Jaz smiled as her pizza arrived and watched as Seb received his – a pepperoni with cheese. It smelt great, but she couldn't imagine anything quite as unhealthy.

Seb pushed aside the knife and fork, grabbed a slice and began chewing.

'You don't look like you're from here,' said Jaz. He didn't reply, so she said, 'Let's play a game. I get three guesses about you. If I get all three right, then you buy me a drink.'

Seb reluctantly put the slice back on his plate. This woman was just not taking the hint. 'And if you don't?'

'I buy you one. Is that fair?' Jaz took a sip of water as she considered her initial question.

Seb nodded, stuffing more pizza into his mouth.

'I think you are new here... in town, I mean,' she said.

'Wow, you must be a mind reader.' Seb sounded sarcastic, but he didn't care.

'That car outside – the Camaro. The DMV plates are from another state. You keep looking at it – I know it's yours. And, like I said, you don't look like a local.'

'It's my car,' he confirmed, a lazy smile touching his mouth but never quite reaching his eyes. 'But *what does* a local guy look like then?'

Jaz shrugged. 'Not like you.' She sipped her drink, a smile playing over her mouth. 'You're military?' She watched him, looking for signs of deceit in his answer.

Seb looked away. 'What makes you say that?'

'I'm rarely wrong... and I'm good at reading people.' Jaz was better than good. Possessed of a natural intuition that couldn't be taught, the FBI agent had made her career on noticing what mattered. With Seb, it was his upright posture, and maybe the hair, which was only just starting to grow out. There was also good muscle on his lean frame. Not gym muscle, carefully constructed in a mirror, but the kind of muscle you get from all-round physical work.

'No,' he said, though he didn't look up.

She tilted her head back, waiting for him to meet her eyes. 'I don't believe you.'

'Okay... until recently, I *was* in the service,' he admitted.

'I knew it!' Jaz looked pleased. 'Yeah, I could tell. What were you?'

'Rangers...' he muttered, and although he looked like he'd say more, he stopped and looked away.

They each ate a few more mouthfuls, and after a while, Jaz said,

'Last guess – you're looking for someone…' She said this in an off-hand way, like it meant nothing. But as soon as the words left her mouth, she had turned *those* eyes on him to see his reaction.

'Why would you say that?' Seb looked at her, again wondering about her ability to read him. Who *was* this woman?

Jaz said, 'When I came in here, I saw folks sitting around, chatting. You were on your own, watching the street outside like you might be waiting for someone to turn up, but you didn't think they would – not really. Then, when I sat down, I saw the look in your eyes that was… distant… tell me I'm wrong, Seb, and I'll buy you the drink. But if I'm right, I score three correct guesses and you owe me a drink.'

He nodded. 'Okay, one drink.'

'I'll have a bourbon and cola,' she immediately said, looking at him with triumph.

Seb signalled Grace and ordered them two drinks. Not wanting to talk too loudly, he decided to move across to Jaz's booth, seating himself opposite her. Grace took their plates, gave an annoyed click of her tongue when she saw Jaz and Seb sitting together, then stalked away.

Jaz took a long, satisfied swallow and said, 'So, tell me, what are you looking for, Seb?'

'My sister.'

'Your sister?' Jaz hadn't expected him to say that.

'Yeah, she's somewhere around town. I'm here to meet her.'

Jaz looked confused. 'So, what are you waiting for? Go see her. Or is she coming here?'

'I don't know where she is, exactly.' Could he tell her that he suspected Angel was mixed up with a biker gang that she was unable to get away from? No – he didn't feel like going over all that with a stranger.

Jaz looked confused. 'I don't get it.' She suspected he was telling just half the truth now.

'We lost contact with each other. I was on deployment in

Afghanistan. Then she wrote me. But her letter didn't say exactly where in Crabtree Cove she was staying.' Seb glanced around, trying not to look at Jaz directly. The story sounded incomplete at best.

'Your sister writes you, tells you she lives here in the Cove but doesn't mention her address? Maybe she doesn't want to see you.'

Seb shook his head. 'No… she wanted me to come. She needs me.'

Jazz wondered what he was trying to say. She wanted to prompt him, but getting more out of him required her to tread carefully. 'That's too bad. I hope you find her.' After a pause, she continued, 'But who actually writes a letter these days anyway? Why didn't she text you?' Jaz swallowed the last of the drink, then set down the empty glass.

'Maybe she lost her phone.'

'So… she could buy another,' suggested Jaz.

'Not that simple.'

'How so?'

'The people she's with… maybe they don't want her having contact with me.'

'So, she didn't *actually* lose her phone then,' said Jaz.

'I guess not,' said Seb. Deep down, he suspected that the gang had taken Angel's phone from her.

'She had it taken off her,' guessed Jaz.

Seb stared, wondering at her sudden shift toward a kind of interrogation.

Jaz wanted the sister's name. Seb's story didn't add up. His solitary presence in the town, a letter telling Seb she needed him, the phone she wasn't allowed to keep, the look Seb carried behind his eyes, which she now recognised as *haunted*… all gave her pause. She said, 'I may be able to help you find her.'

Seb leaned back, wondering how Jaz could possibly assist.

Jaz regarded him closely, could see the cogs turning in that pretty head and a hint of something else in his eyes – which might have been the beginnings of *hope*.

Aware of his indecision, Jaz needed to invent something that would spark his interest without giving away her real identity. She said, 'I work for a phone company. We can trace phone numbers, use phone towers to ping the locations of cells. I don't even need a phone number. All I need is her name.' It was a necessary deception, she told herself.

'But she has no phone,' Seb reminded her.

'The last time she *had* a phone – in *her name*, we can see where the calls came from.'

'You can?'

Jaz nodded, then shrugged as if to say *no big deal* and pushed her glass around the table with a finger as she waited. She tried not to look up at his face, then waited some more. She wanted that name, and then she would also get Seb's last name too.

At last, Seb said, 'Straeker. Angel Straeker.'

'Okay then.'

Seb spelled the surname. 'Are you going to record that or something?'

'It's all up here,' she said, tapping a finger to the side of her temple. 'You will have to give me your number, so I can get back to you.'

'I don't have one,' he said.

Jaz shrugged. 'It's up to you.'

'No… I really don't own a phone right now.' Seb slid from the booth, went to the counter and paid his bill. After he came back, he stood near Jaz, then took Angel's photo from his wallet. Holding it out so she could see the image, he said, 'It's important I find her.'

Jaz stared at the image for a moment. 'She's pretty.'

Seb replaced the photo in his wallet.

'Where can I find you, if you have no phone?' asked Jaz, leaning back.

'Oh, *around*… for a few days… maybe even a few weeks,' said Seb. He would stay until he found Angel, and that could take a year for all he cared. 'I'll run into you somewhere, Jaz. This town's pretty small.'

She wanted him to stay a bit longer, but she couldn't think of a way to make that happen. 'Okay, Seb, if I find anything out about Angel, I'll come find you. You take care.'

Seb nodded, walked away, and as he reached the sidewalk, he paused. Looking back in through the front windows, he half-raised his hand in farewell, then wandered away into the night.

CHAPTER 5

Setting off down the street, Seb continued to play the conversation with Jaz on a tape loop. She said she worked for a phone company. Why would she risk losing her job just to help a guy she'd only just met?

There was a party down the road, inside a high-walled garden. As he passed, he walked around a couple using the shadows of a tree to hide their amorous liaison. They were locked in an embrace, tongues shoved halfway down each other's throats. He thought of Jaz again, wondering where their conversation might have led if he'd stayed longer, and they'd had a few more drinks together.

She was a distraction that he didn't need right now, he mused, continuing downhill, under humming streetlamps, the inky expanse of the bay growing closer. Bathed in dappled moonlight, it was so flat that the stars seemed to float within the waves.

Near the harbour, the streets flattened and he was drawn toward pulsing music. Rounding a street corner, he arrived at a bar and some motorcycles parked just outside. He paused before the four machines, examining them. They were Harley-Davidsons. He stood, just staring at them. Then he looked across at the bar, where a sign swung on a rusted chain, proclaiming in faded letters, *Crab Shack, live music*.

Throbbing heavy metal, an indistinct murmur of raised voices, a faint whiff of tobacco and whisky could not have drawn him in more than if he'd seen Angel standing there in the doorway.

Seb entered the bar. There was a band, relegated to a darkened corner, perched on a black-painted stage, power cords running around them like worms. To his left was a rustic bar, crowd packed around it, desperate for their next round. He paused, going instead to his right, toward a single pool table where a group of men were strutting around with pool cues, the game a chance to demonstrate their skill, attract a female or simply win some cash. Here, at last, he found the owners of the bikes. Four bikes for four men, and like their machines, they were slight variants of each other – long, uncombed beards, lank, greasy hair and leather vests stretched over pot-shaped guts. They didn't look very dangerous unless he was likely to catch a disease called *stupid*.

Seb approached, squeezing between mingling groups, cologne and perfume clouding the way in unseen miasma. Gathered around sticky tables, the slightly inebriated chittered, smoked, laughed, all at a volume that hoped to rise above the band.

He wanted to take Angel's photo from his wallet and walk up to the bikers, interrupt the game, ask them about her, get them to tell him what they knew and, if necessary, beat it from them. Instead, he took a seat on a stool and watched the game. As they circled the table, Seb noted that none of the four seemed to be wearing official Dagon's Riders colours or insignia of any kind.

He was also aware of three other guys standing nearby, arms folded, looking impatient. These were clean-cut boys a year or two out of high school. They stood in a group, sipping from beer cans clutched in milk-white hands that had never seen a blister or corn. They wore impeccable jeans with tears placed in just the right locations, designer jackets and hair mussed up in a way that took three types of product. Seb suspected they had been waiting to use the table and their impatience was turning to agitation.

The bikers seemed aware of the younger men but were finding the situation amusing. Something was going to happen. It didn't take long.

The black ball disappeared down a corner pocket, then two of the bikers shook hands and one handed over a small wad of cash.

They lobbed the pool cues onto the table, but as the three waiting men stepped forward to retrieve them, the other two bikers snatched the cues back up.

The music was booming so Seb couldn't hear exactly what passed between them but he saw a biker shove one of the younger men back, sending the guy into a knot of people dancing.

The guy fell, entangled with a woman in a skin-tight, leopard-skin dress, her massive, platform high heels somehow ending up over her head. It looked worse than it was. The two were helped back to their feet by the dancers as the four bikers laughed, slapping their hands on their knees, doubling over, making a big show of the mirth they had created. That should have been it. If the kid was smart, that would have been it.

Instead, the guy, feeling like his carefully refined image had been sullied, came hurtling back, right into the biker's right-cross, which ended the charge abruptly. The kid spun and dropped hard.

The four bikers used pool cues, each stepping in and taking turns at pummelling the young guys, in a way that was playful rather than deadly. Those on the floor backed away, and the rock band kept playing an imitation of The White Stripe's *Seven Nation Army*.

Seb noticed two bouncers watching from across the room. Neither bothered to step in to stop the beating. Seb began to move from his stool. One of the bouncers – solid, bald, goateed – shook his head in warning at him.

Seb had seen bar brawls before, had seen punch-ups in his unit. But he had never seen bouncers just stand back and allow such a one-sided contest.

The three young guys, now with some new tears in their jackets and jeans, were attempting to extricate themselves, dragging their knocked-out friend along the wooden boards of the dancefloor. But the bikers, having found a new sport, followed slowly, in an arc, making it clear that the festivities were only just beginning.

Seb hunched, perched on the stool, heart beating a little faster.

Until now, he had been content to watch. The three young men had made a silly play, and they had earnt some trouble.

A woman near Seb put a hand on his arm. 'Can't you do something?' She looked terrified. Others in the crowd watched with silent wonder and a few gave drunken cheers.

Perhaps it was a *pack* mentality or the *tough guy* image. Maybe it was a few too many beers or a feeling of superiority, but whatever the combination, the bikers wanted to keep the confrontation going.

Seb took a deep breath, abruptly stood, stalked to the table, picking up a cue stick as he swept by. He hefted it, found its balance, moved toward the brawl. The solid, thicker end would make a good club, even if the cue snapped.

Now the four bikers had surrounded the two upright men, had landed two more punches that had sent a few teeth skittering across the floor like little white dice. Seb predicted they would start using their boots any second.

Use *controlled aggression*, he thought. *You can't afford to go bat-shit crazy on these guys and accidentally kill someone.* Reaching the first biker, the one who had started it all, Seb hit him over the head, snapping the pool stick in half. In the same fluid motion, he bent, scooping up the heavier, thick end.

The biker, heavy-set and dazed, turned, just in time for Seb's fist to explode into his bearded face. He spun to the floor, eyes rolling up. Seb wasn't that big, but he had played a lot of baseball and had a powerful arm that, when uncoiled, was like a snake striking.

Seb swapped the pool stick cudgel to his right hand. The three remaining bikers turned on him, grinning wildly, amazed that someone dared to interfere.

The band kept playing like nothing was happening, as the crowd pulled back, forming a space around Seb.

The bouncers still seemed unwilling to intervene, though one of them – a tall man with gold earrings – was moving around the bar to get something. Seb hoped it wasn't a gun. That would take this to a new level.

Now was a good time to stop. Seb was willing to let it go. But they came charging toward him. Seb cracked the cue against the head of the middle biker. He stumbled, eyes rolling back, legs suddenly not under him anymore.

But the remaining two were on Seb, grappling him, forcing him to drop the stick. Seb smashed his elbow into the nose of the closest biker, which at least loosened his grip. But the other biker was free to punch Seb in the side of the head. Luckily it was a glancing blow that only stung. It would have knocked him out had it landed on his jaw.

'We're gonna fuck you right up,' he snarled with rancid breath through a blood-stained moustache, trying hard to stand.

Seb stepped back, giving himself more room, ducking a second wild punch from the biker who had already managed to hit him. Glancing sideways, Seb saw the tall bouncer on the phone behind the bar.

He needed to resolve this quickly. Moving forward, Seb feinted with his left fist and then executed a swift kick to the groin.

The crowd gave an 'oohhh', either at the pain the biker was now in or the use of what might be considered *foul play*. That only left one now, and Seb grinned, allowing some expression to show. 'Who's fuckin' who now?'

'You're one stupid bastard,' growled the remaining biker, pulling a long bowie knife. Seb backed away slowly, watching the knife sway this way and that in the biker's meaty hand.

Someone in the crowd, at the front of the circle, kicked the snapped stick across the floor to Seb's feet. Seb swept it up and held it ready. The knife-wielder reversed the blade, holding it in a stabbing position. He rushed Seb, who caught the downward thrust on the stick and allowed the biker's momentum to pitch forward past him.

Now Seb was behind him and he smashed the cudgel hard across the back of the biker's knees, buckling them. There was a howl of pain. With the cue ends, Seb affected a chokehold. Dropping the knife, the biker desperately used both hands to claw at Seb's grip. Seb choked him, felt the guy black out and allowed him to slump to the floor.

Not hesitating, Seb started for the front door, seeking to join the three young guys who had already made it outside. But a hand took his arm and swung him around. It was the bald bouncer, and Seb reflexively brought up an arm to block a punch that was never thrown.

'Not that way,' the bouncer said, fighting to be heard over the band's next song. The guy shook his head and said, 'Follow me.'

Seb hesitated, but sensing the bouncer meant well, he trailed him back through the crowd, past the bar and into the kitchen.

Pausing, the guy said, 'Man, that was funny!' He clapped Seb on the shoulder. 'Those assholes are always kicking ass in here. No one has ever done that to them before.'

'Who are they?' asked Seb.

'You don't want to know, man.' The bouncer shook his head, his earring glittering. 'They run with some bad people, some real bad people.'

Seb resisted as the bouncer took his arm and headed toward what Seb assumed was a rear exit to the bar. 'Hey, I got to know who they are!'

The bouncer paused as they reached the back entrance. He opened the door to an alleyway, dirty and crowded with garbage cans overflowing with scraps, and empty beer bottles. He looked outside and satisfied that no one was waiting, turned to Seb. 'They were, my friend, Dagon's Riders. You just made some enemies, brother. They'll want to know who you are.'

Seb hesitated, then said, 'If they ask... tell them you think I'm the new guy living out on the coast road.'

31

'The hell I will. Why would I do that?'

'Because I need you to, okay?'

The bouncer looked at him quizzically. 'What are you trying to do, man?'

Seb grinned. It had just occurred to him that finding Angel would be easier if they simply came to him. Worse case, they would rough him up, and take him to their chapterhouse. At least he would know where Angel was or find out what had happened to her.

'You better go!' He pushed Seb into the alley, then slammed the door shut.

Seb walked briskly back toward his car, avoiding streetlights, keeping to the night shadows under trees and storefronts. He felt in his pocket, found the keys to his car still there, and took a breath he had been holding. He touched his head tenderly. Had the guy worn a chunky ring on that hand?

Driving back through town, he tuned to Bay Radio, now cranking some hits from the nineties, and although he did not recognise the song, he turned it up. By the time he hit the first curves of the coastal road winding back toward his bungalow, Charlie J was casting her spell, her voice huskier than he remembered it. *Good evening, listeners, and welcome to another late night with Charlie. I'll be spinning some more vinyl for your listening pleasure… with some stuff you may not have heard before…* Seb smiled, thinking of the four bikers he had *put down*, and then wondered if he should start carrying his Beretta with him from now on. The last thing he expected was to have a knife pulled on him.

Then Charlie J said something at the end of a song that caught his attention, not because of the way she said it, but because it seemed a bit out of place. *Don't stay out late tonight. There's some bad folks in the Cove.* The next song started, and he heard Charlie J say softly as it began, *The boys are back in town*, speaking over the opening few familiar guitar riffs of Thin Lizzy's hit song.

Seb slowed, swung his car off the road and into the driveway of the bungalow, killing the lights and engine as he pulled up outside the house. He reflected on what the DJ had said and thought it odd. *Don't stay out late tonight. There's some bad folks in the Cove.* Along the road below, coming fast, but heading toward town, he heard the motorcycles, the distinct throaty roar of Harley-Davidsons. Then as they approached, through the dense foliage, headlights swept past in the blink of an eye. He guessed that he heard three or four bikes, riding close together, almost in formation.

Leaving the car, he approached his door, slipped the key into the lock and then Ripley was jumping on him, licking his hands. 'Yeah, yeah, it's good to be home.'

*

Having found some tea bags tucked away in the back of the cupboard above the stove, Jaz made a cup of Darjeeling. She picked up the laptop, went out onto the balcony and settled, resting it across her knees.

While she sipped, she connected to the FBI database and used a general search term for *Angel Straeker*. A single line of data came back. There was only one Angel Straeker, and the date of birth roughly matched the age she thought Angel might be.

She clicked the link – a second screen opened, showing that the subject had a criminal history in two states. There was a conviction relating to theft and a similar record for burglary. For both crimes, she escaped jail time.

There was also a red flag attached to her name, relating to a warrant for failing to appear on a court date. She navigated to the current BOLO and opened a page showing a mugshot closeup of an attractive, dark-haired young woman. It matched the photo that Seb had shown her. In the photo, Angel looked like she had aged, and now had a hardness around her eyes.

Jaz reflected on Seb, how he seemed to be holding back on

something. Any other guy may have tried to stay on, drink some more, maybe even try to come back to her place. But he had left, abruptly, now she thought about it. Seb had been super distracted, enough to ignore the signals she had been putting out. His sister, who could well be missing, was definitely his sole consideration.

Jaz pulled up three separate internet search engines and began a stream of keyword searches using *Straeker, Angel Straeker* and *Seb Straeker.*

Links populated the screen, mainly to a bunch of social media platforms. She scrolled down, reviewing the results and discarding the useless information.

She found an old news item from ten years ago, showing a vehicle on a snowy, mountain road, wedged under a truck. Jaz began reading the article.

Jeremy and Rhona Straeker were pronounced dead at the scene...

The evening became chill, and she took a blanket and draped it around her shoulders, unwilling to leave the balcony and the patchwork of stars above her head.

Jaz started to fill in the blanks. The parents were killed in the wreck. Angel, about fourteen, and Seb, about twenty-four, are suddenly left alone in the world. Seb turns to the army, and Angel begins a downward slide into... *what?*

She closed out of several open internet pages and navigated back into the FBI database. Taking a screenshot of Angel's face, she pasted it into a newly created file and named it 'Straeker.'

Then she began typing some notes about Angel, based on the conversation she had with Seb. *Angel Straeker. Age: about 24. Might be missing in or near Crabtree Cove. Known associates possibly preventing contact with her. Only known relative: Sebastian Straeker.* Biting her lip, she paused. *Is she in close contact with Dagon's Riders?*

For Angel's sake, Jaz hoped not. She saved the file on her desktop and considered what else she could do right now for Seb. In the apartments below and around her, she could just hear a TV and the soft murmur of a couple talking quietly as they listened to a local radio station playing some old tunes.

Closing the laptop, she sipped the last of the tea and found it had gone cold. As she was about to go inside, the throaty hum of five or six motorcycles grew. She stepped up to the railing, trying to gauge the direction of the sound. From the hills behind her, following the coastal road into town, they appeared, headlight beams sweeping before them, leaving the riders in a cape of darkness. Their silhouettes hinted at hard helmets, boots and coats. Then they were gone in an instant, travelling at speed toward the docks.

In the bathroom, brushing her teeth, thinking about Seb and Angel, she considered what Seb had told her. It was all about data, and gathering the whole picture. Seb had more information, and she needed it.

Staring at the mirror, she said, 'You should have asked more questions, dummy.'

CHAPTER 6

Seb woke, realising he had left the windows to the room open. His dream was, as always, about the night his folks had died in the car wreck on a mountain road, skidding into a truck on an icy bend. But tonight, Angel was also in the carnage, and he dreamt that she too had perished.

On the bedside table was a small, old-fashioned lamp, and beside it, his Beretta lay within easy reach. Across the bottom of the bed, Ripley lay stretched out on her back, sleeping peacefully. He estimated that it was between three and four a.m. On bare feet, in boxer shorts, he walked to the kitchen and opened the fridge to pour himself cool water. He listened, hearing only the distant sounds of the ocean.

Returning to the bedroom, he brought a clock radio from the kitchen countertop. Ripley was awake now and staring at him. Her tail wagged.

'Can't sleep either, huh?'

He placed the little radio on the bedside table beside the lamp, then tuned it to the same station he had found in the car. He was hoping to hear some quiet tracks that might lull him back toward sleep and was rewarded with a song Charlie J had called *No Stars* by Rebecca Del Rio. He was drifting to sleep once more when Charlie J's voice purred across the airwaves. *If you're awake, welcome to the late session, where we play only the best music with fewer interruptions. At this time of the night, I accept requests, but that doesn't mean you creeps out there can just call me up to get off.*

Seb smiled and wondered if Charlie J had received a few of *those* types of calls. If she looked anything like her voice, she would look amazing. He drifted back to sleep as the next set of songs mingled with the sounds of the wind in the trees.

But then Charlie received a request from a caller, and she must have forgotten to turn off the microphone that broadcast the conversation.

'Listen, bitch, if I find you, you're fucking dead!' snarled the voice.

The song was trailing off when Charlie J replied, 'You can't tell me what to do, asshole.'

Seb's eyes snapped open. Ripley growled.

The caller, voice dripping anger, said, 'If you think you can get away with saying anything you like about us, think again.'

Maybe, just maybe, Seb thought, Charlie J had left the microphone on, deliberately transmitting the conversation publicly to everyone.

'Do you have a request?' Charlie said. 'Everyone is waiting to hear what you want.'

The caller must have realised he was being telecast over the radio. 'Fuck!' There was a pause, then, instead of hanging up, he doubled down on the vitriol. 'I'm going to rip your guts out, you slut.'

Click. Charlie J hung up on the caller. She now paused, taking time to compose herself. Seb pictured her, taking some deep breaths. He sat up, listening.

Then her voice came back, and it was as if nothing had happened. *You heard it right here, folks. He's gonna rip my guts out.* The music started, and the tracks kept coming, one after the other. Charlie J was in no mood for any more calls. Seb lay, wondering what had triggered the creep's call. What had the guy said? *If you think you can get away with saying anything you like about us, think again.*

Seb rolled over and fell asleep. His dreams were of Charlie J, but she looked like the woman at the pizza shop – Jaz. Then she looked like Officer Benson. He had the strangest dreams, one after the other. But his final dream left him feeling cold, of Angel, riding along a darkened street, looking back at him from the back of a motorcycle, her face sad, not seeming to recognise him when he called her name. Then she was gone, disappearing into a bank of mist. He called her name, but she didn't answer.

Ripley was licking at his face to wake him as sunlight streamed into the room. His head ached slightly where he had been clipped in the brawl the night before, and his mouth felt ashy. More than anything, he needed to pee.

In the bathroom, urinating, he became aware of knocking on the front door. By the time he'd finished, the knocking became a banging, which increased in volume and tempo.

When he eventually arrived, he opened the door a crack to see who it was. Officer Benson was close by, and another officer – this one male, very tall, name tag *Webster* – stood back from the door, leaning casually against the railing of the front porch.

'I'd like you to step outside, Mr Straeker,' said Benson, her eyes hidden behind those mirrored aviators she favoured.

'I bet you would,' muttered Seb, opening the door and ambling out onto the porch, his boxers hitched to one side, scratching his unshaved face. 'What's this about?'

Benson paused, looking him up and down, 'Did we wake you?'

'What gave that away?' Seb rubbed his eyes with the back of his hand.

Benson smiled, casually pushing her aviators to the tip of her nose. Her appreciative gaze wandered to Seb's flat stomach.

Webster said, 'We had an incident at the Crab Shack last night, Mr Straeker.' He paused, looking at him for a reaction. Seb said nothing. Then he continued, 'There was some kind of... altercation. Would you like to tell us what happened?'

Scratching his head, then rubbing sleep from his eyes, Seb said, 'I don't know what you're talking about. You must have the wrong guy.'

'You sure?' asked Webster. He had not moved, other than to fold muscular brown arms in front of his chest. 'The witnesses say it was some guy that was new in town, some guy they had not seen before, and the description sounded a lot like you.'

Seb's eyes narrowed. He placed his hand in his chin with mock, exaggerated thought. 'Well, I ate pizza last night, and then I came home. I assure you that if I had some altercation, I would recall that.'

'So, you were in town last night?' asked Webster.

Ripley came trotting out, wagging her tail.

Benson looked at the dog and smiled. 'Oh, aren't you a cutie.'

Seb, feeling the breeze off the ocean, now creeping inside his boxer shorts, asked, 'Is that all? I just woke up and I have things to do. Yeah, I have to...'

Webster continued, 'Because if it was you that got in that fight with those bikers, you should know that they won't let it go. Nope, they *will* come looking for you until they find you.'

'Not that it was me, or anything, but isn't that why we have you? I mean, it's up to you to protect people like me.' Seb added a belated smile.

'Yes, Mr Straeker, it is up to us to protect and serve. That's why we are here now.'

'I thought you might be here to arrest me.'

'Not this time,' said Webster. 'No – this time you get one warning, and one only.'

Benson said, 'Maybe we could look at the bikers. They beat up some boys pretty bad last night too.' She looked at Webster, and Seb could see that the comment was not appreciated.

'Well... you *could* arrest them instead,' said Seb, his smile evaporating. 'I mean, it sounds like *they* broke the law.'

Webster came closer and stood just a few inches from Seb, peering down. 'Don't get smart, Mr Straeker. There is a... balance in this town right now that we enjoy.'

Benson edged forward and Seb thought that she might try to get between them. Then the tall cop continued, 'It would be far easier for us to arrest you and remove you from harm's way than to try and arrest a whole motorcycle club.'

Seb nodded. 'Motorcycle *club*, is it? I would have said motorcycle *gang*.'

Webster's hands were now on his hips, and he faced Seb squarely. 'What is it, exactly, that you do, Straeker? I mean, what are you doing in the Cove? Clearly, you have no occupation.'

Seb shrugged, noting that the polite 'mister' had been dropped.

Webster continued, 'If I was to look at you closely, do a background check, what would I find?'

Seb said nothing, but he gave the barest shake of his head.

Webster stared at Seb for a long time. 'You listen hard to what we are saying, Straeker.' Webster left the porch and strode toward his cruiser.

Benson followed her colleague but stopped at the foot of the porch steps. Quietly she said, 'Maybe you should leave town.'

Closing the door, Seb watched through the window as the police cruiser made a U-turn and disappeared up the driveway.

Later, Seb made breakfast, every now and then pausing to look at the front driveway. Lobbing a couple of bacon rashers to Ripley, he wondered if he should consider a fallback position, somewhere to lay low if he lost control of the situation. The rental advertisement had mentioned something about *additional workspaces set on acres of land*. Glancing out the kitchen window at the rear of the property, he couldn't see much. Just a clothesline and lots of trees. Maybe the advertisement had been wrong.

Seb investigated the rear of the property. The lawn needed mowing, and he could see a thick line of trees marking the beginning of a forest. Walking out of the sunlight, he ducked his head and stepped into the edge of the tree line. There was no path, and Seb simply walked in a straight line from the house. Ripley stayed near, her snout twitching, tail swishing. The dog went forward at a quick trot, and he hurried to keep up. 'Ripley – wait!' But the dog seemed to have already explored the land around the house and seemed to know where she was going. He lost sight of her through the shrubs.

'Hey, girl, where are you?'

The dog suddenly reappeared, her tail wagging. Then she was away again and Seb slipped through the same bushes. He followed a track that led away on a steady angle up the hill. Dappled light made its way through to leaf litter and ferns. After a few minutes, having walked another hundred yards, the trail ended in a small clearing. At one side lay an old shack, half shrouded in trees, its roof covered in dead leaves. The door squeaked open and he pushed his way through a spider web. Inside, the bare floorboards, sagging in places, groaned as he walked on them. Around the dim room, old tools sat on brackets – axes, shears, a hammer and all manner of jars of screws and nails.

He looked around for something that could illuminate the space. There, on a bench, he spied an oil lamp. Now, he just needed some matches or a lighter. But there was nothing. His eyes adjusted slowly, discovering a room set out more like a man cave than a garden or work shed. On one side of the room, he saw a chair and a coffee table with a radio on it. 'This isn't bad, hey, girl?' Ripley brushed against his leg and lay in the middle of the floor on a dusty, faded rug. 'Yeah, this could be useful.'

Returning to the bungalow, he gathered a few things. Not having a backpack, he placed an overnight bag on the bed and threw in some spare clothes. In the kitchen, he located a box of matches and a few tins of various foods, and after a pause, a can-opener. He looked at Ripley, who had jumped up on a chair and was looking at him curiously. 'Let's hope it doesn't come to this,' he said.

He returned to the shed, this time lighting the lantern and having a better look around. There was a window at the rear, covered in a layer of caked-on dust. He placed the bag on the floor in the middle of the room. At one side, under a pile of empty wooden motor oil boxes, there was a small wood heater, its flume disappearing out the side wall. 'No bed,' he grunted as he began moving the crates to one side so that he could get to the wood heater. Satisfied that they could stay in the shed if needed, he wondered now what to do with the Camaro. If the bikers came, not finding him in the house, they would likely trash the car. He needed to move it somewhere or risk losing it.

Snap.

Outside, he heard a stick break. It was unmistakable. He pulled his Beretta, stepped to the window and peered out. Two kids, each around fifteen years old, were stepping around the shed, talking in low voices. The girl, a blonde, gave a nervous giggle. He returned the handgun to his belt and walked outside.

'Well, what do we have here?' asked Seb.

'Shit,' said the boy. He looked at Seb from beneath a mop of black hair that fell over his eyes.

The pair froze. Seb spoke into the silence. 'Any reason you are on my land?'

The boy looked surprised. 'Your land? This is the Spiegel's place. I could ask you the same.'

Seb smiled. The kid was fast to find his tongue, and although the girl elbowed him in the side, he pushed out his chest and lifted his chin so that Seb was eye to eye.

'Where the hell did you come from?' Seb looked out at the heavily wooded area around them.

The kids glanced at each other. Then the girl said, 'Mister, there are tracks all over these hills. Over there'—she pointed over her shoulder, further into the woods—'is a track that takes you all the way from the back of the Tanner's place to the Ocean Road.' Again, she pointed, past the bungalow.

Seb followed her gaze, then relaxed. 'You gave me a fright is all,' he admitted. Then Ripley, sensing everything was okay, came trotting out of the shed, wagging her tail. The girl fell to her knees, delighted at the new arrival, her hands rubbing the dog's ears. They seemed to be saying hello again rather than meeting for the first time, thought Seb.

'This is Ripley. She likes you. I'm Seb, by the way.'

The girl smiled, 'I'm Gab, and this is Kelt.'

'There are trails all over these hills, you say?' asked Seb.

'All over,' confirmed Kelt.

Sensing the kids wanted to leave, Seb backed away, allowing the pair to depart. He watched as they continued down past the bungalow, heading, Seb thought, for the bay itself. These kids were locals, born and bred, and obviously knew all the trails. They also expected to be allowed to trespass on private property.

Seb made one more trip from the house to the shed, carrying a few items that might make a stay in the shed more comfortable. The last thing he did was hang a blanket over the window, making it impossible to look inside. Satisfied that he had a decent place to hide out if needed, he returned to the bungalow.

CHAPTER 7

az overslept. She discovered that her next dining option would be brunch, so she took her backpack with her laptop stowed inside. Three more texts had come from her boss, Harvey, enquiring politely about her vacation, which she ignored.

She found a café-bookshop located in an old warehouse near the docks, along a narrow alleyway where the bricks had been painted over to try and blot out graffiti. She liked books as well as coffee, and the two together were her idea of heaven.

In the glow of her laptop screen, she reviewed, one by one, the faces of the twelve she considered victims, the ones never located. She paused at one – the youngest of them – Rhys Prescott, a twelve-year-old boy, snatched from his bedroom. The age and the circumstances of the abduction, or disappearance, depending on who you spoke to, had caused more than a stir in the community. The boy was from a town less than seventy miles away, south along the coast from Crabtree Cove. The local cops there decided that without a body, the boy may have just up and run. The Prescott parents were never convinced. That was seven years ago. To this day, they had not changed his room. He would be nineteen now, if he were alive. They still placed photos in local papers, asking people to contact them if they had information. It was desperate, thought Jaz. But she knew she would probably do the same thing.

Her thoughts were interrupted when a boy of around fifteen returned, carrying a coffee. He set it down in front of Jaz with a smile. Jaz closed the laptop to prevent him from seeing what she had been viewing.

'Thanks.'

'You're welcome, ma'am,' he replied.

'Do you have a section on local history?' she asked him.

'Huh?'

'I am looking for books on your town. You know, most towns keep some old books around that talk about the town's history.'

'No, I really couldn't say.' When he straightened, he said, 'Maybe check the library.'

Leaving the café-bookstore, moving back up the hill away from the docks, she walked east toward the edge of town. She arrived at the town's municipal buildings, made up by the courthouse, the local jail, the police station and the town hall. It was in the town hall that she located the public library, on the second floor.

'Can I help you, miss?' The voice from behind the counter came from a very short man. His eyes seemed large for his face, but it could have been the thick lenses in the glasses.

'I'm interested in your local history section.'

The librarian looked at her blankly for a moment. 'Who are you?'

'Is that relevant?'

'I am sorry. I've never met you before. I've never seen you around town.'

Jaz gave him a long, cool look. 'I'm doing a little research.'

'About the Cove?' He looked amused. 'Nothing ever happens here. What are you looking for exactly?'

Jaz smiled, though her eyes narrowed. 'Maybe I'll know when I see it.'

'I see,' he said.

'Do you?' she asked.

He smiled now and pointed at the far corner of the room, past rows of books. 'We have a small section, written by local historians. It's over there.' He disappeared into a back office.

Passing along dusty shelves, she found the books to be decades old, mainly out of date and largely untouched. The few she found on the history of the town were old too. Flipping through them, she found black-and-white photos of the main street with captions under them. It was all early settlers, standing and sitting around in groups — bearded men, women in white dresses holding babies or camisoles, but nothing of substance. Jaz was not really sure what she expected to see, but it was disappointing.

Then she found a single PC, sitting on a desk in the corner. When it booted up, she explored the local hard drive, which contained folders on a range of topics including 'cooking and food', 'politics and religion' and 'health and medicine.' It seemed that while the library had not purchased many hard-cover books in recent years, it had managed to collect a number of electronic publications.

Glancing up, she found the librarian watching her. He quickly looked away when Jaz lifted her gaze toward him. *Nosey little fucker*, Jaz breathed to herself.

There was a folder called 'Crabtree Cove'. Opening it, to her satisfaction, she located a subfolder called 'Newspaper Archive'. The archive was extensive, covering the town's one paper — *The Cove Tribune*. The collection went back to the 1930s, with someone having painstakingly copied hundreds, if not thousands, of newspaper images. She skipped to the folder containing newspapers from the eighties, deciding to begin her browsing in that decade. She began flicking through, her eyes rapidly scanning. Then she opened the next date, and the one after.

Hours went by as she trawled the archive, not actually knowing what she was expecting to find.

Using the search terms *Dagon's Riders* and *motorcycle*, she received some hits.

The few newspaper articles returned in the search about the gang were good news stories. Carefully contrived, the articles showed bikers visiting sick kids with toys, local gang members trading leather jackets for fishing rods, smiling in black-and-white photos outside of local diners, or simply posing with their bikes. Each story was short and meant little. But it was the underlying message that was consistent – *these guys are our friends.*

Returning to her methodical browsing, she noticed that several dates were missing from the collection. For such a meticulously collated archive, it was strange that some editions were gone, as if on those dates the newspaper simply didn't bother to publish. Clearly, that must be wrong. She made a note of the missing edition dates, though it meant nothing specific to her enquiries. Jaz had a habit, formed over years of collecting information, to note anomalies.

One of the last editions of the paper showed a front-page article welcoming the new police chief. The article was short and showed a large photograph of a woman in her fifties, posing with several police officers.

The piece espoused Donna O'Brien's experience as a local law officer in several other counties. It discussed her appointment by the town council, who said they were delighted that she had accepted the role. Jaz skipped several paragraphs to where the chief talked about her plans for the position and her background. It was all very straightforward, thought Jaz. The last paragraph caught her eye though. The journalist had said, *Many local residents are hoping that O'Brien's appointment will breathe new life into the now cold investigation of the youth, Eric Winters, found deceased nearly two years ago...*

Jaz hadn't seen anything about any missing kid. That would have been front-page news. Jaz calculated that the paper (five years old) was referring to events from two years before that. That put this kid's death at seven years prior. She consulted her notes. The papers from February 26th through to March 15th, exactly seven years ago, were not in the archive. That *was* odd. Now, she opened the folder again and double-checked the archive. The newspaper editions for that period were definitely missing. She opened the next available record, the March 16th edition, and entered new keyword terms for *Eric Winters*. Nothing came back for the search. She sat, thinking, brow furrowed.

The librarian called to her, 'Everything alright?'

'You're missing some editions,' replied Jaz.

'Are you sure?'

'Quite certain.' Jaz noted down the boy's name in her laptop, and his age at the time he was killed.

'We're closing now,' called the librarian. The lights switched off and the library became dim. Jaz gathered her things and headed for the exit.

As she left the town hall, Jaz was surprised to discover that the sun was nearly setting. Not wanting to be outside in the cold evening air, Jaz hurried.

When she arrived back at her lodgings, the old landlord, Clem, was sitting on the front steps of the apartment block. He was smoking a cigar, taking in the air. He had on another of his loud Hawaiian flowery shirts, clearly not feeling the chill.

'Evening,' said Jaz as she passed him.

He looked surprised that she remembered his name. 'Good evening...'

'Jaz.'

'Jaz,' repeated Clem. 'I'm getting forgetful as I get older,' he muttered.

'It's okay.' Jaz sat beside the old guy, smelling the sweet scent of cigar tobacco mingled with a sharp-smelling cheap aftershave. He looked surprised. 'have you heard of a boy called Eric Winters?'

Clem's face went still, his eyes betraying his answer. 'No... why do you ask?'

'Are you certain? He died, around seven years ago.'

The old man nodded slightly, as if his memory was slowly returning. 'I'm not sure where you would have heard about him.' He looked displeased that the subject had been raised.

'So, you do know about him. What happened?'

Clem hesitated. 'Well, no one really knows. I would rather not talk about it. It was a bad time. He had an accident.'

'An accident? But there was some kind of criminal investigation,' said Jaz.

'Was there?' Clem turned away from her and blew out a long trail of smoke. In that moment, Jaz realised that he had no intention of saying anything more. She stood and walked back inside, leaving the old man to his thoughts.

In her room, she locked the door, slid the chain into place and took out her laptop.

She switched on the old TV on, dispelling the silence within the room. A western that appeared to be made sometime in the 1950s was showing. Sitting in the armchair, she watched as the cavalry charged across a dusty plain, firing six-shooters. For some reason, the picture was a little fuzzy. Having watched some TV the night before, she didn't understand why the reception was bad. She stood and adjusted the rabbit-ear antenna until the image on the screen sharpened.

The movie kinda sucked though, and she was distracted. Who was Eric Winters and why did the incident get removed from the library's archive? Why did his name, or the thought of what happened to him, still upset some people?

*

As the sun dipped below the horizon, Seb moved his car, driving the Camaro into the tree line behind the house. Darkness fell. He left all the lights off inside the house, bar one – a lamp, which illuminated the kitchen in a soft glow. As he stabbed the chops, flipping them over to sizzle in the pan, he considered the situation.

Sooner or later, the Dagon's Riders would rock up – maybe tonight, maybe tomorrow or the day after. His plan, *half-baked*, but the only one he had, was to avoid them but then follow them back the way they came, back to their clubhouse or wherever they were staying. For the plan to work, he needed them to find him. Perhaps the bouncer at the Crab Shack would do as asked and send them to find Seb.

The approach along the coast road was easier to observe when the house remained in darkness. Headlight beams would be seen for a mile or more and the sound of engines would carry easily if he left the TV off.

But Seb wanted the radio on. Keeping the volume low, he discovered that his favourite radio host – Charlie J – was not yet on the air. Instead, a guy with a raspy voice was cranking out some old rock tunes from the sixties and seventies. Seb took out the Beretta and sat it on the bench. Humming along to *Take It Easy* by The Eagles, he served up two plates, then sat at the kitchen table.

Ripley sat across from him, and as soon as he put the plate in front of her, she began to eat, food dropping on the table and spilling on the floor.

'You're disgusting, you know that?'

After dinner, his thoughts once more turned to Angel. He bet that she was still running with the gang. Blown along by circumstance, never quite in control, but ultimately a survivor, he hoped his sister would do what was needed to stay safe.

He piled the dishes and the pan in the sink and poured a bourbon into a glass. Settling down in the front living room, the house in near darkness, cradling the glass with the radio quietly playing in the background, it wasn't long before Charlie J's smooth voice came over the air.

Good evening, Crabtree Cove. It's Charlie, and do I have a playlist for you tonight…

Seb smiled simply because he liked listening to her voice. She was steamy and sensual. *God, I need to get laid*, he thought. He thought first about Jaz, her exotic good looks and easy manner, but then returned to Benson, her smoky, direct stare and *the way she moved.*

A few songs played before Charlie re-joined her listeners. *This next track is for our new friend in town, the one who likes to break pool sticks. If you're listening... you know who you are.*

The song that came on the waves began and Seb immediately recognised the song *Private Eyes* by Hall and Oates. He listened to the tune, joining the chorus as it began.

Had word gotten around town about the bar-fight? Then there was the song choice – *Private Eyes*. Was he being watched? He thought of the cop, Guyatt, parked outside, down the road, in the middle of the night, watching the bungalow just a couple of nights ago.

The song ended and Seb stood near the radio so that he could clearly hear Charlie J. *For those of you night owls, you're listening to Charlie J, rocking it until midnight.*

Seb went and showered, then changed into his second pair of jeans. Walking by the kitchen, he scooped up the Beretta, the weight of the handgun in his palm reassuringly familiar. He checked the time – it was 11:17. He wanted to go to bed, but he felt too awake. He put on a t-shirt, one of his army-green ones, and some sneakers. Pouring another bourbon, he settled down in the lounge chair, waiting for his favourite radio host to talk to him again. Somehow, he felt that the night was not yet done with him.

CHAPTER 8

Clyde Miller stubbed out a cigarette, not caring that no more than three feet away from him, beside the bowser pump, a sign said *STRICTLY NO SMOKING WHILE PUMPING GAS.* The area around the road was dead flat for as far as he could see, both north and south along the interstate. To the west, in the distance, across a rugged plain, was a line of sharp hills. A road just past the truck-stop branched off in that direction. The exit had a sign beside it, lit by an old streetlight. He could make out the faded painted cartoon-like drawings of a man fishing, kids swimming and beside them, a pin-up style woman in faded yellow bikinis, leaning suggestively to one side. It said: *23 miles to Crabtree Cove. Come and play.*

Glancing inside the diner, Clyde noticed a few long-haul truckers eating a late-night meal and talking to a pair of waitresses in uniforms, and hairdos that belonged in a 1950s sitcom. He finished pumping the gas and moved his car into a parking bay. No sooner had he switched off the ignition before a hooker tapped her knuckles on the glass. Clyde had seen her approach in the rear-view mirror moments before, and so was not surprised when her heavily made-up face leant close to the glass.

'Not interested, honey,' he said before she said a word.

He watched her slink away and then got out and locked the door to the black Chevrolet Malibu. The gas station doubled as truck stop, with a good-sized diner. Everything was styled in a retro way, or maybe it was simply run down, not having been updated since the pace had been built. The tables were all edged in polished

52

chrome, the chairs faded orange vinyl, with splits here and there. Clyde went to the counter and as he waited for service, lit another cigarette. The clock on the wall showed that it was around a quarter past midnight.

'Excuse me, sir, there's no smoking in here,' said the older waitress.

'I didn't know,' said Clyde.

The other waitress said nothing, but her eyes flicked up toward him and then away again. She was much younger, and still had the look of woman that could see a way out of her current existence. Her hair was pinned back and she carried herself in an upright kind of way.

Clyde took a long pull on the cigarette. As he exhaled smoke, he said, 'I'd like a coffee.'

The older waitress glanced at the truckers. There was three of them, all lined up along the counter, putting serious strain on their stools. Clyde followed her gaze, noting the plaid shirts, the jeans that showed too much bum-crack, and the close attention paid to their plates. They didn't even look up.

'There's no smoking in here,' repeated the older waitress, her eyes hardening.

'Does anyone in here tonight care if I smoke?' said Clyde, turning slightly to look at the other men in the diner.

Clyde was built like a prize fighter. He had a tattoo of a rattlesnake rearing out from the top of his white, pressed, business shirt, along the top of his neck toward his hairline. He wore a deadpan expression that hardly ever changed. The truckers seemed to instinctively avoid his gaze. No one said a word.

The older waitress must have seen something in Clyde's eyes, for she shut her mouth and poured the coffee. The young waitress went to the kitchen, and Clyde lost sight of her. The three truckers continued to avert their gaze and just kept silently shovelling in the bacon, sausages, grits and beans that were piled up on the over-sized plates.

Clyde sipped the coffee and smoked his cigarette. 'Any of you fellas ever go into Crabtree Cove?' he said to no one in particular.

A bearded guy, the one closest to him, said without turning. 'Ahh, nope. I stick to the interstate.'

The other two nodded in agreement.

Clyde believed them. 'I have to go there.'

The waitress and the three truckers said nothing. They didn't want to know why he had to go there. But when the younger waitress emerged from the kitchen, carrying a fresh pot of coffee in a glass urn, she said, 'I think you will like it,' and smiled.

Clyde would have smiled back, but he did not want to frighten her. She seemed like a reasonable kid. 'What's it like?'

'You never been there?' she said, ignoring the flashing eyes of the older waitress.

'No,' said Clyde. 'I take it you have.'

'Yeah, it's nice,' she said. 'What do you want to know? I used to live there.'

'Why is it nice?' Clyde asked her.

'I don't know,' she said, refilling his cup. 'Now I think about it, it is hard to say. The Cove is peaceful, and there is a pier. The people are friendly... mainly. There are lots of nature walks through the woods. There are streams and lakes, and it's real pretty...' She trailed off because of the intense way Clyde was staring at her.

Clyde's hand suddenly reached out and took her wrist, making the older waitress gasp. Before the young waitress could pull away, he pressed a hundred dollars into her palm, closing her fingers around the money. He smiled. 'That's for the coffee, and the gas.' He abruptly walked out to the Chevy.

Clyde swung the car toward the exit and followed a straight road toward Crabtree Cove, and the line of hills that slowly grew through the windshield.

About halfway across the plain, he crossed a train level-crossing, the tyres making a thump as he drove over the rails. He glanced about as he drove, the road still dead-straight. Low tufts of grass and only an occasional stunted tree gave the landscape a desolate edge. He noticed in the rear-view mirror some headlights. They were far off, perhaps as far as the gas station he just stopped at, near the exit from the interstate.

The moon appeared from behind some drifting clouds, casting the land in silver. In the distance, twin, glittering eyes of several coyotes appeared. They watched as his car sped passed them. In his rear-view mirror, the headlights had gained. Then Clyde realised that they were motorcycle headlights, riding in a tight cluster and moving fast.

Before long, the road was tilting upward, and he was climbing into hills. Almost immediately, he was driving through woods, swerving around hairpin turns. From behind, he could hear the motorcycles as they neared him. Rounding a bend, he spied a driveway into a private property. Slowing down, he pulled into it, killing the lights.

Moments later, the three motorbikes zipped past, throttling and howling as they climbed higher up the hilly road. He waited. Satisfied that he was alone, he took his phone from the console and opened the last text message. The attached photo was an old one, and the guy could look a different now. It showed a handsome, middle-aged man, hair just starting to gray, neat beard, reclining on a deckchair by a pool in yellow swimming shorts. Draped around and over him, three gorgeous girls, barely dressed in bikinis held cocktails, and smiled for the camera. Under the photo, the words – *his house in Crabtree Cove.*

The guy's name was Stirling McTaggart. He was a bigwig in the area, a local mafia man some might have called him. He had made deals with the wrong people, or something like that. He flicked through some more pictures, showing McTaggart with some guys on motorcycles. One of them, a tall Nordic-looking guy looked to be at least 6'5". Clyde was told that in McTaggart's arsenal was a gang of motorheads calling themselves Dagon's Riders. He had no time for these guys. He wasn't even sure he respected them enough to be wary of them. But even he understood that if you came up against enough guys in one place, you could soon get in trouble.

He deleted the pictures from the phone, and switched on his motor and lights before turning back onto the road toward the township. He had no idea where to find McTaggart. The intel suggested he resided in a mansion in the hills near the town somewhere. That was all. The road switched back and forward, and soon he had a view of the ocean. In the late night, under moonlight, the sea seemed bleak. He could make out, below the cliffs, white breakers smashing onto rocks. Glancing at his phone, it showed just one bar for reception. This town really was the back of nowhere.

Clyde coasted into the grid pattern streets of Crabtree Cove. Nothing moved. It was now after two a.m. and the town seemed to slumber. He drove down the main street, under streetlights that cast pools of yellow light amongst the deeper, larger pools of darkness.

Closer to the dock area, a group of goths stood near a narrow doorway in-between shopfront which may have been the entrance to a nightclub. As he neared, a neon sign showed *the Underground*. He could just make out the distant thump of bass, reverberating from a basement. Stark white faces with black lipstick turned and stared at him as he coasted past. Their accusing eyes reminded him of faces looking up from the bottom of freshly dug graves.

'Where's the funeral?' he called. He smiled, but their expressions remained emotionless.

Selecting a park near the pier, away from any ambient light from the town, he switched off the motor. As salt air washed over him, he breathed deeply. The tide was in, dark water slapped audibly around the pylons. Nothing to worry about, he adjusted the seat so that it lay all the way back. Within minutes of closing his eyes, Clyde was asleep.

*

Seb had drifted to sleep, listening to the calming, soulful voice of Charlie J. With a start, he came awake, his military training kicking in. In the distance, but closing, motorcycles, more than he expected. The Beretta sat under his feet where he sat in the armchair, having slipped to the floor. It took a moment to locate it. Ripley was sitting in the middle of the floor, her gaze on him, ears pricked forward. 'Let's go,' he said, and headed for the door.

The dog followed immediately, aware it seemed of the coming danger. Seb exited through the kitchen via the back door and locked it behind him. 'Holy shit,' he said to the dog as they hurried across the yard, 'can you believe these assholes.'

Seb and Ripley stopped a few yards in under the trees, hidden in darkness, and waited. Revving engines filled the night, and Ripley cowered slightly before Seb put his hand on the back of her head. 'It's okay, girl,' he soothed, though his voice was inaudible above the engines. He could see the headlights of several bikes, high beams, shining into the house, as the riders continued to rev the engines.

Three men, nothing more than dark silhouettes at first then clearly visible as they moved into the moonlight, strode to the back of the house, seeking to block any chance of escape. Their leather vests with grinning skull motifs left him in no doubt as to who they were. At the back door, they waited, crouched on either side. Seb thought he could see one of them holding something – a bat, crowbar or a sawn-off shotgun.

The bikes continued revving for a good minute before falling silent. Had they thought he would panic, and attempt escape out the back door? Not seeing any lights come on in the bungalow, they decided to go in and bring him out from wherever he was cowering.

Inside, lights flicked on and Ripley growled before Seb again reassured her with a rub behind her ears. 'Steady, girl,' he breathed.

He heard crashing, things breaking, and he wondered what might be left unbroken inside as the gang went from room to room. Every light in the house was on now, and a golden glow cast into the yard beyond. Seb watched now, able to easily see every biker in each room. A loud argument began as they failed to locate him.

The three at the rear of the house had gone inside too and left the backdoor wide open. Then a huge guy, with shoulder-length, almost white hair, came and stood at the back door, looking out at the yard, his gaze slowly wandering around. It was uncanny, for Seb believed the guy was staring at them.

In Afghanistan, during night operations, Seb often used infrared goggles. Only with that sort of kit could the giant blond have seen Seb. His throat dry, Seb inched back further into the safety of the darkness under the trees.

There must have been close to twenty gang members in the house. His plan to follow them suddenly seemed foolhardy. He had underestimated their reaction. He looked for Angel, but he didn't see her and although he glimpsed a female or two in their ranks, they bore no resemblance to his sister.

When he retreated another ten yards, Seb slowly and carefully picked his way toward the shed where he had set up the hideaway. Ripley had left him quickly, glad to be away from the bungalow. Every now and then, Seb turned and watched the path he had followed. The ambient light from the bungalow was gone. He had no idea what the gang was now doing, or if they had left the house, but he felt that to stay close to the house was to invite disaster.

Arriving at the shed, cloaked in utter darkness, Seb found Ripley already inside, lying on her belly. He entered and quietly shut the door. If the shed had been hard to locate in daylight, at night, it would be all but impossible to find. He settled down on the floor and listened. He heard nothing – no sound of footfalls on leaves or twigs, no voices, nothing at all seemed to carry to him in the night.

After a while, he heard the distant cacophony of around twenty motorcycles roaring away again into the night. He settled back on the rug, smelling the mustiness and lantern oil. Ripley curled in beside him, her side pressed up against him. 'We'll wait here.'

He looked at his watch. It was 3.21 a.m. He slowed his breathing, allowed his mind to empty, and then fell fast asleep, pretty certain that the night was now done with him.

CHAPTER 9

A tapping on the window near his face caused Clyde to come awake. It was barely dawn, and it took him a second or two to adjust his eyes, to blink away the blur. Officer Guyatt was standing nearby, staring in at him. Two police cars, one parked beside him, another behind, had hemmed him in. He brought his seat to an upright position, at the same time rolling the window down so he could talk to the officer.

Then a light shone in his face and he blinked. Guyatt reminded Clyde of a kid at school he used to bully. His wire-framed spectacles and weedy physique marked him as someone Clyde immediately dismissed as a lesser being. But the cop had his gun drawn, forcing Clyde to pay attention.

Two more cops, one on the other side of the car wandered up, looking nonchalant. Benson's hand never strayed far from her piece. She was standing nearby, listening.

Webster waited at the back of his car, parking Clyde in. He had his trunk lid up. Clyde knew they often stowed their shotguns in their trunks.

'What seems to be the problem... Officer'—he saw the name on the badge—'Guyatt.' Clyde said this only because he thought that's what they expected to hear.

'You can't sleep in your car, in the town limits,' said Guyatt.

'Well, I'm not sleeping now,' pointed out Clyde. He stretched his neck. Sleeping in a car was never comfortable.

Guyatt stared at the rattle-snake tattoo. 'Step out of the vehicle.

Place your hands on the door.' Clyde hesitated, then placed both hands on the open window frame.

Benson stepped in and opened the door as Guyatt trained the torch and his pistol on Clyde, who swung his legs around and exited the car.

'Turn around, and place your hands on the hood, sir. That's right, and spread your legs,' said Guyatt, kicking Clyde's legs further apart. Benson remained silent and walked around to the other side of Clyde's car, bent and looked inside. Webster suddenly came into Clyde's view, a shotgun in hand.

'I'd rather she patted me down,' said Clyde, his eyes on Benson, taking in the way her uniform hugged her compact, tight frame.

Webster was reading the plates, noting them down. Being a rental, Clyde had no problem with them checking them. 'I assure you the car is mine,' said Clyde.

'Did we ask you?' said Guyatt. He performed a quick search, patting Clyde down in a matter of a few seconds. He came away with Clyde's knife, which had been hidden in a sheath inside the left calf. 'Look what we have here.'

'I suppose you think I have a body in the trunk too,' said Clyde.

'Do you?' said Guyatt. 'Let's take a look. But you stay where you are.'

Clyde stayed in the position he had been placed. But he craned his neck to watch Benson open the trunk using the keys he had left inside the car on the console. She opened the trunk and came away with an overnight bag, which she placed on the ground. Then she went back and looked carefully inside the trunk.

'Nothing,' she said. 'Just a spare tyre.'

'Open the bag,' said Guyatt.

'We don't have cause…' began Benson.

'Webster, you do it,' said Guyatt.

The tall cop unzipped the overnight bag and rifled through it. 'Nothing here.'

'What the fuck are you doing?' said Clyde.

'You from Boston?' said Guyatt. 'I think I hear an accent.'

'No shit,' responded Clyde. This earnt him a solid blow in the ribs. It was a good hit, but Clyde rode it with a grunt. He had taken worse, much, much worse.

'Put your hands behind your back,' said Guyatt.

'I hope you know what you are doing here,' said Clyde, smiling. 'Sleeping in your car is not a big deal, right?'

'Shall we add *resist arrest* to the charges? Put your fuckin' hands behind your back – now!' Guyatt ordered.

Clyde put his hands behind his back and felt cuffs click into place. They felt tighter than he remembered. Benson gave a small shake of her head as she folded her arms, and leant against the car, mouth tight. As Clyde was escorted away, Benson watched with curious eyes.

*

Seb woke, rolled to his side and found Ripley there. She looked at him, like she needed to pee. Letting her out of the shed, he followed the dog out and found the morning dim and grey. Low, pregnant clouds hovered close to the tops of the trees. He stalked back toward the bungalow, wondering what he would find. As he neared the tree line, he was relieved to see that the house had not been torched. He crouched, putting his hand on the dog's back. 'Stay!'

Seb edged around the perimeter, coming to his Camaro. Inspecting the vehicle, he found it untouched. Taking a deep breath, he walked directly toward the house, crossing the yard as quietly as he could, Beretta in a two-hand grip. He sidled up to the edge of the house below the kitchen window and peered inside.

Entering the house through the kitchen, gun up, he cleared the room – left and right. No movement. The TV lay smashed on its side, lounge chairs were broken, the fridge was pulled over and its contents had been spilled all over the floor.

Someone had taken a dump on the loungeroom floor. He walked into the bedroom and found the sheets in tatters, strewn across the floor. He stalked back to the lounge and crept up to the window facing the porch. Seb peered, his eye on the corner of the frame. Out front, parked in the trees beside the driveway were two bikes. A pair of booted feet stuck out from the base of a tree where someone was reclining, facing the road. He'd seen one guy, but two bikes. So there was at least one more biker somewhere close. He slowly backtracked through the house to back door. He peered out the back. Ripley waited for him in the trees, her ears pricked forward.

Then he heard the toilet flush. 'Hey, do you think this guy will show?' the voice was pitched for someone in the house.

Seb stepped from around the corner and the biker's eyes widened. Seb landed a punch, the startled eyes in a hairy face taking the full force in the nose. His head snapped back, he stumbled, his half-buckled trousers going down around his knees. Seb followed quickly, caught the guy with a knee in the jaw as the biker was about to fall on his ass. He landed, fully stretched out, his pants around his ankles, already out cold.

Seb resisted the instinct to depart, instead peering out the window toward the front. The other guy was still there, half asleep, probably wishing he had a morning coffee and a cigarette.

Seb considered going out there, ambushing the guy, but he couldn't see where that would lead. He turned back and went to the laid-out biker, checking his pulse to make sure he was breathing. Then he rifled his pockets, found a few bucks, took them and stuffed them in his own pocket. The jacket had a badge. It said Dagon's Riders. In the jacket pocket, he found an old, cheap-looking cell phone. This could be useful, thought Seb, taking it. If Jaz could use the phone to maybe trace where this guy had been, he could perhaps get a line on where the gang was hiding out.

Then he considered, just for a moment, calling the cops and

asking for Officer Benson. He went to pick up the phone off the wall, but found it in about six pieces, lying under the fridge.

He pulled the biker's cell, began to dial, then stopped. The image of Officer Guyatt, standing out front, leaning against the police cruiser with a cigarette gave Seb pause. If the bouncer at the Crab Shack had not given the gang his whereabouts, as he'd requested, and instead kept such information to himself – then there was every chance that a cop had tipped them off. He thought then of Webster, the tall cop, leaning on the porch rail, drilling him for information, perhaps looking for an excuse to arrest him.

Seb left the house. He disappeared into the tree line, striding deeper into the woods, Ripley trotting at his side. By his calculation, he could walk to town in an almost straight line over a period of perhaps eight or ten hours, finding enough fresh water along the way to make the exercise possible.

No one would look for him in the forest, and when he made it out the other side, he would find Jaz, hand over the biker's phone, and ask her to make enquiries about where it had been used. His plan to track the bikers to their lair remained, but now he would approach them without them even knowing he was coming.

*

When Jaz woke, she wandered down to Lucille's diner for breakfast, laptop stowed in her backpack. She grabbed a window seat in a booth, then ordered coffee and breakfast. She was able to access the internet and within seconds was bringing up search results for *Eric Winters* and *Crabtree Cove*. Several of the links were either old, or dead, but she found a result that gave her some more information.

The dates from the newspaper more or less coincided with the dates in her notes. The article showed a school photo, of a kid smiling at the camera. He looked happy. There was a second photo, taken from a distance, showing two cops standing near a body, partially covered by a tarpaulin. In the corner of the photo, Jaz could make out the edge of a railway track. She recalled passing a railway line some miles inland, between the town and the interstate highway. What was the kid doing so far from town? She read the article.

> *Police have confirmed that the body of a teenage boy, located on a remote section of rail, was that of Eric Winters. Eric was last seen three days ago when his parents reported him missing to Crabtree Cove police. Sources close to the investigation have indicated that his injuries were consistent with having been hit by a train.*

Jaz took a sip of coffee, mumbled, 'What the fuck,' and continued reading.

'Everything okay?' asked Lucille, looking up from her crossword.

'Everything's fine,' replied Jaz.

'I hear you are staying in a room at the lodge. I know Clem quite well,' said Lucille.

Jazz looked away from the article. 'You do?'

Lucille's said, 'Clem and I go back.'

'Did Clem say anything about our conversation last night?'

'Yes, he said you mentioned Eric Winters.'

'So, what happened to the kid?' questioned Jaz.

Lucille took a long breath. 'I don't really know. He was one of three kids we lost that year. Two ran away and never showed up again. It was assumed they just took off.'

'Two kids run away and another is found dead?' said Jaz.

Lucille bobbed her head. 'Uh-huh, that's right. You know, Eric came in sometimes. I liked him.' Lucille paused, and Jaz could tell that she was recalling something. 'Eric's parents never stopped asking questions. They were never happy with the way it was handled.'

'How so?'

Lucille leant forward, her face near to Jaz. 'They said he was killed. And my husband, Joshua, he's always believed that boy was murdered.'

'Go on.'

'Crazy old fool. He thinks everything is a cover-up, like in the movies.' Lucille seemed embarrassed to discuss it further and went back to the crossword.

But Jaz, thinking of the missing newspaper editions, wasn't about to let the subject rest. 'What do you mean – *a cover-up?*'

Lucille came and sat across from Jaz. Lowering her voice, she said, 'Nothing really. Joshua talks nonsense half the time and twaddle the rest.'

Jaz became aware that Grace and the other waitress, Lola, were chatting instead of serving. They seemed excited by something. Jaz tried to listen in. She heard something about a fight and the Crab Shack.

Lucille looked up, also having overheard part of their conversation. 'We had a guy come in here a couple of days ago… or was it yesterday? Anyway, word around is that he got himself in a brawl at the dive down near the docks.'

'The Crab Shack?' asked Jaz.

'Yeah. It's a place where the bikers go sometimes. The girls here think it was a guy that Grace knows.'

Jaz looked at Grace, deep in an animated, whispered conversation with Lola.

'I don't think Grace actually *knows* Seb… not really,' said Jaz.

'Do you know him?' asked Lucille.

'If it's the guy I think it is, yeah – we met.'

'He beat some bikers up. Did a fine job of it,' said Lucille. 'I think he's… *bad news*, that one. How can you be in town barely two days and get in a fight? And to top it off – a fight with a gang. What's he thinking?' Lucille's disapproval was, however, delivered with a certain admiration.

'How indeed,' said Jaz, now aware that Seb had some obscure link to the bikers.

'Your friend… Seb. He should be careful,' said Lucille.

'Speaking of him. I wanted to ask you something related,' said Jaz.

'Shoot,' said Lucille.

Jaz considered, then abruptly opened her laptop and swung the screen to face Lucille. 'Do you recognise this woman?'

Lucille looked, noting the FBI insignia at the top of the screen. She looked at Jaz, eyes suddenly narrowed, hesitated, and then said, 'FBI?'

'The woman – look at her face.'

'Is she a criminal?'

'That's beside the point,' said Jaz. 'Look harder. Tell me if you have seen her around town.'

Lucille stared hard at the screen. 'She's a pretty girl... unusual looking.'

'Have you ever seen her around? Has she come in here? I bet nearly everyone comes here at some point,' said Jaz. 'I bet you see every new face. Is she familiar?'

'Is it important?' asked Lucille.

'It could be,' said Jaz.

Lucille looked at the photo for a long time, then shook her head slowly, her brow furrowed. 'I don't think I know her.'

Jaz looked disappointed.

'Do you mind if I show one of my girls that photo? I know it's a mugshot, but it could help. I recall Grace talking about some girl or other. Maybe it was her.'

Jaz sat back, deflated, but nodded.

'Grace, could you come over here?' called Lucille.

Grace approached, taking off her apron. Looking at Jaz, she frowned. 'I saw you at the pizza shop. You were with that guy.'

'Seb, his name is Seb. Don't worry about that now, Grace. I have something you need to look at.' Jaz turned the screen around and showed Grace the photo of Angel Straeker, taken at a police station around two years before. 'Do you know this woman?'

At first, Grace shook her head, as if just knowing someone who could be in trouble might somehow get her into trouble too. Then, under Lucille's watchful stare, the girl said, 'I met her a few times.' Grace noticed the name beneath the photo. 'It's her, she said her name was Angel.'

Jaz closed the laptop. 'Who was she with?'

Grace shrugged. 'I remember they were a strange bunch. All black leather, boots… big coats.'

Jaz felt something flutter in her stomach. She shifted in her seat. 'What else do you recall?'

'I met her in here one day and we chatted. Then I met her later, a couple of times.' The waitress looked uncomfortable.

Jaz said, 'What is it, Grace?'

'Her group was all guys, and then just her. It was kinda weird, I thought. One of them tried to get me to leave the nightclub, to go for a ride on his bike, out to the woods somewhere.' Grace was starting to recall the evening in greater clarity. 'Angel cornered me in the bathroom and made it clear that I shouldn't go with them.'

Jaz leant forward. 'Go on.'

'Not much more I can say. I was pissed. Why should Angel have all the fun?'

'But you didn't go, did you,' said Jaz.

Grace shook her head. 'Angel told me to stay away from them. I think she was in some kind of trouble.'

'How do you know that?'

'Well, she said so.' Her eyes rolled. 'She gave me a letter to post. She said it was for her brother. Slipped it to me when we were in the stall, in the bathroom.'

'Here?' interrupted Lucille.

'No, at the Underground.'

'What's the Underground?' asked Jaz.

Grace's face lit up. 'It's this awesome place down the street. They play a lot of grunge, and death metal and…'

Lucille interrupted, 'Does your mamma know you go to that place?'

Jaz held up a hand to cut off Lucille. 'You were in a nightclub or bar called the Underground and you met up with Angel. She gave you a letter to post?'

Grace was nodding, though her face had gone red with embarrassment. She would have been underage to be in a bar.

'Can you describe the people Angel was with?' asked Jaz.

'Is this the time or place?' said Lucille. She stood up, greeting a couple of more customers walking in off the street. Then she turned back to Jaz, and said quietly, 'You could have said you were with the FBI.'

Jaz had more questions. But she stowed her gear inside the backpack and looked at Grace who seemed stuck between wanting to talk to Jaz, and the expectation that she should be waiting on some tables. Jaz waved her away. 'Grace, we need to talk later about Angel.'

The girl looked confused but hurried away to fetch the coffee pot from the kitchen.

CHAPTER 10

Seb and Ripley followed a trail through deeply wooded hills, with steep ridges and sharp, deep gullies. Crossing occasional creeks, Ripley and Seb drank from clear water flowing across smooth stones.

By midday he had met no one. On a high ridge, looking back toward the bungalow, Seb paused and scanned the surrounding land. On a distant piece of trail, several figures appeared, stepping out from the cover of trees. Several more came, coasting slowly on dirt bikes. One of them pointed in his direction and waved. There was a glint of sunlight reflecting off what Seb assumed were binoculars. He heard the whine of the bullet just in front of the crack of the rifle. A piece of bark flew off the tree to his left and Ripley yelped in fear and danced sideways, ducking her head.

Seb turned and ran, Ripley beside him. The ridge was steep and they were only halfway up as a second shot rang out, kicking up dust at his feet. They crested the hill and started down the other side. Dust swirled and loose gravel made their charge down the narrow trail treacherous.

They moved down the ridge, leaving the open trail, seeking the shadows between the boles of trees. Enveloped by branches, they provided good cover but slapped at his face as he pushed through the dense woods. It didn't matter now how many there would be. He knew before he left the forest, he would kill, for now they meant to kill him.

Picking his way over uneven earth, a ranger now in his element, he realised that the situation, if not the enemy, was familiar. Hissing wind rustled through pine needles, shredding the silence but masking his footfalls. Ripley instinctively stayed near, her eyes never far from him.

He stopped, crouched low in the undergrowth and pulled out the tourist map he'd stowed. Scanning it, he realised that the trail he'd just left wasn't even marked. 'Come on,' he urged the dog.

Seb ran, hard, wanting to put as much distance between the gang and himself as possible. The further they went before the next contact, the less likely he was to be dealing with the whole group. In the distance, he could make out the high-pitched whine of several trail bikes as they throttled along the trail.

For two hours, he could hear the dirt bikes spread out all around him, circling and zipping around the trails. Sometimes they stopped and he guessed they were listening for him, waiting for him to step into view and show himself. *That isn't going to happen, dumbasses.* Seb was crouched in a pocket of trees, Ripley lying on her belly nearby, panting.

'We know you're out here, motherfucker! Come out and play!' The shout came from a distance. There was a suggestion of other voices too, but they were indistinct. Seb waited patiently, breathing hard. There was no way these clowns would find them without stumbling blindly onto them. If he had stayed off the trails, his tracks would be impossible to locate for any but a skilled tracker.

'Tonight, you won't have anywhere to hide. We won't stop until we have you, man.' The yelling held a fanatic edge.

Seb moved away again, hunched down, keeping his profile from silhouetting to the hunters. He stumbled onto a narrow creek with knee-deep water running through it. Crouched there, hiding and looking pale were two youths, and Seb recognised the pair instantly. These were the two he'd caught trespassing near the bungalow the day before. Huddled together, Kelt raised a finger to his lips as Seb walked across the creek, making sure of his footing on the mossy stones. Ripley lowered her head, took a drink and then trotted to Gab, who hugged the animal fiercely, burying her face in the dog's coat.

Kelt, tense and angry, eyed Seb accusingly. 'They're looking for you,' he hissed.

Seb nodded. 'Do you know where we are?'

'What did you do?' asked Kelt.

'It doesn't really matter, does it?'

The kids just stared at Seb. Then Kelt said, 'You have no idea who they are.'

Seb said, 'We need to get away from here – quietly. I'm sorry you're here, in the middle.'

They seemed frozen to the spot. Gab glanced at Kelt, and a look passed between them. Then Kelt said, 'I guess you can come with us. If we follow the creek down this hill, it meets a swing bridge, and we can take a trail all the way to my place. If we keep out of sight, we have a good chance.'

Seb nodded. 'It's me they want. If they find us, I want you two to run. I'll cover you, okay?'

'We will, don't worry. But they won't want any witnesses. If they kill you, they will kill us too. So, all three of us should stick together.'

Seb wanted to disagree with Kelt, but the kid made sense. 'Okay, let's get moving.'

For about an hour, they picked their way over loose stones along the edge of the creek, following a slight gradient downhill, ducking under low branches, and trying hard to be quiet. They could hear at least three trail bikes in the distance and for a while, it seemed like they may lose the pursuit. But then the trail bikes came close again. Abandoning caution, they hurried as fast as they dared, feet slipping occasionally on mossy stones along the stream bank.

The cell phone that Seb had taken off the biker began to buzz loudly. 'Goddamit,' he hissed, fumbling in his pocket to turn it off. Kelt and Gab stopped and looked at Seb, dread in their faces.

'Over here!' came a shout.

Seb swung on Gab and Kelt. 'Run!'

Kelt and Gab looked once at Seb and took off, at as close to a run as the stony stream bank would allow. Ripley went with them, seeming to understand that she should follow.

Seb slid the handgun behind his back, tucked loosely under his belt. He walked calmly in the direction of the shout, hands raised. Emerging from the trees into a small clearing, he found a biker standing barely thirty feet away, a cell phone in his hand.

The guy wore a leather vest, the Dagon's Riders motif surrounded by a dozen other patches. The beard and hair were as wild as the glint in the guy's eyes. Seb recognised him as the guy he had choked out on the dance floor at the Crab Shack. But it was the revolver, held loose, that drew Seb's eyes.

The biker smiled. 'Just enough bars to get a call out. Maybe you should have left the phone, buddy.'

'Yeah... what now?' Seb shrugged. In his head, he was counting, giving Ripley, Gab and Kelt time to get clear.

'Now you get fucked up,' he snarled. The buzz of approaching trailbikes filled the air though he couldn't yet see them. 'We know who you are man, we *know*.'

'Who *am* I?'

'No use pretending... fucker... not now.'

Seb stared. What was this guy going on about? He'd beaten up a few of their guys, but so what?

The biker grinned and Seb noted several missing teeth. 'If we kill you out here, nobody will ever find you.'

'So, just so we are clear,' said Seb, 'you *are* threatening to kill me?'

For an answer, the biker pointed the gun at Seb's face.

Three trail bikes burst from the undergrowth and slid to a halt in a tight arc around Seb. Two riders' faces concealed behind black visors, dismounted, bringing up automatic handguns, which they pointed at Seb. The third sat and watched, still on the idling bike.

The first guy took a photo of Seb on his phone and sent it to someone. 'I don't know who the fuck you think you are, man, but you sure as hell made some stupid fuckin' mistakes. You had the chance to leave, and man... you should have.'

'Did you get my good side?' Seb taunted because he wanted them closer.

'Get down on the ground and put your hands on your head, fucker,' said one of the riders, voice muffled by the helmet.

Seb said nothing. If their intent was to kill him immediately, shots would already have been fired. He needed them even closer, and so he remained standing.

'We were told to bring you in alive, but dead is okay too,' said the bearded one, face split by a toothy grin.

One of the faceless bikers walked up to Seb and struck him as hard as he could in the stomach. Seb doubled over, coughing, going to his knees.

The other rider stepped close and punched Seb in the side of the face. 'That's for making us look for you, asshole.'

They were both close enough for Seb to smell them, feeling very confident that the job was done. Seb was down on his knees having taken two decent blows. With clothes soaked in sweat and a face red with exhaustion, Seb's dull eyes glanced around as if seeking a way out. He projected defeat. Feeling beside him in the grass, his right hand closed over a large, slightly larger than *fist-sized* rock, as his left hand grabbed the crotch of the nearest leather-clad biker.

He grabbed, found what might have been a pair of balls, and squeezed for all he was worth. The howl was high and immediate. The biker fell away as Seb used his right hand to bash the stone into the side of the other rider's helmet, sending him stumbling sideways, pistol dropping from loosened fingers.

The third biker, the one who had been watching, brought up the gun, still astride the chortling machine. A shot rang out, the whine of the bullet close.

Seb ducked instinctively and stepped between the two bikers, one holding his privates in a doubled-over pose, the other dazed, stumbling to the side. Seb closed on that one, using his body to shield him from the shooter. The next shot rang out and hit the dazed biker in the back of the leg.

Seb threw the stone at the one on the bike, making the guy duck, the bike sliding awkwardly out from under, the idling motor kicking the bike onto the ground as the break came off. He stepped away from the bike, taking the pistol in a two-hand grip.

Seb dived, rolled, felt two shots kick up mud near his face, and reached for the Beretta at his back. He felt a bullet rip through his left shoulder as he returned fire, his first shot left of where it needed to be, the second one a heart shot that dropped the shooter instantly.

He was done fucking around. The bearded biker started running across the clearing in the opposite direction. Seb raised the gun, took aim, felt the finger tighten, realised he wasn't in a warzone and then allowed the guy to disappear into the trees. One of the two remaining bikers was removing his helmet. It was the one that had been shot in the leg, and Seb saw that it was, in fact, a young woman. Her long blonde hair flowed out as the helmet came away. Dazed, she limped along, looking for her discarded pistol.

'Don't pick it up,' warned Seb.

She dropped the helmet and moved a further few feet, now dragging the leg that had taken the bullet.

'Leave it!' Seb growled.

She reached for the gun, snatched it off the ground and turned toward Seb, pistol coming up.

Crack. Her body snapped sideways as the bullet punched through her centre mass.

Seb lowered the Beretta. The rider toppled over.

She slumped, face to the sky, and Seb could see that she was still breathing. Her delicate nose had a small diamond stud through it. Bubbles of blood dribbled over her lips painted with hot pink lipstick, staining her chin. When she looked up, Seb knew that she would bleed out within minutes. 'I said to leave it.'

She said something, but he couldn't quite hear it. Seb bent forward, taking the gun from her limp fingers. 'They'll kill you and everyone you love,' she managed weakly.

The other biker, the one with the busted nuts, was crawling away slowly, gun discarded. Seb watched him go. He was heading for the stream. Seb pulled out the photo of his sister from his wallet and showed the dying woman. Her eyes were glazing over and she could not focus. 'Have you seen this person? Look at it.'

But the eyes were fixed now and reflected the blue of the sky above. He left her lying there and walked past the other corpse, heading in the rough direction that Kelt, Gab and his dog had gone. Seb realised that his shoulder was bleeding, and he might need a doctor.

The shadows of late afternoon in the trees were deepening. Gold sunlight and gently rustling leaves made the scene of death seem surreal. He would have to find Gab and Kelt, and ask them everything they knew about the gang. Maybe they could tell him where to find the gang.

CHAPTER 11

The cell, on the ground floor of the police building, was open on one side with bars running from floor to ceiling. Through a cell window, as the evening shadows deepened, Clyde watched as Webster went through his rental vehicle from top to bottom. Now he had the trunk open and was unloading the spare tyre.

Clyde had gone through fingerprinting earlier in the day, after being charged with *disturbing the peace, possession of a concealed weapon* and *resisting arrest.*

He relaxed onto the bench, knowing that there was absolutely nothing to be found in the car. His tools of the trade were not in there.

'Do you normally lock people up for sleeping in their cars?' asked Clyde, pitching his voice loud enough to carry to Benson.

She looked up from her computer monitor, staring, mouth thin.

'Do I get a phone call?' Clyde had no one he wanted to call, at least not yet. But he wanted to see just how far he could push the local cops before they cracked. Benson ignored him, though Clyde saw that her eyes tightened. Maybe she did feel at least a little bad that he had been picked up and charged with some bullshit offences and thrown in a cell. But she remained quiet, unwilling to say anything.

The weasel-faced officer, Guyatt, was making coffee, and he walked over to the cell, holding out a cup to Clyde. But as Clyde got up and reached through the bars to take the cup, it was dropped on the floor. 'Oops, sorry, Mr Miller.'

Clyde said nothing. He sat down again on the bunk and folded his arms. This all felt wrong. There was no way they knew he was coming, was there? If they did, why hadn't they charged him with something else more serious or contacted the state police? What did they suspect?

'There is no one with your name that matches your description in the criminal or prison database,' said Benson, who was now cleaning up the spilt coffee.

'That is not surprising, because I haven't been in any trouble,' lied Clyde.

She pursed her lips. 'Your DMV records appear correct too.'

'Yeah,' agreed Clyde.

'Not even a parking ticket,' said Benson.

Clyde smiled.

'This seems to be too perfect,' said Benson.

'What can I say? I am a careful driver.'

Benson returned to her desk and sipped her coffee. 'What are you doing in the Cove?'

'Sight-seeing. I was travelling along the interstate, and I felt like a change of scenery,' said Clyde.

'That's bullshit,' chimed in Guyatt, his gaze falling on Clyde.

Clyde wondered what it would be like to strangle him. Perhaps he would get the chance. 'Do I get a phone call?'

No one answered him.

The phone on Guyatt's desk rang and the officer picked it up. 'Guyatt here.' Clyde watched the cop's face. The guy looked at Clyde and smiled. 'Yeah, I have him here. He isn't saying anything... yet. What do you want?' Guyatt nodded a couple of times even though the person on the other end of the call could not see him agreeing eagerly. 'Okay, whatever you say.' He glanced once more at Clyde and placed the phone back in the cradle.

Abruptly, Benson left her seat and picked up her desk phone. She handed the phone through the bars into the cell, the spiral cord stretching just far enough. Clyde took the phone. 'Make your call. Tell me the number to dial.'

'What are you doing?' barked Guyatt.

'My job,' replied Benson. She turned back to Clyde. 'What number?'

'Do you know the number for a pizza?' asked Clyde.

Benson blinked. 'You want a lawyer? Or do you want to call a relative?'

Clyde smiled. 'I like pepperoni.'

Benson withdrew the phone as Guyatt came and stood beside her. He glowered. 'Did I say he could call someone?'

'Do I give a shit what you say?' said Benson.

Clyde could see the disgust she had for her colleague.

Guyatt leant against the bars, ignoring Benson now. 'You want a pizza, tough guy?'

Benson sat down, looking troubled. Clyde now knew which cops were straight and which were bent.

Guyatt crossed his arms over his chest and said, 'When those prints come back, we will know who you really are. Nowhere for you to hide then.'

'You should let me out, and I won't sue your asses. I will pay whatever fine I have to pay and be on my way. You can't hold me without cause.'

'Let him out,' said Benson. She stood.

Guyatt's hand shot out and he pointed at Benson. 'Stay put, Benson. This asshole isn't going anywhere yet.'

'Who was on the phone?' she demanded.

'Chief O'Brien,' said Guyatt. He left the room, heading for the car park to talk to Webster.

Benson picked up the phone and dialled the last number. '*You have reached the message bank of Chief O'Brien.*' She slammed down the phone

She looked at Clyde. He stared back at her, face unreadable. Then Clyde said, 'Your pal is a piece of work. I don't think he likes me.'

'Officer Guyatt is no *pal* of mine,' she said. She looked outside, could see Guyatt stride up to where Officer Webster was pulling everything out of the trunk, including the lining. 'What do you think they will find in your car? A gun, or drugs?'

'Nothing. I don't know who you think I am,' said Clyde. 'How long can you hold me here?'

'By the law, we shouldn't be holding you now,' admitted Benson.

'Maybe you should let me out,' suggested Clyde.

Officer Benson sat at her computer, biting her lip. She stared intently at the monitor, as if the answer to her problems were hidden there on the screen.

CHAPTER 12

After the diner closed, Lucille had insisted that Jaz should accompany her back to her house where Jaz could continue to question Grace about Angel.

Seated in the backseat of the Ford explorer, Jaz looked out at a blur of trees. Lucille's husband, Joshua, frequently glanced at her from the rear-view mirror with clear, blue, eyes that shone from within a sun-kissed, wrinkled brown face. His large, calloused hands grasped the steering wheel firmly. Though unkempt, his white whiskers leant his face a wise sturdiness.

Sharing the backseat with Jaz, Grace sat glued to her phone, chewing gum loudly. Jaz wanted Grace to tell her everything she could remember about Angel and the people she was running with. What would have happened if Grace had gone with them, on the back of a bike out into the woods? Angel had intervened, which meant she was not a victim, but something else.

'Does my mom know where I am?' asked Grace.

'You have a phone, you could call her,' said Lucille from the front passenger seat in a deadpan voice.

The girl nodded, and said, 'Am I in trouble? Are you really FBI?'

Jaz smiled. 'No, Grace, you aren't in trouble. And yes, I am an FBI agent.'

'Where is the rest of your team?' Lucille's husband spoke up only occasionally, but when he said anything, it was to the point. Jaz had not met him until more than twenty minutes before when he had pulled up outside the diner, but she thought him likeable. 'Shouldn't you have more people as backup? Are you undercover?'

'It's just me, I am afraid, Mr Corbett. The leads I'm following…
let's say that they are mine right now. Just mine.'

'Mr Corbett was my father, young lady. I'm Joshua. You call
me Joshua.'

'Call him Joshua,' said Lucille.

Pulling into the leafy driveway, they exited the four-wheel drive
and stood in the front yard. The forest loomed close to their house.
Jaz sensed a hush falling as dusk shadows grew toward total darkness.

Joshua pointed. 'No neighbours for a few hundred yards. And
behind our property, the forest extends for miles until you eventually
get to the ocean. There are some beautiful lakes and streams in there.'

'Nice place,' said Jaz, assuming such a comment was needed. It
had a slightly overgrown appearance but the lights glowing from
within made the place seem a little less brooding.

'Let's get inside. I have a feeling that we need to discuss your
leads, Ms Freeman,' said Joshua.

'Mom says I can stay for dinner,' said Grace, pocketing her phone.
She had been standing off to one side having a whispered conversation.

They went up a few steps onto a wooden porch before opening
an entry where shoes sat in an orderly row. Hooks with umbrellas,
coats and hats sat near a lamp. Jaz removed her shoes, kicked them
aside and followed Lucille, Joshua and Grace into the living room.

The kitchen was well-appointed. Jaz climbed onto a stool at the
kitchen island as Lucille poured three glasses of red wine. 'What
is that smell?' said Jaz.

'That… my FBI lady-friend, is slow-cooked beef-brisket.' Joshua
smiled, sipping some wine from his glass. 'That has been cooking
for hours,' he said, a twinkle in his eyes.

'Smells amazing,' said Jaz.

'Don't you go pumping up his ego too much,' said Lucille.

'A handsome man that cooks too. You have done well, Lucille.'
Jaz took a sip of the wine.

'He's okay, I guess,' said Lucille.

Jaz looked over at Grace. The teenage waitress had planted herself on the couch in the room beside the kitchen and was texting. She wanted to start grilling Grace as soon as possible. She had to coax the cell out of her hand before she could start an interview. Jaz moved across to the couch as Grace looked up.

'Is Gabrielle home yet?' asked Lucille.

'Gabrielle?' Jaz turned.

'My daughter,' said Lucille. She looked at Joshua. 'Is she in her room?'

Joshua's blue eyes looked up at the ceiling. 'I can't hear Gab up there.'

'I hope that boy isn't with her,' said Lucille, her face suddenly creasing.

At that moment, a dog came trotting into the living room, tail swooshing from side to side. 'I didn't know you had a dog,' said Jaz with delight.

Joshua's eyes narrowed. 'We don't.'

The dog was busy greeting everyone when two youths burst into the room. One was a young girl, perhaps fifteen, the other a boy of maybe the same age. They looked sweaty and frightened, thought Jaz. Joshua said, 'What's wrong, Gab?'

'Daddy...' she stuttered and burst into tears.

'What happened?' said Joshua as Lucille hurried over to her daughter's side and enveloped her in her arms. Grace stayed put, though her phone was now put aside.

'Where have you two been, Kelt?' asked Joshua, turning to the boy.

The boy's eyes were wild, and he had to swallow several times before he could answer. 'We ran into a bit of trouble, sir.'

'Just tell us what happened,' said Lucille.

The boy swept a trembling hand through his sweaty hair and took a deep steadying breath. 'The bikers found us in the woods...'

Jaz looked up and came to her feet. 'What happened?'

'We came across a guy... and her.' Kelt pointed to the dog. The bitch sat and looked at them, head tilted to the side. 'The bikers were hunting him.'

'Wait… hunting?' asked Jaz. 'What do you mean, hunting?'

'They were after him, a whole bunch of them. Some of them were on trail bikes.' Gab sniffed. Grace was watching and listening, her eyes wide.

'Where is this guy?' asked Joshua.

'Seb's still out there somewhere,' said Kelt. 'We had to leave him. The bikers found us, and Seb went to meet them while we escaped.'

Jaz was listening, her eyes glued to Kelt. 'Seb? Where did you last see him?'

Kelt looked at Jaz. 'The stream running down off the main ridge beside the western trail. I could get back there if I had to, easy enough.'

Jaz went to a window and looked out at the forest. It was already dark outside. A sudden wind was now hissing through trees, breaking the silence that had fallen on the room. 'You said the guy was *Seb*. Are you sure?'

Gab nodded, still holding onto her mother. 'They would have killed him. We heard some shots.'

Jaz said, 'We should call the cops. They need to know about this.'

'Aren't you the police?' said Joshua.

'This isn't my jurisdiction,' replied Jaz, taking out her cell phone and punching 9-1-1.

'Wait,' said Joshua, his hand on her arm.

At the other end of the phone, there was a female voice. 'This is Crabtree Cove Police.'

Jaz looked at Joshua, his hand now upon her arm. He looked at her, trying to convey something with his eyes.

'Hello, hello…?' the police officer was calling into the phone.

Jaz hung up. 'Any reason, Joshua, why I shouldn't be talking to the police?'

'Police… no… Cove Police on the other hand…' Joshua trailed

off. 'Isn't that why you are here, Ms Freeman? If you completely trusted the local police, you would be talking to them about missing people, instead of us.'

Jaz pocketed her phone. 'We need to get out there and find Seb.'

'What about dinner?' asked Grace.

'Shut up, Grace,' snapped Lucille.

*

Officer Benson slammed the phone back into the cradle.

'What's the matter, they didn't want to talk to you? Go figure.' Clyde assumed a knowing look, leaning back against the wall and sitting on the bunk.

Officer Guyatt was still on duty but he had gone on patrol, taking one of the cruisers. Tyrone Webster had gone home for the evening.

'It's bad enough I have to babysit your ass without you speaking to me. Why don't you shut up for a while, Mr Miller?'

'You sure are polite. Call me Clyde. We could be friends.'

Benson looked at him briefly. 'You set off some alarm bells around here when you turned up in town, Mr Miller. My colleagues seem to think you pose a threat.'

Clyde shrugged, trying hard to maintain a cool exterior. But Benson could see that he was feeling increasingly agitated the longer he remained in the cell.

Clyde sat down, his eyes never straying far from Benson, wishing he could convince her to allow him to leave. He still needed to meet his contact and he was already hours late.

'I don't know why, but my boss seems to think you are some kind of trouble.'

'You spoke to your chief?' asked Clyde.

Benson looked at him but said nothing. No, she had not spoken to Chief O'Brien. Guyatt had said that he had. She didn't know whether he had or not, but Guyatt was her senior and she had to at least pretend to listen to him.

'Why don't you let me out?'

'That is about the tenth time you have asked me, Mr Miller. Why would I change my answer now?' Benson got up from her desk and walked away, heading for the kitchen and another coffee.

Clyde watched her leave the room, wondering how the hell he was getting out. He stood, paced to the narrow window, stared between the steel bars. His rental car sat in the lot outside the station, the contents having been rifled through for a couple of hours. He didn't like the way things had gone, not one bit. How the hell had they known to expect him? How did they know *anything*?

The phone on Benson's desk rang again, and after about the fourth ring, Benson strode into the room and snatched it off the receiver. 'Cove Police.' Then she listened, her face hardening with concentration. 'Say again.' She jotted something down, the pen scratching over a notepad. 'Got it.' She reached for her gun belt, which was hanging over the back of the chair, and fastened it in place.

'Where are you going?' asked Clyde.

'Relax, Mr Miller. I will bring a pizza for you on my way back.'

'From where? You can't leave me here alone.' Clyde got up and stood near the barred door.

'I have a bit of an emergency, Miller. You stay put.' She smiled at the joke and left through the front door. Clyde watched her move quickly to a police cruiser, the last one parked out front. She put the siren on and the lights flared as the cruiser sprung away, tyres howling. Clyde watched her go, his face expressionless. This, he did not like.

CHAPTER 13

As night settled, a hush fell. The moon disappeared beneath the canopy and shifting cloud, forcing Seb to pick his way carefully. With no sense of north, south, the direction of the ocean or the town, with a bullet wound in the shoulder as a persistent distraction, Seb became lost.

He'd been shot once before, and this time he'd also been lucky, for the bullet had been a *through and through*, missing bones and organs.

Knowing that the forest was not vast, that if he kept moving in any direction, he would eventually cross a road or find a trail, he kept moving.

After wandering in this fashion for several hours, he heard distant voices. He followed their muffled conversation until he knew exactly where they were. Edging forward, willing his eyes to adjust, he crept toward a hollowed-out dell, where gold light flickered in the trees. Seb peered over the lip of a natural depression, seeing a trio huddled around a small fire.

Leaning on the dark side of a tree, close to the edge of the clearing, he listened to their conversation.

'Give it here.' A young woman sounded annoyed.

'Wait your turn, bitch,' said a young guy, voice slurred.

'Hey, man – that's my girlfriend,' said a second male voice.

'You tell me that she ain't a bitch,' said the first guy.

'No, but you can't say that to my girl,' responded the second guy.

'Listen to you two, whining and shit. You call me the "bitch"?'

Seb ambled from his concealment, probably looking a little less attractive than your average homeless bum. The girl, in her late teens, a beret tilted on her head, visibly stiffened, while the two young men looked up at him with eyes that seemed out of focus.

'I need to get to town,' stated Seb.

'Is he real?' said one guy, starting to stand up. His jeans were low on scrawny hips and he struggled to pull them up level with his underclothes.

'You know him?' asked the guy still reclining on the ground.

'Nah,' said the really scrawny one, shaking his head with great exaggeration.

Seb nudged the guy on the ground with his boot. 'I need a doctor.'

'He's bleeding,' said the girl, backing away a step, as if she might catch something from Seb.

'Man, you're in the woods, there's no doctors out here,' said the reclining guy, and he began laughing.

Seb licked his parched lips. 'Give me something to drink.'

'I got some bourbon,' volunteered the standing guy. He looked warily at Seb.

'You're a *dumb shit*, aren't you,' said Seb.

'He just wants some water,' said the girl, now hurrying to her backpack. She returned and handed Seb a plastic bottle.

'What are you doing out here with these two losers?' asked Seb, taking a long pull on the bottle.

She smiled. 'One is my boyfriend, and the other is my brother.'

'Ever get them mixed up?' asked Seb. The words were out before he could think to keep them in his head.

She frowned and snatched the bottle back. 'You sure have a smart mouth.'

'Where am I exactly?' Seb demanded.

'You're deep in the woods,' she said, like it was some kind of secret. 'No roads for a few clicks.'

'Which way is the coast?' Seb asked.

She looked confused. 'Over that way.' She pointed to her left. 'No, hang on – that way… maybe,' , pointing back behind her.

'Fuck,' breathed Seb, rolling his eyes. 'I need someone to look at my shoulder.' He sat heavily on the ground near the fire, the two men now sitting across from him.

'Let me look,' said the girl. 'I'm Codi, by the way.'

'I'm…' Seb howled as Codi prodded the wound with her fingers.

'Did that hurt?' she asked.

Seb glanced at her, breathing deeply. After a minute, he said, 'The bullet went right through. Has the bleeding stopped?'

'Yeah, I think it has – almost. When I prod it, it bleeds.'

'No more prodding, Codi,' said Seb. Then, 'Do you have a way out of here… a car?'

'We don't have a car, mister,' said the guy reclining on his elbow. It was the one she said was her brother. He was holding a bong, and he took a long inhale before saying, 'You might die out here tonight. Only way out for you is to walk.'

The two boys laughed, but Codi shook her head sadly.

'You see a dog?' asked Seb. They looked at him, faces vacant. 'Or two kids – names are Kelt and… I don't remember.'

'Nope,' the three said in unison.

There was a sudden gust as a breeze rustled in the branches around them. It began to drizzle, drops already dampening their clothes and hair. 'We're all going to get wet pretty soon,' said Codi.

Immediately, rain fell, hissing and spitting into the fire. Seb levered himself up from the ground. The trio gathered their gear into a single pack that Codi was made to carry, then started to move, slowly at first, then faster, like they needed their batteries charged.

Seb called after them, 'Where are you going?'

Codi at least cast one last look at him over her shoulder before she disappeared.

Seb followed them, but soon they were as insubstantial as ghosts drifting through the trees. He suspected that they had a car somewhere, perhaps a tent or maybe even a caravan. There was no way they were out here, so deep in the woods without some kind of shelter.

*

Benson had really punched the police cruiser hard along the coast road to get to Seb's house as fast as possible, telling herself that she didn't even like him that much.

In a spray of dust and gravel, she slid to a halt directly in front of the porch. The twin beams of the cruiser's headlamps showed the remnants of a front door hanging precariously from one hinge. 'Jesus Christ!' she said, peering at the house.

The place looked deserted. No lights shone from within. It looked like a murder scene, she thought, though she had never attended one. Sliding out of the car, leaving the headlights trained on the front porch, she peered inside. Despite the car's lights, there remained black cavities within the yawning door and windows that could be concealing anything. Pistol drawn, torch in the opposite, Benson advanced up the steps and called, 'Police officer! Is anyone here?'

No one answered as she stepped over the threshold, flicking the torch left and right. She listened and couldn't hear anything at first. The night was so still that she realised she could just make out the crashing surf a few hundred yards behind her. Benson moved swiftly, the pistol tucked just behind the torch, watching her corners, sweeping the house from the living room to the kitchen and back down the hall to the two bedrooms, then finally the bathroom. Believing the house was empty, she let out a breath.

She wanted to radio back to base and ask for assistance, but she knew no one was back there. Only that creep, Clyde Miller, stowed tight in the lock-up. He was supposed to have someone with him at all times. So many protocols were being ignored lately.

She lowered the weapon, taking in the scene. The place had

been thoroughly trashed. The call had come in from a muffled voice, saying that Seb Straeker was in trouble, that his house had been ransacked. That was an understatement, thought Benson. But where was Seb? Had he been snatched? Webster had tried to warn him that the gang would not rest until they had payback. But there had to be more to this. This was 'overkill'.

Benson returned to the cruiser and snatched up the radio. 'Guyatt, come in. Guyatt, *where are you?* I need assistance!' She waited. There was the hiss of static. Benson threw down the radio and stalked back around the house, past the clothesline and a shed.

The forest loomed in front of her, a dark mass, yielding nothing to her sight. When she paused, she could hear the hum of crickets, the rhythmic, unsettling, tocking of frogs. She trained her torch along the edge of the forest, searching for Seb or his dog.

Walking around the property, the torch beam eventually found Seb's Camaro parked under trees within the edge of the woods. As she examined the car, a breeze sighed into the leaves around her, then stiffened, swaying the branches and filled her nose with the fresh scent of rain.

*

The figure crossed the police station's car park, head bowed slightly, hoodie pulled up around the face. In contrast to the fleece jumper, the trousers seemed all wrong, with perfect creases and conservative, polished black leather shoes. Aware of the possibility of cameras placed around the facility, he walked straight into the police station, pausing for a moment to look at the squad room, at the empty desks and finally over at the cell where Clyde was sitting on the edge of the bunk bed, looking a little nervous.

'Who the fuck are you?' said Clyde, standing and walking to the bars, fingers curling around them. He didn't like this much, no – not very much at all. The cop had left in a hurry, leaving him exposed. It felt like a set-up. Anyone could just walk in here and, well, do whatever they wanted with him.

At last, satisfied the place was devoid of police, the figure pulled back the hood exposing a clean-shaven, dark-haired white man in his fifties. 'My name is Father O'Malley.'

'Excuse me, Father, for I have sinned,' said Clyde grinning.

'Yes, I am sure you have, Mr Miller,' came the immediate reply.

Clyde froze. 'So, you know me?' His grin melted away.

Father O'Malley began looking around the office, looking for something or someone.

'Did you get them out of here?' said Clyde.

'No. That wasn't me, I'm afraid. That's why I am here though. To try and get you out.'

'I don't understand,' admitted Clyde, now mindful to avoid swearing. If there was a type of person he would be polite to, it was a priest. As a kid, Clyde had eaten at more soup kitchens run by the church than he could remember.

O'Malley was running his hands over and under the desks, looking for a lock release button on the cell. None could be found. It appeared that the Cove Police Station was firmly settled in the 1950s, and the cell would likely only release with a good old-fashioned key. 'Do you know where they keep their keys?'

Clyde looked at the priest. 'You're really here to break me out? I would be in your debt.'

'Yes, you would be. When I pay for someone professional, I expect to be getting a professional. Yet here we are.'

'Jesus...' began Clyde.

'Watch your mouth,' snapped O'Malley. Opening another set of drawers, his face lit up. 'Here they are.' The priest reached into a deep filing cabinet and came out holding a set of keys.

'Hurry up.'

'Yes, yes.' The priest crossed the room, his eyes locked on the keyring, trying to figure out which key was needed. He stopped at the cell door and went through each key, one at a time, concentrating.

'You okay, Father?' asked Clyde, noting a slight tremor in O'Malley's hands.

'I'm fine... but none of these are the right key.'

'What? You're kidding.'

'Here, you look,' said the priest, handing over the keyring between the bars. Clyde took them and began a methodical test on the lock from his side while Father O'Malley walked quickly to the window and peered out at the car park, as if expecting an imminent arrival. 'They will be here soon. I was watching from across the way. When Officer Benson departed, I guessed they had special plans for you.'

'*Special plans.* You have a way with words. You mean they will kill me,' said Clyde.

'I would say so. You would not be their first. Others have gone missing in this town not long after meeting our police force. Are you having any luck with those keys, Mr Miller?'

Clyde said, 'Why did you hire me ? What did McTaggart do to you?'

'Do you always ask your employers these questions? Do you care why?'

'No, not usually. But I've never been hired by a priest either.'

O'Malley crossed from the window and went to the bars where he stood close to Clyde. 'Bless you, my son. Give me the keys. They should not know that I, or anyone else, has been here. That's vital.'

Clyde reluctantly handed over the keys, his shoulders slumping. 'Are you leaving me here? Is that why you blessed me? You know they will kill me.'

'They will, I think. I have only a few minutes at most. They will come here knowing Benson is away somewhere.' The priest crossed back to the desk where he had found the keys and returned them to where he'd found them.

Clyde's face had paled. 'They somehow knew I was coming.'

'They listen in on everyone here. Maybe they heard the call I placed. But I doubt they know my voice, otherwise I would not be standing here before you now. But yes, somehow, they guessed you were here for McTaggart. Did they find a weapon in your car?'

Clyde shook his head.

O'Malley nodded. 'I have to go, now.'

'You're just leaving me?'

'We all have to die one day, Mr Miller. Don't be afraid.' The priest reached into his coat, under the hoodie, and withdrew a very small, compact .22 pistol. Clyde backed away slightly. But the priest reversed the gun and handed it through to Clyde. 'Take this. They won't know you have it. Perhaps you can get out of this yet, Mr Miller.'

Clyde took the gun. It felt tiny in his hand. 'Where the hell am I going to hide this on me?'

O'Malley paused and then removed his belt. He handed it through the bars. 'I assume they took your belt when they put you in there.'

Clyde accepted the belt and began threading it through his trouser loops. It barely fit him. Then he tucked the gun into the belt, at his back, and pulled out his shirt so that it covered it.

O'Malley nodded once and then headed for the front door. He paused, and said, 'Mr Miller, if you do manage to get away, you should come to the church. You will need to lay low for a while.'

The priest turned on his heel and pulled up the hood before stepping back out the front door and walking beneath the first of several security cameras. Striding away across the car park, he barely made it to the street before the police cruiser came into view and swept by.

Standing close to a large elm tree, hidden from view, on the opposite side of the street to the police station, O'Malley watched as the police car pulled in close to the entrance. Officer Guyatt climbed out, and beside him, a man in dark leathers, carrying a large revolver. The pistol, nickel-plated, glittered in the low light.

A few minutes passed before a handcuffed Clyde Miller was marched out the front doors with Officer Guyatt leading the way toward the police cruiser. The biker followed close, his pistol jammed close to Clyde's back as they pushed him into the back of Guyatt's car. Slowly, the cruiser pulled away from the car park. Although its headlights shone toward O'Malley, the black hoodie helped the priest melt into the shadows of the treelined street. The car turned in the direction of the city centre and coasted away.

Heart thundering, O'Malley left the police station in his wake. The almost full moon was now shrouded with shifting clouds. He detected the faint, fresh scent of rain on a sudden breeze as he hurried for the church, knowing he had at least tried to give Clyde a chance.

*

The Ford Explorer's high-beam headlights cut into the woods on either side of the dirt road. In the middle of the backseat, Kelt sat peering through the windscreen, giving directions toward where he thought they had last seen Seb. He tapped Joshua on the shoulder as he told him to pull over.

'So, where from here?' asked Jaz.

'In there.' He pointed to the left, up a ridge, into dense woodland. There was no path that Jaz could see.

'In there?' she repeated.

'What? Are FBI agents scared of the dark?' said the youth.

Jaz turned a steely gaze at the boy but said nothing. She popped the door handle and climbed down from the seat, as Joshua went to the back of the vehicle and opened the hatch.

'Why on Earth did you not want me to call the police?' said Jaz. She felt uncomfortable about hanging up on the cop who had picked up her call.

'Around here, well, not all the police are one hundred per cent trustworthy,' said Joshua, returning with two torches. 'This is all I have,' he said as Kelt came to his side.

'Be that as it may...' began Jaz.

'No, Ms Freeman... Jaz. You don't know everything I know. You haven't lived in this town. Trust me when I say that you need to limit your interactions with local law enforcement here.' Joshua handed Jaz a large metal torch. 'These things are heavy. They can make a good club, if needed.'

Jaz smiled and patted her jacket, where the snub-nose .38 was holstered. 'I have something better.'

'This way,' said Kelt, and he led them away into the trees, walking in what he hoped was the direction of the stream bed where they had left Seb.

'We have a lot to talk about, then,' replied Jaz.

'I suppose so,' said Joshua, his voice calm.

They had only gone about a hundred yards when they found a trail, barely three feet across, leading up a steep incline. Jaz shone her torch up that dirt track, noting that the beam of light was quickly lost in the dense foliage.

'We go that way about a mile and cross a ridge. On the other side, we come to a creek. We follow it along...' Kelt paused, his face creased. 'For maybe another half a mile. That's where we left him.'

The breeze that sprang up around them was cooler, the night suddenly feeling deeper, the woods wilder than only a moment before. 'Let's go,' said Jaz, and she strode out in front, her torch sweeping out in front. In silence, they followed the trail.

CHAPTER 14

As the drizzle turned to rain, Seb trailed the trio, using their muffled conversation as a guide. Soon, their shadowy silhouettes became ghosts, their voices detached. After that, he heard only the patter of rain.

He'd lost them.

His head now light with exhaustion, pain radiating from the wound in his shoulder, teeth clenched, soaked through, he put one foot in front of the other in the direction he thought they had gone. Pausing twice beneath large trees in the hope of finding a dry place, he felt large drips make their way onto his head. The wind picked up, chilling him.

He came awake, slumped sideways against the bole of a tree, chilled and stiffening. The glowing numbers on his watch showed 12.22 a.m. Estimating that the three potheads had disappeared at least two hours before, he set off once more into the night.

Around fifteen minutes later, treading carefully, he saw what he believed was a torch beam but then realised it was actually a distant light. He stopped and listened but heard nothing but the hiss of rain on leaves.

The light winked in and out of view several times over an hour as he crossed low ridges and muddy gullies.

Walking from the tree line, he emerged near a cabin beside a grey lake. Nearing the two-storey, rustic lodge, he noticed a narrow jetty over a rain-pocked lake. At the edge of the cabin, his footsteps squeaked on old wooden porch boards. At the back, a covered awning gave him his first shelter from the rain in hours.

Light shone from beneath the crack of the door, and he crept to a back window and glanced into a kitchen. Nothing moved inside.

As the back door was unlocked, he stepped inside, feeling warm air. Opening the fridge, light spilt into the kitchen. He popped a beer and drank, froth bubbling down his chin. There was a half-eaten sandwich sitting on the bench near the sink. Seb picked it up, sniffed it once, then practically inhaled the meal in three bites.

He crept along a narrow hall past a laundry and an office before finding a large, open lounge with a stone fireplace. The fire was glowing red, chunks of wood crackling above the hiss of rain on the lake outside. He had found the source of the light that had guided him.

Around the fireplace, the trio were motionless in various poses, reclining on overstuffed sofas. They had fallen into a deep sleep, satisfied with their surroundings, the weed having provided a further state of relaxation. Codi had paused only to remove her beret and boots, which lay discarded on the rug.

Seb ignored them, instead moving to the stairs, climbing into the darkness, seeking his own refuge. Hopefully, a place where he could think and rest.

Halfway up the stairs, at a landing, he paused, eyes drawn to a framed painting. It showed the figures of silhouetted wolves, sneaking out of a darkening forest, stalking a frontiersman. The man seemed completely unaware of the wolves, for he held his musket down at his side, rather than at the ready. Seb wondered then if he could be compared with the frontiersman. But perhaps he was the wolf.

The second floor was in total darkness, and it took a minute for his eyes to adjust as he snuck along the carpeted hallway, glancing into each bedroom. At the end of the hall, he found a bathroom. He entered, closed the door, and turned on the light. Stripping out of his sodden clothing, he kicked it into the corner of the room. The mirror afforded him a good view of the bullet wound. It was high on the shoulder, neat and round. Blood seeped from it in a thin watery trail. He nearly feinted just then, feeling the floor tilt slightly. He allowed himself to slump onto cold tiles, before running a hot shower and crawling into it.

He must have dozed for when he woke, the water cascading across him was only warm. He turned the faucet off, exited the shower and listened carefully. The house was still. Opening the bathroom vanity, located behind a mirror, he found toothpaste and mouthwash. Rifling through the cupboard below the sink, he found cleaning products, and stashed at the back of the cupboard – a first aid kit.

Examining the gunshot wound in the mirror, he poured an alcohol-based antiseptic directly over the hole. Then, straining, he tipped it all across the exit wound on the back of the shoulder. A low groan escaped him despite clamping his mouth around it. His head swam with pain and he wished he had some whisky.

Now the hard part. He threaded a needle and began stitching the holes closed. He had done this to other soldiers once or twice in the field. His hand trembled, but he managed to close the front wound within a few minutes. Twisting to look over his shoulder into the mirror, he closed the exit wound.

The stitching complete, he selected a large gauze pad from the medicine kit and stuck it down over the whole area. 'Looks like shit,' he mumbled before turning off the bathroom light and slowly opening the door.

As Seb crept quietly from the bathroom and into a nearby bedroom, a hint of light made its way from the rooms below. There were shirts hanging in a closet. He slipped into one, feeling stitches pull tight. He manoeuvred into some *skinny* jeans, feeling dry and warm. Pushing the quilt from the bed and spreading it on the floor near the window, he was confident that from the doorway, a person would see only an unmade bed.

Seb lay down on the floor, in the narrow gap between the bed and the window and within moments, the sound of heavy rain lulled him into a deep sleep.

*

Jaz, Kelt and Joshua retreated to the Ford Explorer but were soaked by the time they got there. A combination of the darkness and driving rain had dampened their belief that they could find Seb. It seemed hopeless to continue the search after one of the torches failed, leaving the trio with only one source of light.

They sat in silence for the first five minutes on the return drive before Joshua at last spoke. 'We did what we could. He's probably *holed up* somewhere.'

'Remind me again why we should not have called the police,' said Jaz.

'You could call them. You could call them now,' replied Joshua, turning his soft blue eyes on her for a moment.

'Keep your eyes on the road, please,' said Jaz.

'You have a cell. You can call them now,' Joshua repeated, his voice as calm as always, despite the challenge.

Joshua had already said that he didn't trust the local police. Behind those gentle blue eyes, Jaz sensed a deep wisdom that she should only ignore at her peril.

'I'm supposed to be on vacation. No way I'm going to the local police as an FBI agent unless I have to. For now, we leave the police out of this. But tomorrow…' She allowed the thought to hang.

'Okay,' replied Joshua, 'I can live with that.'

Kelt had slumped back in his seat, the dark-haired youth silent and sullen. He had not liked the idea of leaving Seb out in the forest in the rain.

'You said something about the locals having their phones tapped,' said Jaz.

Joshua nodded. Keeping his eyes affixed ahead on the road, he switched the wipers up to full speed as the rain drove against the windscreen. 'There is a lot you don't know. There have been stories told, by people that I trust.'

'Tell me,' said Jaz.

'Where do I start?' said Joshua. After a few minutes of silence where Joshua must have been thinking about where to begin, he continued, 'There's this rich guy, McTaggart, who lives outside town. He seems to run things around here.'

Jaz turned her eyes on Joshua. 'Never heard of him.'

Joshua smiled. 'Yeah, that's the point I guess.'

'What are you not saying?' said Jaz.

'Tell her,' urged Kelt.

'Tell me what?' said Jaz.

But Joshua shook his head, and said, 'Let's wait until we get home.'

*

The gun barrel thrust hard into his back again, shoving him forward once more. Clyde Miller walked just ahead of the biker with hands cuffed in front of him. He looked around at the warehouse, expecting to see more bikers. But they were alone. Guyatt had left them at the entrance, locked the door behind them, then sped away.

Clyde could see several boats on the back of trailers, sitting in neat rows. The ceiling was twenty or more feet above them, made of corrugated iron and old hardwood. At the far end of the warehouse, a sliding door was open, revealing a concrete boat ramp and a grey waterline. Clyde assumed the biker would shoot him here and then take a boat out into the harbour beyond to dump his body, weighed down with an anchor chain. It was a good option, thought Clyde. Bodies could resurface, after a while the decomposition making them bloat. Fish would eat him soon though. Clyde shrugged at the thought.

'You going to tell me who sent you? I can make it quick,' said the biker. Rain drummed on the iron roof as they strolled toward the far end of the warehouse where the concrete ramp and the waterline waited for them.

'I *was* invited here,' said Clyde.

The biker, at least four steps behind him, replied, 'Now we get somewhere. Who was it?'

'I was surprised to know myself. You see, these types of deals are done with a high degree of...' Clyde searched for the word. 'Anonymity.'

The biker's hard-heeled boots echoed on the concrete. Clyde listened, judging that the guy was around ten feet behind him – not quite close enough to catch him unaware.

Clyde continued, 'Yeah, last person I would have guessed.'

They reached the ramp. A small boat sat there, in a couple of feet of water, waiting. They were alone. Clyde turned and faced his executioner. The guy was shorter than Clyde but wore Cuban heel biker boots that gave him a few inches. He had a goatee, and hair pulled back from his face in a ragged ponytail. The nickel-plated revolver, a .357 Colt Python, was pointed at Clyde's chest. The weapon would buck like a motherfucker when fired. The recoil was fierce, but it would put a big hole in anything it hit.

'I'll tell you, on one condition.'

The biker was still, and he watched Clyde carefully. At last, he said, 'Name it.'

'Cigarette,' said Clyde. 'I get a smoke. Then I tell you who paid for the hit. Then you do what you got to.'

'Do you think everyone about to be executed asks for a cigarette?'

'No, not everyone,' said Clyde, with authority. 'In my experience, they usually grovel, and whine, and cry. Sometimes they piss themselves.' Clyde smiled, forcing calm.

The biker's eyes were flat. He shrugged, then took a packet of cigarettes from his pocket with his left hand and lobbed them in front of Clyde. Then he fished a lighter from his jeans pocket and dropped it on the ground.

Clyde crouched and fumbled with the packet of cigarettes, the cuffs jingling. Placing the cigarette between his lips, he tried to light the cigarette. But he deliberately fumbled the zip, saying, 'This thing doesn't work.'

The biker shrugged. 'Not my problem.' He took a step back, putting a little more distance between them. The big revolver remained trained on Clyde.

Clyde tried to use the lighter, again and again, but he could only get a spark. The cigarette wouldn't light. 'This isn't going to work like this.'

'Tell me who sent you.'

'When I smoke this, I'll tell you. You won't believe who it was.'

'I don't have all night, man.'

'You take these off, so I can light this?'

'Do I look dumb?' said the biker.

'You have a gun big enough to blow a hole in an elephant. You scared of me?' chided Clyde.

'You need to tell me who sent you.'

Clyde held up his wrists, the cigarette clenched between his teeth. He spoke around the cigarette. 'Come on, I just want a smoke.'

The biker took the keys to the cuffs from his pocket and lobbed them to Clyde who caught them in mid-air. 'Thanks.'

The cuffs came off, and Clyde dropped them carelessly at his feet with a clink. He made a show of lighting the cigarette and drawing in a long, enjoyable breath. When he breathed out the smoke, he relaxed on his heels, hands on his hips. 'God, that's nice. They wouldn't give me a smoke all afternoon.'

'Pigs,' said the biker, smiling.

'Yeah, would it have killed them?' said Clyde. 'Just a smoke. That bitch cop...'

'Who sent you?'

'I haven't finished my cigarette.'

'I don't care. It's time.'

'Don't you want to know? Your bosses sure as hell want to know. What happens when they send the next guy?' Clyde backed away a step.

The biker stared unblinking at Clyde. 'Get on your knees.'

'Oh, you want to shoot me in the head?'

'Who sent you?'

Clyde went to his knees as the biker came closer, the colt's barrel a black hole. 'These deals are done at the end of a phone. There is a go-between in case *shit happens* and the cops find out stuff they shouldn't.' Clyde grinned. 'You know, the son of a bitch visited me in my cell. Yeah, when Benson gets called away, he walks in, cool as you like, right into the station.'

The biker was listening now. He lowered the gun just slightly.

Clyde continued, 'Yeah, this priest, he just walks in. Can you fuckin' believe it? A priest. He tried to find the keys to the lockup, but they weren't there. Instead, he had to settle on giving me something.' The biker looked genuinely interested now. Clyde's hand had snaked behind his back and under his shirt. He gripped the .22 and dove sideways onto the ground, his arm coming around.

The python boomed, the shot going wide, the pistol recoil massive. As the biker corrected his aim, the hitman tracked the pint-sized .22 onto his target's forehead. Clyde squeezed the trigger. There was that smaller sound of a pop and a neat hole appeared in the right cheek of the biker.

Clyde scrambled up as the python boomed again, the hand of the biker spasming, the bearded face going blank. Clyde fired three more rounds into his target's chest, making sure he went down.

Clyde scooped up the colt python and tucked it in his belt. Then he dragged the biker by his boot heels toward a boat that was moored at the bottom of the boat ramp. He walked down the ramp a few steps until he was up to his knees in seawater. Cursing, because Clyde really liked his shoes, he climbed onto the boat.

Through the opaque screen, wind and rain, the visibility toward the bay was poor. Clyde found the keys to the boat in the ignition. There was plastic sheeting lying in the small, forward cabin. Clyde returned to the body and set about wrapping the corpse, taking care to not get blood on his shoes or track his boot prints through it. 'This was meant for me, huh?'

He hauled the body to the back of the boat and flopped it over the edge, where it landed heavily, causing a slight rocking. Climbing into the boat once more, he used an oar to push further away from the boat ramp into deeper water. Satisfied that the propeller was well clear of the concrete, he switched on the ignition and taxied out into the harbour with rain sheeting down around him.

*

Benson returned to the cruiser, parked in front of Seb's bungalow. The patrol car was warm and dry. She watched the heavy drops bouncing off the windscreen, and once more radioed base. 'This is Benson, pick up.' She waited, but there was just more static.

Returning the radio in its cradle, she turned on the ignition. Where the hell was that asshole Guyatt? Benson swung the car around and powered back onto the coast road, accelerating back along the blacktop, switching her wipers up to full so that she could see the road.

She considered the voice that had called in the tip that Seb was in some trouble. Could it have been Guyatt himself? She guessed she was ten minutes out of town, and pushed the car's limits, using the high beam to illuminate the road ahead. The trees on the sides of the road were tall and dark, flitting past in a blur. Lights from Crabtree Cove appeared to her right. Turning her emergency lights on, she cruised into town, well over the speed limit, aware that Miller had been left alone for a couple of hours.

In the police car park, she killed the lights and engine. Normally she would expect to see him standing at the window, peering out into the car park. But he wasn't there. Maybe he was on his bunk bed, lying down or something. She strode up the couple of steps and in through the foyer, then into the squad room. The place was dead. She looked straight into the lockup, and... Miller was gone.

She crossed to the cell, looked in, bending down to see if he was under the bunk bed. 'Okay,' she said aloud, though no one was there to hear her.

She examined the admission register, just behind the counter and flipped open the book. At that moment, she heard the toilet flush in the men's room and a few seconds passed before Officer Guyatt walked out into the room. Benson relaxed and turned her eyes back to the book that she had just opened.

'We had to let him go,' said Guyatt.

Benson read that Guyatt had signed Clyde Miller out. 'I thought you were "hot" to keep him in here?'

'His lawyer called. Made some threats. Chief said to *let him go*. I argued against it but was overruled.' Guyatt took a seat at his desk and switched on his computer.

'I called here barely twenty minutes ago. I needed some back-up,' said Benson.

'I might have been in the *John*,' replied Guyatt.

Benson stared at him. He was *full of shit*.

Guyatt continued, 'I was busy. I had to get his car out of the compound out back and bring it around. He gave me some more lip about unlawful detention. You know how it is.'

'I could have been in trouble. You didn't pick up.' Benson remained standing, hands on her hips.

Guyatt stared at her for a long moment before he said, 'I'm sorry, Benson. But here you are, and you're okay. Where were you anyway?'

'Up at the new guy's house. You know, the one that was having a little run-in with the bikers. Sebastian Straeker's place has been ransacked,' said Benson.

'Straeker? Yeah, I remember him – the jogger. Well, you play with the bull...'

Benson cut in. 'You get the horns? Aren't you concerned?'

Guyatt shook his head. 'He'll turn up.'

'How do you know that? He could be dead,' said Benson.

'Are you worried about your new *boyfriend?*'

Benson opened her mouth and closed it again. She stared at Guyatt. Guyatt stared back. Her animosity toward him was undisguised. She had always tried to hide that. Not now.

'You know, Guyatt, I always thought you were *by the book*. Now I know you're just some *dumb asshole.*' Benson walked to her desk and sat.

Guyatt smiled. 'You better file a report on your *boyfriend* Straeker. He's probably left town though. He wouldn't hang around knowing those guys are after him.'

Benson pictured Straeker's car parked on the edge of the woods, hidden deliberately out of sight. In the morning, when the rain stopped and by the light of day, she would check it out properly. Maybe Straeker was dead, and his car may hold a few clues. Or perhaps he was still in town and had every intention of returning to his concealed car. She would not mention either possibility to Guyatt. Something was *off* about everything that had happened today. She glanced out the window, at the heavy rain, and wondered where Seb was right at that moment. She had a terrible feeling that he could well be dead.

CHAPTER 15

To some it was the graveyard shift, and others referred to it as *the wolfing hours*. Seb knew this time of night well, as many an operation would launch between two and three a.m., targeting enemy encampments. Afghanistan, under starlight and the freezing air of their mountains, came flooding back with barely a thought.

Hearing footsteps on the stairs, he came fully awake. He rolled sideways, stifling a groan as the stitches in his shoulder pulled. Then, tucking himself hard against the bed, he waited.

The footfalls reached the top, heavy rather than cautious. They paused for a moment, and then slowly made their way up the carpeted hallway. Seb pulled the Beretta and cocked the hammer. The stalker had stopped and was listening. The silence grew.

After a while, Seb heard the treads continue, then the door was pushed gently open. The stalker was at his bedroom door because Seb could hear breathing, just the barest hint of it. Whoever it was paused, looking at the unmade bed. The treads continued to the bathroom, and the door squeaked open. The light flicked on, and it shone down the hall a little. Seb cursed, recalling that he had left bloodied gauze in the bathroom, and discarded wet clothing.

The intruder walked quickly back down the hall, down the stairs, thumping two at a time. Then Seb heard raised voices in the rooms below and realised that the kids in the lounge were in some kind of trouble. Codi tried to scream before her cry was clamped off.

'Where is he?' The voice was loud, and it carried in the night.

Seb slowly got to his feet and walked quietly to the door of the bedroom, glancing around the corner to the stairwell. Nothing moved and so he crept forward, the Beretta poised. He stopped at the top of the stairs, leant sideways, straining to get an angle. The living room was not visible, but he was close now.

'I don't know, man. There *was* a guy… out in the woods.' The kid sounded terrified. Seb recognised the voice as one of the trio he had met in the woods, but any hint of the lazy, tripped-out tone was absent. He was stone-cold sober, and shit scared.

'You had him here. Don't lie to me, boy,' came a deeper voice.

'I ain't lying,' began the kid.

Bang.

Seb flinched as the gunshot echoed in the confines of the house. A body made a *whump* as it hit the floor. Seb wondered which one it was. If he went down the stairs now, fast, he might surprise them, but he didn't know the positions of the remaining kids. And he didn't know how many enemies were down there either. Calculating the risk, finding it unacceptable, Seb waited.

'That's what happens, bitch!' said another voice.

'Tie her up, and let's have us some fun,' said a woman.

The deep voice came again. 'This didn't need to happen this way. I'm sorry for the loss of your friend but lies won't be tolerated. We're on a schedule. I don't wish to be here for long. The man who used your bathroom upstairs, to clean and stitch his wounds – where is he now?'

The remaining boy spoke, 'I know you think we're lying, but *please* listen to me… to us. We came here stoned off our heads, and we smoked more, and then… we fell asleep. If he came in here, we never saw him. I promise I am telling you the truth.'

There was a long pause. Then the female intruder said, 'He's lying.'

'Fuck no, I'm not lying!' He began sobbing. 'I swear I am not lying!'

The deep voice cut over him. 'I think I believe you.'

'I think we should have some fun, and then later, you should let me waste him. Let me *please*,' said the woman, almost sensually. Seb thought she sounded *sexually* excited, like she was slowly getting off on the idea of killing.

Seb retreated slowly along the hallway, looking in each room. One of the bedrooms had a single bed and posters of hot-rod cars on the walls. Over the bed, proudly displayed, a double barrel shotgun had been mounted. It looked old, perhaps an heirloom, but Seb could see that it would probably function. Snatching the gun off its brackets, he began scavenging for shells, knowing that it would only be a matter of time before the intruders came upstairs and searched every damned square inch of the second floor.

Seb heard them coming – more than one. He couldn't find any shells. A cord was hanging from the ceiling, and in the darkness up there, the barest outline of a trapdoor. He jumped, grasping the cord, held on to it, landed with a thump. Yanking it, the trapdoor in the ceiling opened, and under its own weight, a wooden ladder fell to the floor with a second thump. Looking up, Seb could see that the attic was blacker than pitch. He put one hand on the ladder, then stopped and wheeled away. On the other side of the bedroom, a closet stood closed, the white doors beckoning. He crossed fast, closing the closet behind him.

A heartbeat later, two people, a man and woman, sprang into the room, handguns extended. Seb watched through the slats, trying to control his breathing. They were dressed in matching leather. The woman was young and severely beautiful, with stark white makeup, blood-red lipstick, and bleached blonde hair, cropped short. She was petite, but her black boots gave her a few inches. The leather suit was tight, almost as figure-hugging as a wetsuit with a crocodile pattern running through it.

Beside her, a hugely muscled guy stood looking up into the blackness of the attic trapdoor. He was built like he worked out every day, but seemed top-heavy, like he would simply fall over if he tipped in one direction or the other. His hair was also bleached blond, cropped very short and he may have been wearing the same makeup. 'I think he went up there.'

'Whatever gave you that idea?' said the blonde woman. She held an automatic machine pistol with a long clip, which Seb recognised as a Scorpion. It was designed for close quarters and would fire incredibly fast in a killing arc.

The last guy to enter the room was a huge Nordic guy with shoulders that wouldn't look out of place on a statue of Zeus. This was the embodiment of a Viking war chief if ever there was one. The night prior, Seb had seen this guy standing in his kitchen door, peering into the night as his crew ransacked his house. He walked to the ladder and peered up. He had not bothered drawing any weapon. He turned to the woman. 'He's injured. He's cornered. He may or may not be out of ammunition.'

'We'll kill him,' she promised, almost breathless, shifting from foot to foot.

'Fuck yeah,' chimed in her heavily muscled companion.

'Don't leave here until it's done. Remove the bodies,' said the giant. Seb watched the Nordic guy leave, and when he disappeared back down the hallway, the blonde woman slapped the gym junkie hard across the face.

'Why did you do that?'

'Because you sicken me, you little chimp,' she said. Her smile was evil.

'That's no answer. You get like this when it's time to kill.'

She put the Scorpion up under his chin. 'You need to wake up. This guy has already killed at least one of ours. He needs to pay.'

'I'll go up first,' he announced.

'Yeah, you will, you muscle-headed freak.'

The body-builder goth walked a few rungs up the ladder, his Glock pistol in his right hand. He was peering into the blackness.

'He would have shot you if he had any bullets left,' said the woman.

'You don't know that,' replied the guy. 'Fuck, I hate this.'

'Will I do it, numb nuts? You are one spineless sack of shit,' she said, a mocking smile playing over her face.

The muscle-bound intruder glanced back once more at her before continuing his ascent along the ladder, very slowly. Seb heard him crawl into the attic. 'It's dark, and there are heaps of boxes up here.' His voice echoed down.

'Look for a light,' she called to him.

'I can't find one,' he responded.

'Can't you see?' she said.

'I'm not one of *them*,' he responded.

Seb didn't move. He was barely breathing. The more he wondered at how many shots he had left in the Beretta, the more he thought it was only one or two. Then, the blond jumped onto the ladder and scampered up into the roof space in a matter of a second. Her voice carried down. 'Where are you, you little fuck? You can't hide up here!'

Seb pushed aside some clothes, discovering open shelves. Arrayed there, in neat order, were a couple of bottles of cologne, a watch, a set of keys and some shoe polish. On a lower shelf, a couple of novels and a bottle of bourbon, and below that, on another shelf, a few baseball caps in various colours.

It was on the very top shelf though, in a steel tray, that Seb located what he hoped would be found somewhere in the room – a clutch of shotgun shells. He snatched up two and loaded the weapon before snapping the breach closed.

Seb considered leaving while the two intruders were scrabbling about in the attic. But he wasn't certain that the tall, Viking guy had left the house. He could still be down below. They were up there for only a few minutes, and Seb could hear boxes being kicked around and a few muffled shouts. Then the steroid junkie came back down the ladder and landed heavily on the floor.

When the woman came down the ladder, she skittled like a spider. She was damn fast on her feet, thought Seb, still peering through the cracks between the slats.

'Where did he go?' said steroid boy.

'If he didn't go up there, and he wasn't in here when we came in…' she began.

Her body language changed just a little. It was enough for Seb to go into a low crouch. The black-clad would-be assassin suddenly brought up her arm and fired a long spraying burst into the cupboard where Seb was hiding. Twenty rounds expended in a heartbeat, bits of wood splinters flying over him, shredding the shirts over his head, spraying bourbon and glass onto Seb's face.

Seb kicked open the door, bringing up the shotgun in a fluid motion. Brass was landing about the woman's feet, tinkling on the ground around her from the magazine she had just expended.

'Surprise!' Seb levelled the shotgun.

The woman froze, as inanimate as Seb had seen her. There was no way that she could load another clip before he could pull the triggers. Seb couldn't miss at that range with a 12-gauge. The blast with the pellet spread would be deadly.

But the steroid boy was pumped up now, and he was not going down easy. He started to bring up his Glock when Seb fired into the guy's chest. Thrown back, he pitched against the wall, blood spraying. When he came to rest, he was staring sightlessly at the ceiling, a gaping wound in his upper torso.

'One left in the breach,' said Seb.

The woman was frozen, though Seb saw her eye twitch.

'Not so tough now?' asked Seb. 'Now I killed three of yours.'

She spoke, 'Please, mister, I wasn't with these guys. They had me do things I really didn't want to. Now I can get away.' Her voice was completely different from everything he had heard coming out of those blood-red lips. She could have been someone else if he had closed his eyes and listened. She was almost parroting how Codi sounded when she was pleading with them.

'When I go downstairs, will they be dead?' Seb asked casually.

Her face was distraught. 'He killed them,' she said, her eyes now on the gym junkie, sprawled in a spreading pool of blood.

Seb could tell that while she was watching him, taking in the unusual situation she now found herself in; she was calculating her chances. He could see it in her eyes. She dropped the Scorpion machine pistol on the floor and waited. Seb watched her, the barrels of the 12-gauge pointed at her, aware he had one more shell available. Seb felt his heart rate slow a little, and he began taking in more details. She had a diamond nose stud and she was beautiful in a strange way. A kind of madness lived behind eyes the precise colour of glacial blue ice.

Seb listened, but the house gave nothing back, remaining as quiet as if nothing had happened in the preceding minutes. The ice queen said nothing but she did not break eye contact with Seb, seemingly willing to wait for him to come around to her way of thinking. The longer he waited to pull the remaining trigger on the double barrel, the more likely she was to survive the encounter. His shoulder ached where he had been shot. He could feel blood seeping into his gauze bandages. The shotgun felt heavy. The silence extended. It might have been just forty-five seconds, but to Seb, it felt like ten minutes.

'What now?' she asked, her voice sounding small and pitiful. Her lower lip trembled.

'Now, we go downstairs and see what happened to those kids,' said Seb. He gestured with the gun and said, 'You go first. You do anything remotely stupid and I'll put you down.'

She grinned briefly, but then returned her submissive face as quickly as the feral smile had appeared. She walked slowly ahead toward the doorway, her hips swinging just a little, tight leather stretched over a perfect ass, knowing Seb would watch her closely. He did, appreciatively, but the shotgun remained trained on her back all the same.

Halfway down the hall, she looked back at him, just to make

sure that Seb was watching, a slight smile on her lips. As she faced forward again, Seb stepped up behind her and hit her a glancing blow on the back of the head with the butt-end of the shotgun. Her legs buckled beneath her and she fell to the floor of the hallway. Seb nudged her with his foot. She was out cold.

He dragged her along the hallway, back to the room where he had killed the bodybuilder. There, he left her and went looking for something with which he could tie her up. He returned with a leather belt, rolled her onto her face and pulled her hands behind her back before using the belt to secure her wrists. Then he found a second belt and tied that around her ankles.

He settled back, taking a deep breath, and wondered who these people really were. And what was Angel doing with them? What in God's name had she gotten into? Was she also running around like a maniac, amped up and homicidal?

Seb gathered together the machine pistol, the Glock pistol and his own Beretta and tucked them into his belt. Going back to the girl, he rolled her from side to side, looking for a place she could keep extra ammunition. He found an extra magazine tucked in each of her calf-length boots. These, he took. The dead gang member, the pumped-up steroid boy, had an extra three clips in his jacket. Seb gathered these too and reloaded the second barrel in the shotgun. Going to the shredded cupboard, he found a coat that was still intact and put it on. He looked down at the woman who hadn't moved or even groaned.

Leaving her, he went back down the hall, down the stairs, the shotgun pointed at eye level. The house was still. Even the rain had stopped, leaving in its wake a preternatural calm. In the sickly amber radiance of a single lamp, two bodies lay side by side on the couch. The two young men were in different positions. One had been shot in the chest, and the other had his throat cut. The girl, Codi... was gone.

Seb searched the bottom floor, going from room to room. Nothing. No one. Through the windows, a lifeless forest waited, grey and still. Seb thought he caught movement in the trees, at the corner of his eye. He imagined departing souls, fleeing the house, perhaps unaware they were dead at all. Stepping away from the window, he had the strong sense that he was being watched. Had he heard something upstairs? He waited, listening.

The sound, muffled, definitely came from the rooms upstairs. Although he had left the crazy bitch trussed with belts, he had not pulled them so tight that the circulation would be cut off. Seb placed the shotgun on the kitchen bench top, listening intently, neck arched up toward the ceiling. He glanced at the wall phone, considering a call to the police. Benson had seemed okay. But the bodies were piling up and he might need to explain his self-defence. A small green light on the side of the phone was on.

He carefully picked up the receiver and listened.

'...that motherfucker... is downstairs.'

'Is he escaping?' Seb recognised the tall Nordic guy's voice.

'No... I don't know.'

'Can you kill him?'

'Of course, I can, Gunther. He thinks I'm tied up.'

'I have new intel. He's not our guy,' said Gunther in a deadpan voice.

Her voice took on a shrill note and she struggled to keep it low. 'We've been chasing him around all day and night, and he killed Rupert... *point blank*, with a shotgun.'

'That's unfortunate, but he's not our guy.'

'You know, I hated Rupert, soooo much, but this guy has to pay for that.'

'We had bad intel. This guy came onto our radar at the wrong time. He seemed like a good fit. Assumptions were made.' There was a long pause before Gunther spoke. 'Krystal?'

'I'm here.' She sounded annoyed.

'Kill him, or just leave. The choice is yours now. He's just some guy,' Gunther said flatly.

'What about the clean-up? There are three bodies here.'

'Doesn't matter.'

'I want him dead. He's going down.'

'Report back when you are done.'

The phone was put down with a clunk. Seb returned his phone gently to the hook. How did she intend on killing him? He had taken her gun. Rupert, the guy who he had blown away, was carrying too. Seb had Rupert's Glock tucked in his belt. What did that leave Krystal? Not much. A bad attitude. Fingernails long enough to be claws. Seb was a soldier and at the end of the day, he would not kill an unarmed civilian. He could leave too. Just walk out into the dark woods, into the rain, and simply melt away. There was no way that she could locate him. And yet... Seb did not want her at his back. He would have to leave before the cops might show, but that was hours away, surely. Seb waited for a minute, thinking. Perhaps Krystal could lead him to Angel. If she could somehow be persuaded, he might learn something important from her.

The house was still, but somehow not as still as it had been. Krystal waited upstairs. She was unarmed but intent on killing him. Seb unloaded the shotgun and left it propped in the kitchen. He took out all three handguns – his Beretta, the Glock and Krystal's Scorpion machine pistol. Removing the clips, he placed them on the benchtop. There had been too much killing. Whatever he did now, it would not involve another shooting. Not tonight.

CHAPTER 16

Although the hour was late, and they were wet and cold, Jaz could not yet entertain the idea of going back to her apartment to sleep. She felt that she was on the brink now of discovering missing pieces to a puzzle that had occupied her for years.

From her earlier discussion with Lucille, Jaz had become aware that the town held secrets. But it was Joshua who seemed to suspect more, and he wanted to talk. She sensed that he had been weighing her, deciding if he could trust her.

Lucille had waited up for them to return from their search in the woods. She seemed disappointed that they had found no signs of Seb Straeker. She wanted as much as anyone to tell him about his sister, and how Angel had managed to pass the letter to Grace. It was an important piece of information that Seb would no doubt have been happy to know. Ripley proved that a dog could look disheartened, for the animal lay on a couch, watching them talk, sad eyes blinking.

They sat in the living room, listening to the rain on the roof, sipping at black coffee as they dried themselves with towels.

'What's going on in this town, Joshua? Earlier, in the car, you were going to unload on me some heavy intel,' said Jazz.

He looked at Lucille, who nodded her encouragement.

Wordlessly, Joshua went to a sideboard and from within the sliding door, he withdrew what appeared to be a photo album. When he came back to the table, Jaz noted that it was a kind of scrapbook. He opened it up, and inside was a collection of newspaper articles.

118

'What've you been doing?' asked Lucille.

'Keeping track of things. I didn't want to worry you, Lucille.'

He turned the book around so that it faced Jaz. The very first page had an article about the boy Eric Winters. This, Jaz knew, was the missing article from the library archive.

Jaz began reading, a smile touching her face. 'I'm glad you've done this, Joshua.'

Joshua smiled back at her, and Lucille sat back, looking at Joshua with a small smile of her own.

'What else?' asked Jaz, eager to turn over the page.

Joshua nodded. 'Go ahead.'

The youth, Kelt, sat in silence, sipping his coffee, both hands wrapped around the mug. He looked wrung-out and pale. Jaz had the sense that he too had something to share with her.

Joshua continued, 'Anything I thought didn't make sense, I kept a copy.'

Jaz began reading, her eyes darting across each article, trying to take in as much information as she could. She could have done with a whiteboard, a pinboard or at least some post-it notes. This was something that she would have liked to map out in some way.

The first article, about finding Eric Winters near the train line, hinted at confusion over the cause of Eric's death. The journalist quoted a police officer at the scene saying that she thought the body had been moved there and the whole thing was staged to look like an accident.

The next article was a small piece about the untimely death of a policewoman who was killed in a car accident outside the town limits. Her name was Jolene Reimers. The article instead focussed on her replacement – a smiling image of a cop called Webster.

'Why do you have this article?' asked Jaz.

'Jolene was the police officer that said the scene had been staged,' said Joshua.

Lucille clicked her tongue in disapproval.

'She also said that the coroner's report was wrong,' said Joshua.

'Is there anything here about that?' asked Jaz.

'No... not directly from her, but you'll see more on that,' said Joshua.

Jaz shook her head but simply turned to the next article.

This one was about the 'untimely' death of the town coroner, a Mr Paul Jackson. Apparently, he had suffered a heart attack after slipping in the shower. He had been pronounced dead at the scene by paramedics.

'So, you're saying that the coroner's report was changed. And next thing, the coroner, Jackson, is found dead? This doesn't prove anything,' said Jaz.

Joshua said, 'Jackson had been on the phone to Eric's mom and dad. He had said that he was being pressured to change the report. He said that Eric was definitely killed... murdered, I mean. He said it was no train that hit him. The initial finding was for homicide. He said he was being told to call it an accidental death.'

'Homicide would mean wider coverage, maybe even nationwide attention,' said Jaz.

'The report that exists... says *accidental death* or *misadventure*,' said Joshua.

'What happened to the first report?' asked Jaz.

'Buried. Burnt... who knows?' Joshua shrugged.

Joshua turned the next page in front of Jaz. This article was about Eric's room having been ransacked. Apparently, some kids had broken into his room and were taking souvenirs of the *dead kid*. Jaz felt sick at reading the details. It must have been a terrible experience for the parents, who no doubt just wanted to be left alone. The kid's room had been rifled and graffiti painted on the walls. Apparently, some items were taken and never recovered. Jaz shook her head, imagining the parents' trauma.

The next article that Joshua had kept related to a very small piece, which had only made it to the back page of the local paper.

It simply said, *Dayton Phillips, a visitor to the Bay, was found dead in his room this morning. It is understood he had committed suicide in the hours preceding his discovery. His relatives are being contacted.*

'Who's Dayton Phillips?' asked Jaz.

Joshua said, 'He was a private investigator.'

Jaz sat forward slightly, her eyes narrowing. 'And?'

'He was hired by Eric's parents, Joan and Ken.' Joshua's blue eyes were fixed on Jaz, challenging her to make the same leap of faith that he had.

'You think that he was killed?'

'What guy comes into town, happens to be investigating the death of Eric Winters, and kills himself? That's ridiculous. And now *they* have a new coroner, someone who they can get to do whatever the hell report they want,' said Joshua.

'Okay....' Jaz said, thinking, 'say this Dayton guy is hired for this purpose. I agree that there is no way that he kills himself when he is being employed to investigate something like this. It would be incredibly *fishy*. But how can you know that is who he was and what he was here for?'

'Joan and Ken hired him. They told me so,' said Joshua.

'Hang on,' said Jaz, her hand coming up, palm out as if to stop Joshua. 'Are you for real?'

Joshua nodded. He looked at Lucille, who was staring back at her husband, wondering when he had started putting this together.

'That's why you don't trust the police, or the phones,' said Jaz.

Joshua nodded. 'There was no way that anyone even knew that Dayton Phillips was in town, or if they did, what he was here to do. The only way is if the Winters' phone had a tap on it. He died on the first night he arrived in town. He was staying in a room two down from yours, Jaz.'

'How?' asked Jaz.

'Blew his brains out with his own gun,' said Joshua.

Jaz went still, and at last nodded. 'Who called it suicide?'

'The police, and the new coroner backed it up.' Joshua flipped the page in the scrapbook.

There were two more articles. One was about a boy who had been found in the woods, another apparent suicide. He was said to be a known drug user and 'depressed'. The final article was about a girl who had apparently up and left town. Her name was Chloe Smyth. The police had said that she had left a note that she was leaving town and not to worry. Her parents were worried, understandably, as she was just seventeen years old. The police said that there was nothing they could do as she had been sighted in nearby communities down the coast and was *happy*.

Joshua said, 'Both those kids were in Eric's class at school. But I don't know much about them. Their parents refused to speak to me.'

'I remember those kids. Such a terrible time. Why didn't you tell me any of this?' asked Lucille, facing her husband across the table.

'You would have thought I was mad. You said I was crazy to believe JFK was killed by the CIA. You always say I'm getting old and senile.' Joshua closed the book. But he wasn't yet finished. He walked back to the sideboard and opened another drawer. From inside, he lifted out a small tin, which may have once held candy or something. But when he opened the tin, he tipped two small devices onto the tabletop.

'What are they?' asked Lucille.

Before Joshua could respond, Jaz said, 'Bugs.'

Joshua nodded. 'One of them was found in the Winters house.'

'And the other?' asked Jaz.

Joshua looked over at the kitchen, and the phone on the wall. The rest of them followed his gaze. Lucille had gone a bit pale.

They sat in silence for a long time, the rain constant, the night pressing in on them before Jaz turned to Kelt and said, 'Kelt, you spoke to me about this guy, what was his name? *McTaggart?*'

Kelt nodded. 'Yeah, Stirling McTaggart.'

'Then how is he tied in?' asked Jaz.

Kelt looked at Joshua, who nodded. A long look passed between the older man and the youth.

Kelt looked back at Jaz. 'Can I trust you?'

'It might be too late for that now, don't you think?'

Kelt looked once more at Joshua, who in turn nodded to the youth.

'It all started with this video,' he began.

'Like a DVD movie?' said Jaz.

'No, like a home movie,' said Kelt.

'Go on.'

'Some kids at school saw it. They said it was messed up shit. They thought that it was fake, and... it was a sick joke or something,' said Kelt, trying to explain.

'But it wasn't?'

Kelt hesitated and then shook his head. 'I never saw it, so I don't know. It's kind of an *urban legend* at my school. The story changes every time about what's on the video.'

Jaz made good eye-contact with the youth. 'What did people say was on it?'

'A party. Well, it seemed like a party. They were drinking and swimming, and there was music,' said Kelt.

'You never watched it? Are you sure?' asked Jaz.

Kelt shook his head. 'No, this is what Eric told his friends, and this is what the rumours say.'

'So, third- or fourth-hand *hearsay*,' said Jaz.

Kelt stopped. 'You wanted to know what was on the video.'

Jaz sighed, and at last nodded. 'Yeah, go ahead.'

'This party was some kind of Halloween party at a mansion. It was cool... topless girls swimming around in the pool, and then...'

Jaz said, 'And then...?'

'People were getting killed – massacred, actually.'

'Are you trying to tell me that this all happened up at the McTaggart mansion?' Jaz had trouble hiding a smile. 'Where is this so-called movie now?'

'It was in Eric's room,' said Kelt.

'And this is what got him killed,' supplied Jaz.

'That's what some kids think. No one talks about it anymore. This happened ages ago,' said Kelt.

'A movie?' Jaz said, her voice dull.

'A video that Eric took.' Kelt could see that Jaz was not convinced.

Joshua spoke now. 'It does sound crazy, right? I can see that you, a fancy big city FBI lady would think this is all… *horse shit*. But you came to us, remember?'

Jaz nodded. 'Yes, I did.' Suddenly, she looked very worn out.

'If you could see the video, would you believe us?' said Joshua.

'You said that Eric's room was ransacked and items taken. I can see that this event occurred. The newspapers printed it. I assume that the rumours about what was in the room led to this *story*,' said Jaz.

'His room was practically destroyed. They took nothing. They were looking for the video,' said Joshua.

'So you say,' said Jaz, her head now in her hands.

'They didn't find the video because it was already somewhere else,' said Kelt.

Now Jaz looked up. 'The video is real? You could have told me that.'

'We're trying to, Ms Freeman,' said Joshua. The older man was looking tired, and a wild look had come into his normally placid blue eyes. 'It was taken by Eric's parents to their priest, a Father John O'Malley. It was handed over before his room was searched.'

Jaz blinked. 'Does he have it?'

Joshua smiled, though without any real humour. 'Is the pope a Catholic?'

Jaz turned to Joshua. 'What's actually on the video?'

'I haven't seen it either,' he said. 'The priest won't show it to anyone. He says it's evil, and it's best that no one outside the *circle* knows anything about it. No one.'

CHAPTER 17

Seb ascended with slow steps, listening carefully. The house gave him nothing, no shifting timbers or creaking boards that might suggest where Krystal was hidden or waiting. She seemed to think she could kill Seb, even without a gun. He wondered how she thought that was a possibility given she was now unarmed.

He reached the top of the stairs, expecting to see her standing there. The hall was still. On either side, bedroom doors were open, just pools of deeper shadow. His eyes had not yet adjusted properly. Somewhere here, Krystal would be ready for him. Was she watching him? He edged up the hall, holding his breath, trying to hear her breathing.

Seb made it to the bedroom where he had left her tied, knowing that she had wriggled loose. He walked in, flipping the light on. She lay there, on the floor, pretending to be tied. He could see that both of the belts were loosened. It was a poorly laid trap. Near her, the steroid junkie was sightlessly staring at the ceiling, the pool of blood having congealed around him.

'I heard you on the phone, *Krystal*.' He looked down on her, hands on hips.

She rolled over and sat up, removing both the belts, looking at him with loathing.

'Get up,' ordered Seb, motioning with his hand.

'You're not armed,' she observed. 'Stupid, stupid boy.'

Krystal leapt to her feet, and Seb was reminded of a dancer or acrobat. He recalled the way she had skipped up the ladder and back down again, so light on her feet. Now she danced forward, aiming a kick at his face. Seb tried to move back, but her heeled boot creased his forehead, snapping his head back. It left him dazed.

'I've never hit a woman,' he growled, now lifting his hands and forming two fists.

'What makes you think you can now,' she snarled and launched a barrage of roundhouse and snap-kicks that were alternatively aimed at his head and groin. Seb retreated, blocking each attempt, but having to move faster with each attack. But then two blows found the mark and he felt air explode from his lungs as he doubled over, holding his gut.

In the end, he was forced to hit her, and it was just a plain old right cross that landed on her chin. She stopped, dazed, a trickle of blood running from the corner of her lip.

'You asshole,' she spat. 'You hit me. What kind of guy hits a woman?'

'Put the restraints back on. I have more questions.'

'You want to tie me up, do you? You like to play those games, mister?' Her voice dropped back into those innocent girl tones that she affected when pleading. Her eyes were now large, and she pouted. She cocked one leg, hand on hip, affecting a pose that was despite everything else, damned sexy. A slight smile touched her lips.

'I know you want to kill me,' said Seb. 'I heard you say it on the phone. But that's not going to happen.'

Krystal bent, her leather pants creasing in a nice way, thought Seb. But as she straightened, he realised that she had taken something from her right boot, something shiny, something he had earlier missed. It clicked, and a blade appeared. Mesmerised, he watched the switchblade dance, from her left hand into her right, and then at him, like a hissing, spitting viper.

He could see that she had used this to kill before. She seemed good with it and very fast. Knife fighting is an art, and watching her move around, she seemed well-versed. He was so intent on the blade that he didn't see the boot lash out and take him in the hip.

It was a distraction only, for the blade swept fast, snicking his neck. Another inch and he would be clutching his throat as he bled out. It was too close a call.

The next thing, she feinted left, then right, pirouetted and leapt onto him, her legs straddling him, boots wrapped around his hips. As the momentum pushed them backwards, Seb caught her wrist as she reversed the blade position to stab at his face or throat. She snarled, and then as he held her wrist fast, her mouth came down where his neck met his shoulder, biting him hard enough to draw blood.

Howling, Seb flung her sideways, propelling her through air to crash into the window frame. Her eyes had a crazed look, and for a moment he could have sworn that she had fangs.

Seb felt the new wound and his hand came away smeared with sticky blood. Looking at her, his blood trailing from her lips and chin, he couldn't believe what she'd done. Her tongue darted along her lips, and the look she gave him was almost sensual. 'Oh yeah… you taste *good!*'

'What sort of freak are you?' He stepped back.

Krystal seemed distracted, seeming to look past Seb. Absently, she used a finger to feel along the edge of her teeth. When she came back to herself, she pouted. 'Can't we play, mister?'

A moment later, her mood suddenly shifting once more, and Krystal came at him again, darting this way and that.

Seb blocked the arm holding the whirling knife. Her opposite leg swept up toward his face. Expecting the move, he caught her and pivoted, using her momentum, then flung her as hard as he could, through air, into the wall.

She crashed into a mirror, shattering it, and lay still. A shard of glass had sliced her cheek. Despite the blood, her wild hair, the odd pose she had landed in, Seb thought her beautiful.

He went to her, belt in hand. This time he would make sure that she had no chance of escaping the bonds. As he neared, her eyes flicked open and he punched her hard in the jaw. Her eyes closed and she lay still.

Seb nudged her and she flopped onto her front. Pulling her arms behind her, he bent both her legs to meet them. With the belt, he pulled all four limbs together and chose a belt hole that gave her little in the way of choices when she eventually woke up. He sat back on the bed, feeling every ache in his body. Bitten, sliced, kicked and shot, it had not been a great day.

CHAPTER 18

The bar was on a quiet back road in the middle of nowhere. Pink and green neon signs on the top of the roof glowed against the early night sky, advertising everything from hard liquor to hot girls.

Angel had ridden into these types of places before and knew what to expect. The car park was no more than a flat patch of dirt and gravel, dotted with weeds and small cacti. She sat astride the motorcycle, her attention split between the bar and a nearby trailer park.

A hundred yards away, the small cluster of pitiful, rusting shacks were arrayed haphazardly around a communal firepit. Angel hated these kinds of places. They attracted the sleazy, the backward, the inbred and, in their case, the plain old nasty.

Unfortunately, it was just the kind of place that her gang preyed upon.

'Let's go,' said Leo, and he swung his leg off the Harley. He was the crew's leader and a sergeant in the Dagon's Riders. Leo walked with a swagger that suggested he liked to think everyone was watching him.

Angel hated that she was his usual pillion. Sitting against him, holding tight as they cruised highways, prowling backroads, she was too familiar with the cologne he wore, the way it mixed with his odd-smelling sweat. His was a chiselled face, that when he was younger, Angel may have found handsome. Now his eyes were too dark, sunken, the skin of his face stretched tight over pronounced cheekbones. Having known him for months, he could have looked like anyone, and she would still have found him about the lowest life form on the planet.

Staring bleakly after Leo, Angel reluctantly swung off the back of his motorcycle. Removing her helmet, raven black hair cascaded, then settled around slender shoulders. She wore black leather. It was shiny, tight and fitted close to everything she had.

The rest of the crew blew into the car park in single file, coats flapping. They parked their bikes near the door in a neat row. At last, their camper van rolled in and with breaks that had a slight whine, stopped across the car park, blocking the view between the trailer park and the bar. With dark-tinted windows and black curtains, it hid its occupants.

Angel judged it to be about two hours after sunset. There were now six of them, with Leo at the head, as they walked into the bar, a fine layer of brown road dust coating leather coats and boots. A long bar with cheap liquor displayed along a shelf lay before them. To the left lay a shabby pool table, and at the far end sat a small stage that had probably not seen a real band in years. A jukebox was playing some country music that Angel didn't recognise. It was as depressing a place as she had ever seen.

Three men and a woman sat at stools, each nursing a beer. They looked up with sleepy eyes as the gang entered. Angel hoped that there would be no one else in the bar and they would be forced to leave empty-handed.

'You folks came in on the right night. Yes, sir, we have some fine entertainment coming your way.' The barman had a dirty cloth draped over his shoulder and hair halfway to his waist that hung limp.

Angel drifted to a table and eased herself into a chair. The three on the barstools crooked their necks to follow her progress. Tall, raven-haired, possessed of a model's body and a pale, *movie star* face, she was the kind of woman that a man like Leo wanted to possess, even if it was only to show her off.

'Whiskies all round,' said Leo, sitting at a stool. The crew of five spread out and found their own places around the bar.

'We can't serve those two, I'm afraid,' said the barman, staring at the two youths that rode with the group.

Little Bear was smiling as the barman said this. He was just a kid, barely old enough to ride, thought Angel. She wondered how he came to be with them. He looked about twelve years of age, but must be older. His real name was anyone's guess, and Angel knew not to ask.

The other kid, the one they called Screamer, was more like seventeen. He wasn't smiling though. It always pissed him off when they questioned his age, which he swore was twenty-one. When Angel had joined the group, both these kids were already there, like old pros.

'Five whiskies,' said Leo. His eyes, sparkling with fire, held the promise of violence. As dim-witted as the barman seemed, he must have seen the devil in Leo's eyes and simply poured five double shots into the five glasses he had arrayed on the counter.

'He's not old enough,' grumbled the older woman from her barstool. She spat some chewing tobacco onto the floor to punctuate her statement. Leo glanced at the mess on the floor and up at the woman. Angel bet that he'd make her pay for the disrespect before the night was done.

Leo turned his face on the old bitch, and she quickly looked away. Then he asked, 'So, when does the party get started here?'

'What party?' asked another patron. This time, an old cowboy with a discoloured hat and a bushy moustache turned to Leo.

'Easy there, Gramps, don't get stiff on me,' said Leo, clapping him on the back.

'I like a party,' said the old cowboy. He already sounded drunk.

'I bet you do, old man,' said Leo. 'Do you like to party, Angel?'

Angel looked at him and rolled her eyes. Her middle finger extended and she flipped the bird, but Leo was already turning away, producing a fat roll of fifty-dollar bills. He slammed it down on the counter. The barman's eyes lit up. He waited only a moment before scooping the cash off the bar. Angel had seen this before. The barman was only a temporary custodian of that bundle of bills. He was just too stupid to know it.

'Free drinks all round tonight for anyone who walks in here,' said Leo.

The cowboy cheered. The other patrons visibly relaxed. Screamer and Little Bear drank the whiskey in a single pull and asked for more.

When Angel came into their gang, attracted by their mysterious ways, drawn by the power they exuded, she found people freer than anyone she had ever met. She had ridden with them for a couple of weeks before they had gone to the Cove.

They had tested her in subtle ways, to see who she was, what she was made of, and how she might react to different situations. On some level, she suspected that she was being evaluated. So she did things that she would not have normally done – just to be accepted. She was both intrigued and flattered.

Somehow, they had decided that she was worthy of joining their ranks. Now, all these months later, she would have done anything to go back, to walk away when Leo had approached her that first night, his swagger assured, a look in his eye that promised a fast life, filled with adventure.

Within an hour, three more people had entered the dive, dragging Angel from her reverie. They were greeted by name by the barman. Angel glanced outside, her peripheral vision picking up movement. A tall, leggy, blonde woman in high heels was walking from a trailer, avoiding cacti as she made her way carefully toward the bar. As she rounded the campervan, Angel noted that the woman had barely bothered dressing in a tight blouse and mini skirt. Here's another stupid one.

Before she could get to the door, an old pick-up truck drove in and halted near her. Another woman stepped into view and greeted her. The second stripper was dressed in a cowgirl getup complete with a white broadbrim hat, long braided blonde hair, tight white matching shorts and leather boots that showed tan legs. Angel sighed, knowing that Leo now had every reason to stay at the bar. Yep, they weren't leaving now – no way.

The cowgirl slipped some coins into a slot, and a Patsy Cline record dropped down in the Wurlitzer Jukebox. The leggy blonde and the cowgirl took to the stage. They danced slowly to *Walkin' After Midnight*, trying not to sweat and make their makeup run. The small bar was close to capacity when another couple of locals came in. Several rounds of whiskey later, the strippers had removed enough clothing to have a few bills stuffed into their panties and boots. Angel could see that the barman looked like he had finally hit the jackpot and that this *shithole* of a place might start paying off.

Looking at Screamer and Little Bear, drinking and dancing on the pool table, she wondered how she would ever escape, or if one day, Leo would simply decide that her role in the crew was no longer needed and shoot her in the head.

Angel waited for Leo's signal, throwing back a cheap vodka and trying not to think too much about how she wished she were somewhere else... *anywhere* else. The two women on stage would be taken, and Angel would live to see another day. She glanced at the strippers, wondering what they had planned for their lives, what they would think if they had the slightest idea that their time was almost up.

Leo glanced at Angel and winked. Angel uncoiled her long legs and walked slowly to the stage, making eye contact with the strippers. She produced a wad of cash as she neared them, showing it to the pair. The strippers paused in their dance, looking at the money and then at Angel.

Looking into their hungry eyes, Angel said, 'This is yours, if you want it.' It had been a similar lie to the one Leo had told her months before, when it was Angel's eyes that had settled on the cash, in another dive, in what felt like another lifetime.

'What do we have to do? I'm not into anything kinky,' said the cowgirl.

'Don't worry – just some entertainment for the boys,' said Angel. 'Follow me outside for some fresh air.'

The two women left the stage, walking close behind Angel, and out beneath the stars.

CHAPTER 19

Sheriff Donnelly drove into the car park, a baseball cap with the word 'chief' printed on the front at a jaunty angle. On his shirt was a silver badge, which glinted in the morning light. From three miles out, he could see the plume of dirty smoke and now he could smell it. Some locals from the nearby trailer park stood in a ragged line talking to his deputy, who looked like she would have given anything to be somewhere else. She had her notebook out and was writing.

Donnelly stepped out of the car and approached the group. He glanced at the bar. It was only smouldering, though the main issue now was the acrid smoke. The local volunteer fire brigade had pulled over to the side and were sipping water from plastic bottles. One or two nodded or waved to him.

'What have you got, Tilly?'

She looked up, squinting away moisture in the corners of her eyes. 'Sheriff, none of these folk saw much, I'm afraid.'

Donnelly walked around the car park, head bowed, looking at the ground. There were some tracks, though the ground was so dry that the tyre impressions were vague and mixed up. There were at least five or more sets of tracks. Clearly, the bar had been busy the night prior. Water, from the fire truck had also destroyed some of the tracks close to the bar's entrance. Maybe one set of the tracks could have been made by a motorcycle. It was just such a mess of criss-crossing tyre treads. He circled back, walking slowly, again glancing at the bar. Part of the roof had caved in. He paused, hand on his hip beside his revolver.

'Sheriff!' called his deputy. Donnelly wandered over to her, his head spinning. Tilly continued, 'There was a campervan parked over there. It was between the front doors and the trailer park.'

'A campervan? Okay.' The sheriff walked on to where the van would have been parked. There was a set of tracks. He could see where the van had arrived and where it probably drove off. Three cars remained in the car park. One was a pickup truck. The sheriff recognised it as belonging to a local woman who sometimes danced at the bar. Taking out his cell phone, he snapped a close-up of the tyre tracks from the camper.

'How many bodies in there?' he asked Tilly, knowing full well that there would have to be at least a few.

'Looks like about seven.'

He whistled between the gap in his teeth. 'Holy shit.'

Donnelly walked to the entrance of the bar, took out a handkerchief and held it over his mouth and nose. He stepped inside, blinking away smoke and fumes, aware that he could be messing up a crime scene, but needing to see what had happened.

The tiled floor was wet, the layer of water mixed with soot and bloodstains. The barman was dead, and he could see that he had been shot in the face. The cash drawer was open and completely emptied. If it had started as a robbery, it had ended in multiple homicides. He looked around but had trouble breathing. He counted five more bodies in the bar, and then another in the men's room. They all looked to be male except one, and she looked like she had been sitting on a stool at the bar. Where was the entertainment? There should have been a stripper to go with the pick-up truck in the car park.

Gulping fresh air as he walked outside, he went and snatched a bottle of water from a fireman. He poured half of it into his eyes and drained the rest in three gulps.

'Sheriff!'

'Yes, Tilly,' he replied tiredly.

'That's Deputy when we are at work,' she replied.

'What is it, Goddamit?' he snapped.

She glared at her partner. 'One of these folks think they heard motorbikes.'

'Yeah, so what?'

'A bunch of them,' she said.

Donnelly strode back to his car and snatched up the radio. 'Jane, are you there, over?'

'I'm here, Sheriff, where else would I be?' came the voice over the radio.

'I want an APB on… some bikers.'

There was some static, and then Jane came back, 'You want an APB on anyone riding a motorcycle?'

'I want those boys up in the next county to keep an eye out for a group of bikers. We had some trouble out here. Get on the phone to the state troopers too. The gang are likely armed and dangerous. We have multiple homicides here at what's left of Henson's bar.'

'Yes, Sheriff,' said Jane.

'And Jane… are you there?'

'Yes, Sheriff.'

'The APB should also include information that we are looking for a campervan,' said Donnelly.

'A camper,' repeated Jane. 'Gotcha, Chief.'

'I gotta go.' Donnelly replaced the radio in the cradle and stood beside his car, his hands on his hips.

Tilly approached. 'Mrs Henson is pretty cut up.'

'Yeah, Travis in there. Don't let her go inside. He's… not pretty.'

'Me? What are *you* doing?' asked Tilly.

'I have to go after them.'

'What… *now?*'

He pushed his cap off his forehead and wiped away sweat. 'That pickup parked over there belongs to Belle.'

'You sure?'

'She's not inside. Her vehicle is right there,' said Donnelly.

'Mrs Henson said Matti's gone. She's not in her trailer.'

'Matti's gone too?' He looked at the bar, and back at Tilly. 'How far in front are they?'

'Five or six hours maybe.' She shrugged.

'I have to go after them.'

'Leave it for the FBI or the state police. This isn't for you to clean up.'

'By the time they get down here, there won't be a trail to follow.'

She shook her head. 'Goddamit, Joe, there is no trail.'

'You know I used to hunt, Tilly. This isn't so different.'

She unfolded her arms and stood a little closer. 'I want to kiss you,' she said.

Donnelly could just smell her perfume. He wanted to kiss her too. 'Not here.' He climbed in the car and closed the door. Quietly, he said, 'You're far too young for an old man like me, Tilly.'

He shifted into drive and headed back toward the interstate, watching Tilly in the rear vision mirror. She just stood there watching him drive off.

When he reached the interstate, the faded stop sign brought him to a halt. He sat for a moment at the intersection. The gravel road behind him was clouded in dust, stirred up by his Ford Mustang. He sat, thinking, staring at the two green and white signs, one pointing north and one south. The southern route extended for hundreds of miles of open plains. It was flat and desolate, dotted with the occasional homesteads.

North, he could see the road slowly climb away into the distance. In that direction, the highway would provide any number of side roads into small towns along the coast. It was almost a coin toss. But the northern route offered many more places to run or hide. He pulled out, turned north, and accelerated through the gears, punching the Mustang hard along the blacktop.

CHAPTER 20

'Wake up,' the voice seemed to whisper beside his ear. Seb jerked from a nightmare firefight on a mountaintop in Afghanistan into another in a cabin beside a quiet lake. Still cradling the shotgun across his knees, sunlight shone directly into his eyes through a side window. 'Wake up,' the disembodied voice had said, but there was no one there, except the two dead stoners, propped a few feet away on the sofa. They appeared to sleep, except for the dried blood that stained their shirt fronts, and pooled on the fabric of the beige sofa.

Stiff and sore, he crept to the back door, holding the double barrel shotgun, then peered out into a still dawn, broken only by the distant cries of birds in flight. Where the jetty struck out onto a lake, a small boat with an outboard motor lay waiting for him. Resisting an immediate urge to simply untie it and flee before anyone arrived, he turned and walked back into the house.

If the cops showed, he would have difficulty explaining himself. The ensuing entanglement would delay his search for Angel. And if the gang appeared, looking for Krystal, there would be more killing.

But Krystal was still upstairs, and with persuasion, she might tell him where Angel was.

When Seb returned to the bedroom above, he found her wide awake. Left overnight trussed like a pig, only a foot from the body of her associate, she stared as Seb came and sat on the bed beside her.

Seb looked down, face expressionless. 'Why should you live?'

Krystal continued to stare at him, mouth tight.

Leaning forward, he nudged her. 'Who are you people?' Getting

139

nothing, he now gave her more of a shove with his boot. 'I know you're not exactly the most normal person I've ever met. But how does someone like you end up with... them?'

Krystal blinked, ignoring his questions, and then said, 'I'm thirsty.' Her spiked hair, pale white makeup and smudged red lipstick mingled with the dried blood on her chin.

'You know, Krystal, you look like one of those Halloween-costumed ghouls. You look like you've been trick or treating. I bet you watched too many horror movies growing up or something. What was it? Something turned you into a...'

'Why are being so cruel to me? I had job to do. That's all.'

'You tried to kill me last night,' reflected Seb, rubbing at his shoulder.

'It was nothing personal.' She wriggled from side to side and winced. 'Hey, these are tight. Could you loosen them?' Her voice was even. She seemed to have retreated from her anger and also discarded the alter-ego teen girl voice she sometimes affected.

'I *could* loosen them. I *could* give you some water.' Seb knew she was a viper – poisonous, deadly and unpredictable.

'I also have to pee,' she moaned.

'I'm not stopping you.'

'You'd do that, to me?'

'I would,' replied Seb, meeting her eyes. 'Where did your friend, Gunther, take Codi?'

'The girl? Oh, she's precious to us. The boys... not so much.' Krystal chuckled softly.

Seb showed her Angel's photo. Holding it no more than a few inches in front of her face, he grabbed her hair and turned her head to force her to look at it.

Reluctantly, Krystal focused on the image and then him. 'Are you here for her?' Krystal suddenly looked confused. '*This*... is about her?'

'Have you seen her?'

'You can go fuck yourself.'

He had not meant to slap her, at least not quite so hard. The blow elicited another laugh and when her eyes turned toward him, focusing on his, he could have sworn that the pupils were elongated and vertical, like that of a snake.

'What the fuck?'

Krystal grinned. 'What's wrong?'

It had to have been a trick of the light because now her eyes appeared completely normal.

Whether it was exhaustion, loss of blood or an overactive imagination, he'd just seen something odd. He continued to stare at Krystal, but her eyes remained human and quite normal.

After a moment, looking amused, she said, 'Say I know her... and say I know where Angel is?'

'Then I let you go.'

Seb replaced the photo, stuffing it back in his wallet. He sat back heavily on the edge of the bed, slumped, his head in his hands. After a while, he said, 'She's my sister.'

'Angel has a brother. *Oh... that's cute!*'

This was taking too long. He wanted to beat the truth from her. 'Where do they have her, Krystal?'

'This is too much... really... too much.' She twisted her face to look at him, showing him a triumphant, deranged grin, because now she thought she had something to bargain with. 'If I don't check in soon, they will come looking for me.'

'I don't care.'

She spat some blood from inside her mouth. 'You think you can kill us all, tough guy? You don't know anything, not a Goddam thing about us.'

'I know that they have forgotten about you. They have better things to do than to come back for you, Krystal.'

But she was intent on taunting him. In a sing-song voice, she said, '*I know where Angel is... I know where Angel is.*'

Seb went to the door. He paused as Krystal continued. 'I know where the bitch is, *I know where, I know where…*'

He turned to face her.

'I know,' she repeated. 'Untie me, and I'll show you. Let me out of this, and you will see her again.'

'Where is she? Where is she right now?'

'Let me loose. Then, I'll tell you. We had a deal.'

Seb slowly shook his head. 'I don't trust you. I wish more than anything that I could.'

'You fucker! I'll fuckin' kill you.' Krystal began thrashing, her body convulsing as she sought to wriggle free from the straps.

Seb left as Krystal's tirade followed him along the hall, becoming a storm of every evil and wicked word that she could hurl at him. Krystal knew Angel, of that he had no doubt. Getting her to tell the truth about where to find Angel might be impossible, knowing that Krystal was a creature of mischief and deception. More talk with that little psycho bitch would just get him killed.

Having descended to the living room, his gaze was reluctantly drawn to the bodies, stiffening with the lividity of death. Staring at the corpses, Seb now believed he was slipping towards a confrontation that might be his last. Perhaps his feet had been set on this path the moment Angel had sent the letter, knowing that he would come for her.

Upstairs, Krystal's frustrated howls of anger took on an edge of panic. He felt a growing urgency to leave. His DNA would be all over the discarded clothing, the bandages he used to clean his wounds and the bedding he'd slept on. His prints would be all over the place too, on every surface he'd touched. And it would be his word against Krystal's. He had no doubt that she would make a more convincing witness than he would.

He took Krystal's Scorpion, her switchblade and his Beretta, and laid them on the table. Loading each gun, he carefully placed them in his belt, front and back.

Krystal's howls again crashed his thoughts. Screaming at the top of her lungs, she launched into another expletive-laden, threatening rant. At the end, she slowly trailed off and began sobbing.

Staring at the two dead boys, Seb wondered why Gunther had not murdered Codi alongside her brother and boyfriend. Krystal had said that she was of use to them. What that use was, he could only guess, though none of it boded well for Codi. These Dagon's Riders were not what he'd expected, not by a long shot. The guys he'd run into at the Crab Shack were your average thug types. But these others who had come after him… Krystal, in particular, seemed amped up on something. If they were using, he wondered, what were they on?

Collecting the shotgun, he glanced upstairs to where Krystal lay trussed. If he really wanted to, he could just kill her. It would be one less loose end. Without her, there would be no witnesses to say that he'd even been there.

For a minute, he stood staring at the ceiling, one foot on the first tread of the stairs, considering the possibility. At last, he unloaded the shells, dropping them on the floor, then wiped the weapon over with his shirt to remove any prints.

Returning to the kitchen, Seb took the phone off the hook and dialled 9-1-1, then tossed it on the countertop. Striding out the back door onto the jetty, he hurled the shotgun into the lake, then untied the motorboat. After two pulls of the rope, the motor coughed to life.

Zipping across the mirrored surface, he looked back at the cabin, picturing Krystal lying in the bedroom. Should he have left her alive to tell her lies? In allowing her to live, was he making a huge mistake?

Looking forward, across the lake, he could see a clearing amongst the trees and angled toward it.

Minutes later, he came ashore, into a parkland. Striding across a lawn with concrete picnic tables, he found a car park at the end of a gravel road. Just one car sat there. It was a small hatchback.

Finding it unlocked, he slid into the driver's seat, smelling weed and other unpleasant odours that originated in the litter of fast food-packets and empty beer cans on the floor. Flipping the sunshade, the keys fell into his lap.

'Geniuses,' he mumbled as he turned the key in the ignition, felt the car stir to life and shifted into gear. Winding down his window, he drove down the dirt road.

Finding Angel was still his biggest problem, but now at least he had some idea about the kind of people she was with. Maybe Benson could help. Being a local cop, she might know where these creeps were hiding out. But how much could he tell her about all the killing? Would she believe his version of the events? He thought about Guyatt, staking out his house, a pile of cigarette butts under a pine tree. Could he trust *any* of the cops in the Cove?

In third gear, the wind in his face, he had the weird feeling that he was being watched. He was sure that if he looked into the backseat, he would see the two dead stoners, pale faces staring with accusing eyes.

He'd already hallucinated twice. The disembodied voice that had said '*wake up*,' and Krystal's serpent eyes. Both seemed all too real, for at least those fleeting moments. The hair on the back of his neck prickled. He was certain that he could feel a presence in the car. Had the spirits of the recently departed attached themselves to him?

Licking suddenly dry lips, then swallowing, he made himself look up into the rear-vision mirror. But he saw only the rear seat, empty except for a pair of muddy sneakers, and a dusting of yellow, stale crumbs.

*

Benson approached Seb's Camaro, picking her way through tall grass and trees. She hoped that the rain had not spoiled any part of the interior as the car's windows had been tightly closed. She hesitated, then smashed the car's window using her truncheon, then climbed into the passenger seat. Examining the interior, she noticed no blood or any other signs of anything untoward. Seb must have parked his car in the trees behind the bungalow, probably to try and hide it from the bikers.

Retreating to the house, she unrolled crime-scene tape across the threshold of the porch. Nothing had changed since the night prior when she had come to the house and found it deserted and ransacked. She had returned partly in the hope that Seb had come back from wherever he was hiding. But he hadn't reappeared, and now she really believed that he was the victim of foul play.

She took some photos of the scene, from outside the house and then inside, where the destruction was evident. There was no blood in there either. If she had to guess, she would have said that Seb had planned his escape and had taken off with his dog before the gang could take him.

Guyatt, and maybe even the chief would say that he had left town, that there was nothing more to be said, or done for that matter. Without a body, there could be no foul play.

She walked out the back one last time and looked into the trees that bordered the property. The forest extended up steep slopes into the hinterland. Not having grown up in the Cove, she had only heard of the trails that crisscrossed the hills between the coast and the town. If Seb had made it out alive, he might have gone into those hills, up into the forest. It was a vast area to search, and she would need more than a hunch to attempt it on her own. Inside, she spent some time looking for Seb's personal belongings. She may need a contact number for a family member. In the main bedroom, she found an overnight bag, its contents upended across the floor. There was just some clothing. No papers, no wallet, no license.

She went back to the cruiser. 'Base? Base, come in,' she said into her radio.

'What is it, Benson?' said Webster, sounding a bit annoyed.

'Sorry, Webster, did I wake you? Any reports yet about a Sebastian Straeker?'

'Nothing. Are you back up there now?' asked Webster.

'Roger that.'

'Boss says you should return to the station and file a report.'

'Saying what? I have evidence that a crime has been committed and a missing victim. Surely, we need to find him. Isn't that what we do?'

Webster sighed. 'Look, the chief says that you have done all you can now. Get your ass back in here. We have work to do.'

'Is the chief in?' asked Benson.

'No, she called in. But she seems to be across everything.'

'Webster?'

'Yeah?'

'Did you see Miller's lawyer last night?' asked Benson.

'Yeah, yeah. Some smartass in a suit came and busted him out. The chief said we had to let him go.'

Benson paused, thinking for a moment. 'Okay, will be back in twenty minutes or so. Not sure what I will put in the report.'

'Break-in and robbery. That's all you have right now.'

'Okay.' She replaced the receiver and started the cruiser. But none of it was *okay*, she thought. Shifted into reverse, her last glance at the house was of the broken front door, and the crime-scene tape.

CHAPTER 21

Dawn was less than an hour away. Under starlight, the pool's still surface looked like a black pit. What the stagnant water concealed beneath the putrid surface was anyone's guess. Angel walked in the grounds of the derelict mansion, wondering about Seb, the note she'd sent him and if he was right now gazing at the same stars?

The campervan had been brought around the back of the house and was parked beside the poolhouse. From the road, passers-by would only see an ornate black iron gate and a long drive up to a desolate brick Georgian house.

She wandered amongst overgrown weeds and an orchard where the fruit was left to rot on the ground. This place was one of the 'holes', as the gang liked to refer to them, a place where they could take refuge and hideout as they traversed the coast. They used many such places, and Angel had been to most of them by now.

Leo came walking out of the mansion, a cell phone to his ear. Angel could hear him as he approached. 'We are a day out. No – we will be there tomorrow night. Two – I got two.' There was a long pause where Leo rolled his eyes at Angel, before saying, 'Sorry, that's the best I could do.' Leo hung up, replacing the phone in his jacket pocket. Angel always watched to see which pocket it went into. Not that it would have done her much good even if she did manage to get her hands on it.

'You better get inside,' growled Leo.

Angel stared at him, then slowly wandered toward the house. It would have been nice to see the daylight, to watch the dawn.

But they were obsessive about being hidden during the hours of daylight. They hated the sun, Leo often referring to his crew as nocturns. They slept during the day and they travelled at night. Soon, if she wasn't able to leave them, to slink away, perform a world-class disappearing trick, she would be one of them and the sun would be a distant memory.

Inside, the wooden floor was covered in layers of dirt and dust so thick that it crunched under her boots. The once-white ceilings were flaking, their ornate mouldings yellowing with age and spotted with black mould. Graffiti was sprayed around the walls in green and orange paint – *Gary was here, 1987* and *Jack fucked Callister, 2012*, as well as a bunch of other unsavoury details someone felt compelled to write for posterity.

Angel descended a steep staircase into a basement. Her eyes adjusted quickly. Belle and Matti sat jammed close together on a sofa. Either side of them sat Screamer and Little Bear, their unblinking gazes glued to the two women's thighs. The flesh on display was visibly exciting the youths. Through mascara-smudged eyes, the two prisoners looked up at Angel as she approached. Angel refused to look at them, instead turning her attention to finding somewhere she could sleep.

Although she couldn't see them, the scent of road dust mingled with leather and sweat told her that the crew were already bunked down in the shadowy recesses of the basement.

She settled into her sleeping bag and spoke to the two women. 'Get some sleep. You have a big day tomorrow.'

'Where are you taking us?' asked Belle.

'Go to sleep. No one knows where you are. No one can help you.'

'Why are you doing this?' asked Matti. She was older and had managed to get a hold of herself much faster than the teenage girl.

Angel did not want to say. Instead, she said, 'Lay down here beside me.'

Screamer placed a restraining hand on Belle's leg as she tried to move. Angel glared at Screamer and Little Bear, and they stared back. The door above them closed, and the darkness became deeper. Leo's two-inch Cuban bootheels announced him as he came down the stairs. He turned his eyes on Screamer and the boy instantly retracted his hand.

'No spoiling the merchandise,' Leo warned.

Screamer's face was a mask of rage for a moment. Angel suspected the youth was on the verge of something terrible. She felt the two women settle in near her, perhaps hoping that she was not quite like the others.

Angel knew the sun was coming up, that somewhere overhead golden rays would be caressing the land. She may as well have been lying in the bottom of a grave, unable to move. She wanted to scream, to wail, to have Seb come and rescue her. Tears settled in the corners of her eyes before overflowing and slipping down porcelain cheeks. She drifted toward an uneasy sleep, thinking about how she could slip away from them, if the time was ever right.

'Why did you take us? Why did *you* trick us?' whispered Belle, close to Angel's ear.

Angel stared at the girl, wishing now that she had not allowed herself to become teary. 'I have my reasons. I was like you... lost. They gave me something to hold on to.'

'Did they trick you, like you tricked us? Or did you go to them, willingly?'

Angel swallowed and shook her head. 'That's none of your fucking business. Go to sleep, or I'll let Screamer come over here and...'

'What? Kill me? Leo said we were too valuable. I heard him.'

'We are all one heartbeat from being *fresh meat*, missy,' hissed Angel. 'I've seen them kill girls prettier than you for saying the wrong thing.'

Belle stared at Angel. 'Why didn't they kill you?'

'Because I will do anything to survive... *anything*. And that includes getting more stupid bitches like you on the hook,' said Angel.

'You're just as evil as those fuckers. I hate you.'

'Well, I hate me too,' whispered Angel. 'But ask yourself – if it wasn't me that lured you into that van, would you have gone with one of the others anyway? You were dead the minute you walked into that dive. Nothing I could do to stop that then, and nothing I can do now.'

Belle began a quiet sobbing, and Matti put her arm around her.

Leo suddenly stood over them, his sunken eyes pits of darkness. 'Shut the fuck up, bitches, and go to sleep.'

Angel wondered if she was worth still saving. Even if she managed to escape, how much of herself was left? Maybe there was only one way out now, a final step, and then she would be just like them. *Could she do it?*

CHAPTER 22

The truck-stop, complete with a diner, showers, gas pumps and a 7-Eleven, was just the kind of place he had been looking for. Donnelly removed his baseball cap and left it on the passenger seat. The star on his chest though, he left be, knowing that some folks still respected a lawman. He was now well beyond his jurisdiction, having crossed four more counties. The night before he had reluctantly slept on the side of the road in the backseat of the car.

It was lunchtime, trucks were parked all over the place and cars came and went with frequency. Around fifty people were in the store, most sitting around in booths eating. Music was playing but the tune was lost in the general hubbub. Donnelly went to the men's room, splashed cold water on his face, combed his hair and walked back into the store. He took a padded stool at the servery and poured a glass of water from a jug.

'Sheriff? But not from around here,' said the guy behind the counter. He was smiling, despite looking hot and sweaty beneath a soiled apron.

'Name's Donnelly.'

'You are well out of your county,' observed the cook, staring at the star on his chest.

'I sure am. I'm looking for some folks that did something... *bad*... back in my town – a little place called Friar's Ridge. You know it?'

The cook shook his head, brow furrowed. Donnelly could see him thinking really hard. 'Nope.'

'You might have seen them.'

'Nope.'

'I haven't told you yet what they look like.'

'Oh, well, I'm sure I haven't seen anyone bad,' said the cook.

'How would you know unless I tell you? You can't tell a person is bad just by looking at them,' said Donnelly.

'Sometimes... I think you can,' disagreed the cook.

Donnelly paused, initially shaking his head, and then nodding, he said, 'Okay, good.'

'I haven't seen anyone bad,' explained the cook.

'Yeah, I got you the first time,' said Donnelly. He glanced up at the menu, which was written neatly on a blackboard. 'Can I order something?'

The cook called over a waitresses and the girl, who looked about fifteen, gave Donnelly an apologetic smile as she took out the notepad and pencil.

'I'm really sorry about him.' She glanced at the cook, and when he moved away toward the kitchen, she smiled at Donnelly.

Donnelly said, 'Can I order some chicken – fried – and a beer.'

The waitress jotted down the order, then said, 'What did those *bad folk* do?'

'They killed some people. And... they took two women.'

'Took? Holy shit. What did they look like?'

'Maybe four motorbike riders... perhaps as many as ten. There would be a campervan with them.' Donnelly turned on the stool and was surveying the room. 'Yeah, there would be a van.'

'Is that it?' asked the waitress.

'That's all I got, right now. You see anyone like that?'

'They came through here alright,' she said.

Donnelly sat up straight. 'You sure? When?'

'Last night. They came in here around two a.m.'

Donnelly allowed her words to sink in. They were travelling at night, he realised. Which meant they were probably laying low during the day.

'How do you know?'

'My friend, Jackie, was on the night shift last night. She talked about them when we swapped over shifts this morning. She said they were creepy and not very friendly.'

'Was there a campervan with them?' asked Donnelly.

'She didn't say.'

'You got cameras?'

She shrugged. 'We do, but... I'm not the boss.'

'Tell me your cook isn't the boss,' said Donnelly.

She smiled. 'God, no.' She pointed to the counter where people lined up to pay for their gas. 'Doris is the boss. This is her place.'

Donnelly looked over at an older woman serving a queue of customers.

He ate his lunch quickly and twenty minutes later, in a backroom office, Donnelly was leaning over a television monitor, watching the interior of the store from a few angles on a split screen. They fast-forwarded to 2.12 a.m. when a group entered the shop. Five walked in, all clad in black leather, coats long and dark. Donnelly could see the two waitresses say something to them. One of the gang looked very young – almost a kid.

'Is there sound?'

Doris said, 'No, just video.'

The bikers took some drinks from the refrigerators and paid for them. Donnelly noted that the two women were nowhere to be seen. He suspected that they could be in the campervan.

'Pause it there,' he said.

The frozen image showed the group leaving the store. There was a good image of one of the group, the one at the front, who might be the leader. He may have been older than the others. He had a chiselled face, hard angles and deep-set eyes. In the corner of the image, the front of the campervan could just be seen, parked outside.

'Look here! I need the plates on this thing,' said Donnelly, tapping his finger on the screen on top of the campervan. 'In fact, I need the plates on their bikes too. Do you have a camera outside?'

Doris smiled but in an embarrassed kind of way. 'Our outside camera is on the fritz.'

'Shit!'

'I am sorry,' said Doris.

'Excuse me, ma'am, I was disappointed. You have been very helpful.' Donnelly glanced once more at the screen, imprinting the biker's face on his memory.

'Did you need a search warrant or something,' asked Doris.

'I don't like paperwork much, ma'am. Look, if it makes you feel any better, I was never here, okay? If I got a search warrant for everything I needed, these types of people would always get away.'

'Okay,' said Doris, looking dubious.

He left her office and strode through the shop, out to the Mustang. He was on track, and not too far behind them. It was no time to give up. Not yet. There were only so many places where they could fuel up and replenish their food. People would notice them along the highways and byways, but only within a short time frame before they forgot about them. He needed to keep up, and a little luck. His cell rang and he answered, 'Donnelly.'

'When are you coming home?' asked Tilly.

'Tilly, you know I have to see this through,' he replied.

'What will you do when you catch up with them?'

'What needs doing,' he said.

'You give them a chance to surrender.'

'You know I will,' he replied.

'I love you,' she said.

Before he could reply, she had hung up.

CHAPTER 23

Joshua drove Jaz back to her flat, staying parked for no more than a heartbeat before swinging the Ford Explorer around.

Jaz darted up the steps to her apartment and slipped inside, her snub-nose .38 at the ready. There was no movement and no signs that anyone had been in there. Closing the door behind her, she started a sweep of the rooms, looking for listening devices.

After a few minutes, finding nothing, she sat in the chair, opened the laptop on the coffee table and went to her email. Nothing from work. She was about to call Harvey when a fleeting memory came back to her – the night when she'd come in, switched on the TV and found the reception had dropped out. She'd adjusted the antennae, getting the reception just right. It seemed odd at the time that suddenly the reception was off.

She wiggled the rabbit ears, examining them, turning them around and upside-down. On the back, held by a small magnet, she found a listening device. Carefully, she put the antennae back on the TV and walked out to the balcony. Closing the sliding balcony door, she called her boss.

'Harvey here.'

'Hey, boss, it's me.'

'Jaz, I hope you're calling to say you're coming back soon. You know we miss you.'

'That's not why I'm calling. I need something.'

'I knew it. You can never just take a break, can you, Freeman?'

'What do you mean?'

155

Harvey laughed. 'I've been down to your office, Freeman. I've seen what you have been working on.'

'My project?'

'Yes, your project.'

'I think I have something here.'

'Yeah, you have *something*. Listen, Freeman, it's time to call it quits and come back to the office. I have some real cases for you.'

'I need your help first, okay?'

'I know you work hard, and I know the cold case work isn't always rewarding, but you have an instinct for it.'

'I know I do. That's why you need to shut up and just listen for a second,' snapped Jaz. There was silence. 'Boss, are you there?'

'I'm here.'

'I need information, as much as you can dig up on a guy called McTaggart – one Stirling McTaggart. Can you do that for me? I have something here, but I don't exactly know what it is,' said Jaz.

'You really think so?' Harvey sounded somewhere between annoyed and intrigued. 'If I do this one thing, will you come back?'

'Something really stinks here, boss. I have some of the picture but I need more.'

Harvey was silent for a while. 'I'll run the name. When it comes back negative, you come back home.'

'Thanks... how long till you come back to me with something?' asked Jaz.

'Give me an hour. Promise me though, that when I find nothing, and it will be *nothing*, you will get your ass back here,' said Harvey.

'Alright.'

'I've never heard of this guy. If he were someone... a big mafia guy, drug lord, or something, I would have heard the name,' said Harvey.

'You may have to go deeper for this one,' said Jaz. 'He's probably connected or at least using an alias.'

'Okay.' Harvey hung up abruptly.

Jaz was sure that she was on the right track. The bug proved that. She sat on the chair on the balcony, feeling bone-tired, but unwilling to go back inside the flat.

She must have dozed off because it was her cell phone that woke her.

'Jaz?' said Harvey.

'What do you have?'

'I don't know,' admitted Harvey. He sounded different.

'What do you mean?'

'Well, you'll be pleased to know that there really is a Stirling McTaggart,' said Harvey. 'He appears to be a chemist – no local town pharmacy guy. No – he's a biochemist,' said Harvey.

'I guess his money came from somewhere. This guy seems to be loaded,' said Jaz.

'He had a company which won some defence force contracts. Those files are all sealed under the official secrets' provisions,' said Harvey. 'And... there are a few other files, which are even more classified. If I was to take it any further, it might sound some serious alarms.'

'Huh?'

'The files are not ours. Nothing criminal exists on him. But there are references to some CIA records. I can't go digging around there without someone up the chain asking why I was looking into this guy McTaggart.'

Jaz sighed. 'This guy can't be CIA.'

'He could be,' said Harvey.

'I suspect he's involved in murder... probably kidnapping. We need to dig up everything on him. The local law here seems to be protecting him.' She waited, but Harvey said nothing. Perhaps he was digesting her words. 'Are you saying you won't take this any further?'

'I didn't say that, Freeman. How bad do you need to know about this guy?'

'How bad do you consider murder, conspiracy and police corruption?' countered Jaz. 'I think he's linked with whatever is going on here. Whatever *this* is, he is at the centre. And Harvey, they bugged me.'

'What?'

'Yep, they put a Goddam bug in my room.'

'Who's they?'

'I don't know for sure – the cops… the gang… I don't know.'

'*Jesus*, Freeman. What have you found?'

'Something big.'

Harvey sighed. 'Alright, what can you tell me? What do you have right now?'

Jaz gave an overview of the situation, starting with the suspicious death of the boy – Eric Winters – around seven years before, to the apparent police cover-up of the investigation. Jaz read from her notes. She mentioned the untimely deaths of the local coroner and a police officer. She outlined the apparent link between McTaggart and the Dagon's Riders gang. Lastly, she admitted that she thought the Dagon's Riders gang were involved in possible abductions and murders all up the west coast over a period of years. She outlined the pattern of disappearances she had suspected were linked to the gang, and how the town of Crabtree Cove was geographically central.

When Jaz finished, Harvey let out a breath. 'I agree we should look hard at McTaggart.' Jaz noted that his attitude had shifted. Now it was *we*.

Jaz could hear him tapping on a keyboard. 'What this is about is anyone's guess. Do not, repeat, do not check in with the local cops. Consider yourself on active duty from now on, in fact, from two days ago. I need a situation report every day moving forward. You seem to be embedded there, so we won't send in a team that will attract attention. There won't be any cavalry, Jaz, just you on the ground, at least for now.'

'I can live with that.'

'I have some contacts I can talk to,' said Harvey. 'But I will need to do some face time with them. I won't risk anything over the phone. This guy is definitely connected.'

Jaz suspected he was talking about some people he might know in the CIA. 'Thanks, Harvey.'

'Are you safe, Freeman?' His question was weighted. If she said 'no,' he might move someone else in to take over the investigation.

She stood, leaning against the balcony rail, considering how Seb Straeker had now seemed to be missing. 'I'm okay. I've got this.'

'Be careful. No unnecessary risks,' said Harvey.

Jaz felt like saying, *No shit*, but instead said, 'Don't worry about me.'

The call ended. Jaz was tired, but on some level, elated.

She went back into the apartment, sat and opened the laptop. In the folder marked *missing*, there were twelve files, each with the case notes and photos. Each file was named separately. She scrolled down the screen – *Rhys Prescott, Gary Waters, Bailey Phillips, Scott Carrick, Jamie Grant, Phil Reece, Chloe Neilson, Judd Filmore, Miley Finch, Mason Smith, Jill Hampstead* and *Julian Monroe*. She opened each file in turn, looking through their photos, and re-reading the case notes for the hundredth time.

Wandering back to the balcony, she slid the door shut. Somewhere, Seb Straeker was either dead or lying low. What should have been a refreshing breeze from the Cove washed over, prickling her skin and creating gooseflesh.

Her cell rang; she answered, 'Freeman.'

'Everything okay?' It was Joshua.

'I have an issue here, but I'm okay.'

'What's wrong?'

'Seems like I made the list. They're watching me. I found a bug.'

There was a silence at the other end, then, 'Can you talk?'

'Yeah, it's in the living room. I'm on the balcony.'

'You need to take care, Jaz. Maybe you shouldn't stay there anymore. You could come to our place.'

'I want them to think I don't know. I'll stay here, for now.'

'But they've been in there. Aren't you worried?'

'I'm confident I'm not blown. All my ID and my computer were with me all the time. They won't know anything about me.'

'Okay then.' He sounded unconvinced.

Jaz felt that time was critical. They needed to move fast before the police decided to pay her closer attention. 'I need to see that video, Joshua,' Jaz reminded him.

'That's why I'm calling. There is a meeting tonight.'

'Go on...'

'Father O'Malley agreed to meet. Do you know where St. Anthony's is?'

'I'll find it,' she said. 'What time?'

'After the evening mass. 9.30 p.m. It's only a few streets from where you're staying.'

'Why can't we go now?'

'It's when everyone will be there. It's the time when a group of concerned citizens can converge on a location without attracting attention,' said Joshua.

Jaz considered arguing the point. 'Okay, Joshua. 9.30 p.m.'

Joshua hung up. Jaz came inside and lay down on the couch, feeling the exhaustion of being up half the night. Within a few minutes, she had once more drifted to sleep.

CHAPTER 24

At exactly 9.15 pm, Jaz exited the flat, rugged up in a coat, jeans and boots. Under the coat, sitting close to her side, the snub-nosed .38 felt necessary for the first time in years. She tried to appear relaxed as she walked the darkened streets, now on a different level of alertness. It was a Sunday night and pretty quiet in the Cove. Following the footpath, she could faintly hear TVs in living rooms, smell late-cooked dinners and the occasional barking dog.

Jaz continued two blocks before taking a right onto the main street into town. A few hundred yards down that thoroughfare, St Anthony's spires rose up, formidable and bleak, silhouetted against the night sky. A police car cruised by very slowly, the interior too dark to see the occupants. It went on down the hill toward the docks.

Arriving at St Anthony's, she found the main doors to the church were wide open, spilling golden candlelight from within. Either the priest was popular or the town was more religious than most for the place was packed. Jaz had been a Catholic or at least had been raised as one. But she no longer believed. In her line of work, she found it hard to think that there could be a God or a God that had all our best interests at heart. She walked in, seeing the service was coming to its conclusion. The priest moved back down the centre aisle, nodding left and right, saying a few encouraging words to the parishioners as he went. The music from the organ and the singing slowly died. Jaz stood awkwardly near the entrance, allowing everyone to file out past her. O'Malley, who had only glanced in her direction must have known to expect her, for he met her eyes and nodded.

Then Joshua was there and he smiled at Jaz as he stood near her. Lucille and her kid were nowhere to be seen. She glanced inside the church, discovering ten people remained, in no hurry to leave. Then O'Malley took Jaz by the elbow and walked her through the ornate archway, and back into the church. He turned and closed the heavy doors with a solid *thunk*, then produced a key, locking out the world beyond. Only then did he introduce himself. 'I'm Father O'Malley. You can call me John.'

'I'm...' began Jaz.

'I know who you are,' he cut in. 'Please come with us.' He strode away.

Jaz walked amidst the group to the end of the hall, close to the altar. On the right was a door, and behind the altar she could see another. But it was to the left that they proceeded in neat order, each person seeming to know where they were going. They went in an orderly single file, like obedient acolytes from a cult, thought Jaz, but dressed in normal street gear. The priest moved a heavy velvet curtain to reveal a concealed door. He produced a second key and unlocked it.

'Everything here is secure,' noted Jaz.

'Everything needs to be,' said O'Malley. He was smiling, but she could see that he was serious.

They climbed a staircase, several in the group using their cell phones to light the way. They emerged at the top of a balcony. Jaz looked over the railing at the church floor two stories below.

There was another doorway, and they passed through it, emerging in a loft. The loft had been converted into a meeting room. In the middle of the floor was a wooden table with a dozen plush chairs around it. A burgundy rug covered most of the timber floor. The roof sloped close to their heads, but on the left and right, small windows afforded glimpses of the town. As Jaz entered the space, she was enveloped by a feeling of charming warmth and seclusion. No one would ever find this place without knowing it was here.

'Everyone, please sit,' said O'Malley.

The group sat, and Jaz found herself seated beside Joshua.

'This is the person I told you about,' said Joshua.

'The FBI lady,' said a woman with a sensuous voice.

'Yes, Charlie,' said Joshua.

'Perhaps I should introduce myself. I'm special agent Jaz Freeman. I work cold cases.'

'Why did you bring her here, Joshua?' said an old man with a bald head.

'I said she should come here,' snapped O'Malley. He held up a hand to head off any further grumblings. There were a few, Jaz noted.

O'Malley turned to Jaz. 'We're a secret group, by necessity.'

'Yes, I think I understand.'

'You might understand a few things about this town, Ms Freeman, but there is much you don't know,' said the priest. He took a carafe of red wine from a side table, which he poured into a glass. 'Can you tell us what brought you to the Cove?'

'I told you...' began Joshua.

'But I want to hear it from her,' said O'Malley.

'I came here, on the trail of a group I suspect of kidnapping, possibly of murder. They are a gang that call themselves Dagon's Riders.'

'We are aware of who they are.' O'Malley met Jaz's eyes, then asked, 'How much do you know of them?'

'I think they could be linked to a number of cold cases I've been investigating.'

'You see,' said Joshua.

'You think you can help us?' said Charlie. She was striking, with long black hair, tied in a ponytail.

Jaz smiled. 'I should hope so. Or maybe we can help each other.'

The priest stood and paced, glancing out the windows as he spoke. 'We meet here, every Sunday after the last mass,' he explained. 'We discuss any new information that comes to hand.

The town's phones, as you know, are sometimes compromised. Occasionally, email is intercepted. The town is watched closely because the lord of the manor has an operation that he doesn't want interrupted.'

'McTaggart,' supplied Jaz.

O'Malley nodded and continued. 'McTaggart has the police in his pocket. He is wealthy… very wealthy. He has an agenda, which I have only glimpsed. And he will kill when he feels the need. His need is… secrecy, and to continue his clandestine operation.'

'How does McTaggart fit with the Dagon's Riders gang?' asked Jaz.

O'Malley's lips curled with distaste. 'They go where he commands, committing every sin forsaken by God.'

Jaz said, 'Kidnapping… killing.'

O'Malley nodded, eyes bright, his voice tinged with righteous rage. 'They steal people away and convey them to him, to carry out his foul trade.'

'What does he do with them?' Jaz

'There are secrets McTaggart guards… has even killed to keep. I've been trying to discover his secrets for years.'

Jaz allowed her eyes to travel the room. The faces that stared back at her were solemn. No one smiled, and no one looked away. Whatever they thought they were doing, Jaz believed they were deadly serious about it.

A second priest entered from another door. Jaz noted that this priest was taller and broader than your average guy, and although he was dressed like a priest, something about him seemed different. Perhaps it was the hairstyle – close-cropped and spiked at the front. He had a jacket on too, despite them being fairly warm in the loft. Jaz thought he might be carrying a gun under the coat.

O'Malley said, 'Thank you, Father Daniel.'

'You're welcome,' said the other priest before he left the room.

'Who was that?' asked Joshua.

'Never you mind, Joshua,' said O'Malley.

'Joshua mentioned you had something to show me – a video,' prompted Jaz.

'We will get to that,' said O'Malley, taking a sip of the wine.

'I'd like to see it,' pressed Jaz.

'All in good time, Ms Freeman.'

Jaz settled back in her seat and allowed one of the parishioners to pour her a glass of red. Patiently, she waited.

'We are in a fight in this town, Ms Freeman. We, this group you see here, and some others... keep watch over the town. We see things that many don't,' said O'Malley.

Jaz waited, her arms folded. She sensed that Father O'Malley had more to say but was procrastinating about whether he could truly trust this outsider before him, this woman that could be pretending to be from the FBI. His paranoia was understandable if half of what Joshua had alluded to was true.

'Can we trust you?' asked Charlie, bluntly.

'You trusted me the minute you allowed me in here. I've been chasing after these guys for years, Charlie.' They all stared at her and after a moment, Jaz continued, 'Look, I want these guys as much as you do.'

'I doubt that,' said O'Malley. 'This is our town, our lives, our way of life–'

'Our children,' interjected an older woman. Jaz looked at her. She stared back, steel in her eyes.

'Charlie here is our means of communicating with each other and with our wider community in a way that stops *them* from overhearing us,' said Joshua.

'When we have something, we need to say to our friends all across the Cove, something that has to go out straight away, I broadcast it,' said Charlie proudly.

'Like what?' asked Jaz.

'When these Dagon's Riders are in town, we play *The Boys are Back in Town*,' said Charlie, quoting Thin Lizzy's hit song.

'The song? You're kidding me,' grinned Jaz.

'And when the police are looking for someone, we mention them on the radio every hour, stating their name and wishing them a happy birthday,' said Charlie.

'No shit,' said Jaz, realising they were deadly serious.

'When we think they are bugging a new house, we play *Private Eyes* by Hall and Oates.' Charlie looked a little embarrassed, but Jaz could tell that the group was proud of their mechanism to broadcast messages to the community that they considered necessary.

'We have other special signals too, and a few code words, but we won't bore you with any more of that,' said O'Malley.

'Clever, very clever,' admitted Jaz. She didn't know really what to think of this little game they were playing.

'But we think they may know what we are up to,' said O'Malley.

'Why do you say that?'

'There have been threats made to Charlie, very direct, very explicit,' explained Joshua.

Jaz glanced at the woman, and Charlie shifted uncomfortably in her seat. 'I move where I broadcast from, all the time,' she said.

'We have a list of people we suspect of colluding too. Some folks can't be trusted. They sold out,' said a bald-headed guy.

'Why haven't you tried to contact the bureau before? Surely that was something you could have considered,' said Jaz.

'And say what? Our police chief is in cahoots with a local rich guy, who we think is a "bad" guy?' said Charlie. 'We need solid evidence for anyone to look into this.'

'Well, I'm here now,' said Jaz.

'Not exactly the cavalry,' said Charlie. 'No offence.'

'None taken,' said Jaz. 'But one call from me, and I can bring in the cavalry. But I won't do that until I have more information. I need something solid. All I have right now is a gang suspected of being in the area when people vanish, some homicides – again – the gang *could be* in the vicinity. I have no solid evidence.' Jaz shook her head, her frustration plain. 'And now I have *talk* about a rich guy called McTaggart, who may or may not be colluding with local law enforcement. I can't go on all this circumstantial evidence alone. I will need to convince my own people that all this is real. A guy like McTaggart could slip out of the noose before it's ever tightened.'

'Which brings us to Eric Winters, and the video he took,' said O'Malley.

'That's why I'm here,' said Jaz, the impatience in her voice no longer concealed.

'I have never shown the film to anyone, not even this group,' said O'Malley.

'Why?' asked Jaz. 'I thought you trusted everyone here.'

'I do. But the images are not something you can unsee, once you see them,' said O'Malley.

'I've seen blood split before, I've seen dead bodies. I can handle it,' said Jaz.

'No, I can't explain it in words.'

'Then maybe you need to show us,' said Jaz.

O'Malley looked at the group, at each person individually. At last, he gave a solemn nod of agreement.

CHAPTER 25

Sheriff Donnelly's Mustang was cruising on a half tank of gas, heading north, the highway angled slightly toward the coast. He'd been thinking about Tilly, missing her, and his optimism at locating his quarry was beginning to wane. He'd given himself just one more night to find the killers before he accepted that they were in the wind.

On the horizon, the glow of a light slowly grew. Within minutes, he was cruising up to a diner. Slowing down, he took a good long look inside. Waitresses and a few customers – but no bikers.

There were a few cars parked, a single truck, but no camper van, and no motorbikes. Maybe he'd missed them, maybe they'd drifted off on some dusty side road. He didn't need the fuel, and he didn't want to stop for coffee or a meal. He looked at his watch. It was close on 10.45 p.m. Slowing as he neared an intersection, his attention was drawn to a sign that said *23 miles to Crabtree Cove. Come and play.* The light on the sign showed a faded image of a man fishing, kids swimming and a cartoon vision of a pin-up woman in a yellow bikini.

Donnelly was considering the exit, wondering, as he had about several other exits before. He'd gone a couple of hundred yards past the exit when he spied several taillights on that side-road, in the distance across a long, flat plain. He slowed to under twenty and stared out at the diminishing lights. Were they bikes? He braked to a crawl, staring hard, and the more he stared, the more he thought they were. He stopped and a truck nearly ran up the back of him. Its air horn blared and it rushed around him onto the verge, spraying dust and gravel.

Donnelly swung the Mustang around in a tight turn and gunned the motor back toward the exit to Crabtree Cove, his pulse just starting to quicken.

*

Officer Benson was alone in the police station, watching music clips on her phone to pass the time. Her feet, crossed on the desk, said *I'm feeling slightly pissed off.*

Nothing much happened in the Cove on a Sunday night. Guyatt, Webster and the others were out cruising the neighbourhoods, looking for someone. They refused to say who or why. Something was up. Her uniformed colleagues were trying to play it cool in front of her, but they were anything but cool. Something hot was under their collars, and it was starting to make them itch.

Chief O'Brien had called her and told her to stay at the station, that she needed to be there. It was an odd command that she had been explicitly directed to remain at the station.

And then there was the matter of Sebastian Straeker. She had filed the report, but nothing more was being done. How odd this seemed. It was as if the chief was happy to forget all about this guy who might be dead and sure as hell qualified as a missing person, last seen a couple of days ago right on their patch. If ever there was a time that she wanted to ignore the rules, if ever there was a time to disobey a direct order, she felt it was now.

Pouring a second coffee, it tasted bitter as she gazed out the window at the car park. She stood, paced, nervous energy and caffeine stimulating her subconscious – ideas and thoughts forming, though she wasn't *there* yet. In the recesses of her mind, she was mulling something over.

'This is total bull shit,' she said, snatching up the keys to the last police car left in the lot. She strode outside, heading for her car.

*

Donnelly pushed the Mustang hard, the muscle car responding with 460 horses, tearing up the narrow road in the direction the bikers had gone, the V8 engine growling.

Somewhere along the middle of the road, he vibrated over a rail crossing. A coyote wandered into his path but as he broke slightly, it shied away, disappearing into low scrub, glittering eyes blinking.

He glimpsed red taillights in the distance, fireflies dancing on a distant ridge, moving in single file, fast approaching a line of distant hills.

Two minutes later, he swerved around a bend and started the climb himself. The taillights disappeared. But they had to be close. If they didn't take a side road, he would be on them in no time. He hadn't thought much about what he would do when caught up with the gang, but these things usually sorted themselves out – one way or another.

Rounding tight bends, the hills abruptly entered the forest, winding around as the road climbed. The car leapt as he crested a ridge, gaining some air before it touched down again. On his right, there was a cliff and the ocean below. He rocketed forward, eyes fixed, owning each bend, closing in on them.

If he was expecting to see the bikes through the trees up ahead, their lights shining, he was mistaken. As he screamed around the next bend, he found the campervan.

They were just in front, finding it hard work in the twisting hills. He slammed on his breaks, the Mustang jacking sideways a little before he brought it into line. Almost kissing the back of the van, he barked, 'Holy shit.' Then easing back, he said, 'I gotcha now, your asses are mine!'

He stayed close, flipping his lights to high beam, jagging the Mustang from side to side. The van seemed to ignore him. He could see some bikers up in front of it, riding in a tight group. One or two had dropped to see what the commotion was. A guy with a spiked helmet shook his head at him.

They think I'm just some asshole trying to overtake them, thought Donnelly. He wound down his window and shoved the beacon onto the roof where the magnet grabbed, then flipped the siren. They needed to know he was police, and that he was not fuckin' around anymore.

Two bikers suddenly braked and then they were on either side. They took a good look at him. The one on the right looked pretty young. He produced a pistol and it fired – *pop, pop, pop*. Nothing hit but he heard the third shot strike the door of the Mustang. The other rider came in close, a sawn-off shotgun levelled at Donnelly's face. The sheriff swerved at him and the gun went off with a loud crack, but the rider had been evading the Mustang and shot high. Donnelly braked too and allowed the bikes to get out in front once more. He could have done with someone in the passenger seat with a rifle or something. He couldn't drive and shoot effectively. *Goddamit.*

Donnelly slowed, following at a distance of just over a hundred yards, keeping their taillights well within sight. The bastards would have to pull over sometime and when they did, he could use his sidearm, and if needed, the pump-action shotgun in the trunk. It was then that the bikes turned off their lights and he had a lot of trouble seeing their exact positions. He heard a few more shots. One struck a neat hole in the windscreen to his left. That was a bit close. He could drill these guys, knock them off their bikes – one by one. The van was kind of in the way though. No – the best course was to follow and be patient. Maybe they would run and leave the van behind. The two women, if they still had them, would be in there. It made sense. Donnelly followed, keeping pace, swerving back and forth, ensuring that a stray bullet didn't easily find the mark.

It lasted like this, a cat-and-mouse game, for around ten more minutes. More shots whined past him as the gang sought to ward him off. Then the road rounded a sharp bend and straightened.

Up ahead, a roadblock came into view. There were red and blue flashing lights, the swirling pattern reflecting off nearby pine trees. One police cruiser blocked the road and another sat facing his direction on the right-hand verge. The campervan had been pulled over but it was on the far side of the roadblock. They had allowed the van and the bikers through but were blocking his Mustang.

Donnelly edged up close on the flashing lights, seeing a state trooper walk out confidently into the middle of the road, his hand held up, the other resting on his sidearm, a holstered automatic.

The second police car, the one pulled up on the grass verge, was a local police car with Crabtree Cove Police printed across the hood. The officer in that car remained in the driver's seat, unmoving. Pine trees loomed up high on either side of the road, dark and still.

'You're a little out of your jurisdiction,' said the trooper. His voice was clipped. He looked down at Donnelly through the driver-side window.

'Those guys you pulled over; they're suspects in a multiple homicide. They may also have two abducted women in the back of the campervan,' stated Donnelly.

The trooper looked back at the van and at the gang that were sitting on their bikes.

'Is that right?' He looked over at the gang, then turned his back and bent slightly to talk close to Donnelly through the Mustang's window. 'How are we gonna play this, Chief?' The trooper was looking at Donnelly's silver star badge, pinned to his left breast pocket at the cap with the word 'chief'. He then glanced at the bullet hole in the windscreen.

'I don't know how you ended up here so fast,' said Donnelly, 'but I'm glad for it. I was having one hell of a time trying to get those boys to pull over.'

'I bet you were. We were already here though, Chief. This is the only road out of the Cove, which goes back to the interstate.

We had a situation in town, looking for someone else as it happens, and we are just setting up some roadblocks.'

'Already here?' Donnelly's eyes narrowed. 'Don't let them go. We need to get inside that van.'

The trooper nodded. 'They aren't going anywhere. But we need to be cool. Wait right here.'

The trooper walked away, heading over to the local police cruiser, and he bent his head and spoke into the car. Donnelly could not clearly see the occupant. Then the local police officer exited the car. It was a big guy. He walked over to the bikers and began a conversation that Donnelly could not hear. They were too far away. The tall cop was standing conversing, his hand on his hips. He didn't look nervous. Donnelly started to worry. This didn't look right. The trooper seemed to be too calm. The local cop seemed to know the bikers. They began laughing. A chill went up Donnelly's spine.

The sheriff sat still, Mustang idling, but his hand went to the service revolver on his hip. He pulled it from the holster and lay it in his lap beneath the steering wheel, across his legs, where he could easily reach it.

Watching the scene before him, he eased the car's gear into reverse, though he kept his foot on the brake. Donnelly was tempted to get the hell out. The Mustang's V8 engine was idling, causing a mist to rise around the car as the warmth from the exhaust hit the chill air.

In the rear vision mirror, he caught movement.

One of the bikers had come around the back of the car, emerging out of the forest, barely a shadow. He had a sawn-off pointed through the back window at his head.

Donnelly slammed his foot onto the gas pedal as the boom sounded. The car shot back over the biker as the rear window imploded with a spray of lethal pellets.

But Donnelly had taken part of the blast to his neck and the base of his skull. He was already dying when he reefed down hard on the wheel, sending him careening off the road.

A heartbeat later, the Mustang smashed into a pine tree at full throttle, the sheriff's boot heel jammed hard on the accelerator.

The state trooper and the local cop came loping over, pistols drawn. To make sure Donnelly was dead, they fired everything they had into him through the windscreen. Then one of them reached into the car and turned off the engine. The swirling lights died.

From within the campervan, Angel watched as they killed the sheriff. She allowed the curtains to close, turned on the two captive women and shook her head.

'What happened?' asked Belle.

'They killed him,' said Angel flatly.

'Just like that?' said Matti.

'What did you think would happen?' snarled Angel. She was angry at herself for having hope when hope had fled a long time ago.

CHAPTER 26

Jaz looked out a window, down on the rooftops of nearby houses and shops. She glanced at her phone, wondering when she would hear from Harvey. They had taken a short recess while O'Malley had slipped away somewhere in the rambling warren of corridors and chambers that made up St Anthony's.

When O'Malley returned, he was holding a thumb drive and a large laptop. The other priest was with him again, with his solid, muscled frame and too-direct stare. Jaz thought he was no more a priest than she was. Without preamble, the group once more gathered at the table, heads bent close to the laptop's screen as O'Malley inserted the thumb drive and brought up the video file.

The file opened and a film rolled. Initially, there was a slight crackle combined with distortion. Then the video cleared. The voice was of a teenage boy. 'Careful, we don't want them seeing us.'

'Is that Eric's voice?' interrupted Jaz.

'Yes,' said O'Malley. 'This seems to be two teenagers carrying out a "dare". They videoed the whole thing on a hand-held camera.'

The video rolled. It was jerky and although dark, Jaz could tell that the kid was climbing the lower branches of a tree. When the kid emerged, the sound of a party in full swing could be more easily heard. Eric was videoing over the top of a wall, from a vantage point in the lower branches of a tree. Jaz guessed that he was perched on the branch, close to the wall.

The image sharpened up and zoomed in on a large crowd of people partying around a pool. It was night, but the area was well-lit by a string of lanterns hanging above the pool and ambient light from a huge mansion and an adjacent pool house.

175

Eric said, 'Wow, look at them.' He breathed close to the microphone. Jaz guessed that the kid was commenting on the young women swimming and splashing around in the pool. They were shouting and seemed excited. Around the pool, lounging about, trying to appear 'cool', a bunch of men and women in business attire. They looked at odds with the girls in the pool. It was like two separate groups were at a party by accident. One was like a sorority house in full alcoholic swing, and the other, a company's executive group drinking cocktails.

The video panned around, mainly focusing on the women, obviously the focus of Eric's adolescent attention. But as the camera came about, Jaz could see the executives clearly.

'Can they see us?' came another voice. This was a girl.

'I don't think so,' replied Eric.

'We shouldn't be here,' she said.

'This is fantastic,' replied Eric.

'For you, maybe,' she said.

Jaz interrupted, 'Do we know the girl's name?'

'Chloe,' said the priest. 'Later that year, she ran away.'

The video paused. Eric must have stopped it. But when it started again, the women in the pool were now removing their bikini tops. Jaz could hear Eric chuckling, getting more excited by the moment. 'Holy shit,' he said.

'This is disgusting,' said Chloe, who was obviously in the same tree as Eric.

One of the businessmen, standing near the pool, waved to someone. Jaz could not see to whom he was gesturing. Jaz hit pause. She leant near the screen. 'Who is that guy?'

'That – is one Stirling McTaggart,' said Joshua.

Jaz eagerly examined the image; now she could put a face to the name. The guy was older, with blond, thinning hair. His build was tall and thin. He looked relaxed and carried an air of authority.

'Where is this being filmed?' asked Jaz.

'McTaggart has a place, a coastal residence. It's just to the north of the town,' said the priest.

'What is that get-up?' asked Jaz. She could see McTaggart was wearing some kind of coloured robe.

Joshua answered first. 'He's dressed like a samurai.'

'He's what?' said Jaz.

'You know what a samurai is,' said O'Malley.

'Yeah, but why is he…' began Jaz.

'McTaggart sees himself as a kind of lord. He has servants, security, a helicopter and his place is like a fortress. As a young man, he studied in Japan for a number of years under an eminent biochemist. His obsession with everything Japanese began there, then grew alongside his wealth and eccentricities.'

'Weird,' said Jaz.

Eric jumped down on the other side of the wall and he panned back toward the party. No one had seen the pair enter the grounds. The teens moved quickly through the garden and paused at a large glass sliding door on the side of the house opposite the party. Through the glass doors, the video showed staff working in a kitchen area, preparing platters of food and cocktails.

'Wait!' said Chloe.

'No way. Look at this place. Let's check it out!' said Eric. The video stopped as a serving girl approached the glass door carrying a large tray of champagne. She was smiling.

When the video continued, Eric and his friend were now inside the house, climbing an internal staircase. They were trying to be quiet, but Eric and the girl could be heard giggling. The inside of the house was a mixture of concrete walls, polished timber floors and sliding paper doors similar to a Japanese traditional dwelling. The teens rushed past a doorway along a corridor where it was obvious that a businessman was in a loud angry discussion with someone over a phone call.

Eric turned a corner and entered a dark bedroom. He walked to the window and looked down over the yard where the party was in full swing. The view of the people at the party was excellent, a downward angle from a second-storey window. McTaggart was surrounded by three or four people that were in deep conversation. Eric turned the camera to the wider grounds. In the distance, the camera picked up a helicopter and beyond, a glimpse of the ocean. There were rows of expensive cars arranged across the lawns. A second house was built close to the edge of a seaside cliff. Although several hundred yards away, the other mansion looked to be old, perhaps a 1920s motel or resort. The camera panned back to the party.

'Look at him, he thinks he's a ninja or something,' said Chloe.

'He's a samurai,' corrected Eric.

'He thinks he is. Lame.'

'Yeah, he's just some old rich guy who thinks he's a samurai.' Eric laughed.

'We should leave, Eric,' she said.

'Not yet. No one is paying the least bit of attention to us. There're so many people here, no one will look at us twice. The servants even offered us some food,' he reminded Chloe.

'Okay,' she said but she sounded nervous.

Jaz hit pause. 'This is all very interesting, but there is nothing here...'

'Yet,' said O'Malley. 'But by all means, Agent Freeman, we can end this here.'

'No, keep it going.'

Jaz watched as the video started again.

The teens, braver by the moment, left the bedroom. Back in the corridor, they filmed a water feature at the end of the corridor, a marble ball seeming to float on a cushion of water. Above the feature, sitting in a bracket, was a katana, intricate and beautiful. Eric reached out and touched the handle.

'Look at it,' breathed Eric.

'Leave it, Eric,' she said.

His hand retracted, and they backtracked away down the corridor.

The film stopped and the screen remained blank for a moment. When it came back, it was obvious that they had entered a completely different area of the house. The sounds of the party, ever-present on the video before this point, were absent.

'Where are we?' said Chloe.

'Below the house somewhere,' said Eric. 'Isn't this cool? What is this place?'

The corridor was dark and unlike the smooth concrete walls of the house, the walls appeared to be an old, dark brick.

Jaz leant forward, now intent on the screen. She wondered how they had managed to get to an area of the house that seemed to be hidden.

Water could be heard trickling. It was very dark.

'Is this some kind of wine cellar?' Eric sounded intrigued. There was a hint of adventure in his voice.

'I don't like this. Can we go? Please?' said Chloe. 'You said you could do this, Eric. You have your proof now.'

'Soon, I promise,' replied Eric. 'I'm just starting to enjoy this.'

They walked on, the corridor dark, the roof low. There were just a couple of lights set beneath metal frames, electric wires running to them along the stone floor. Then another voice was heard. 'Who's there?' *It was a small voice, and it wavered. A girl.*

Eric stopped, and the camera panned to the left. 'There's a door,' said Eric. *They held the camera up to a small opening. Slowly, the camera corrected as the lower level of light was processed. A face appeared and Eric's girlfriend screamed in fright.*

'Help me,' said the woman. Her face was close to the bars. She was filthy and her head looked to have been shaved. 'You have to get me out of here,' she gasped.

'Fuck,' blurted Eric. *The camera kept rolling, but he panned away for a moment, jerky and wild.*

'Get me out, you gotta get me out,' she implored.

Eric turned the camera on her again. 'What are you doing down here?'

A second face appeared at the barred window. It was another young woman. Then a third face pressed close; it was a young man. They began at once, begging to be freed, talking over each other. 'Get help, get us out, help us,' one voice on top of the other.

'I will,' said Eric. 'Where are the keys?'

'Kid, hey, kid,' repeated one of the women. 'You need to bring the cops. Get them out here as fast as you can, tonight, okay?'

'Why are you here? How long have you been here?' asked Chloe.

The camera switched off. When it came back, they appeared to be in the same dark underground corridor. This time, they stopped at another heavy door. This one also had bars on a small window. But the door was steel, set with hinges that were as heavy as those on a bank vault.

Eric's voice had changed. He now sounded like he was in a heightened state of fear.

'Is there anyone in this room?' asked Eric's girlfriend. The camera flicked over her momentarily but her face was lost in deep shadow. Eric filmed the door, then edging close, he filmed inside the room. A figure could be seen lying on a bed in the middle of the room. No, not a bed, a slab of rock or something.

'Hey, you in there,' called Eric. The lens zoomed and the camera adjusted to the low light. Although very grainy, the image of a face turning to the camera was clear. Zooming in, the face did not appear human. The eyes, terrible and sad, were animal-like. The irises were vertical slits. When it opened its mouth, it had fangs, that were serpent-like. It hissed, in what might have been despair or warning. As a scream sounded from Eric's girlfriend, the camera joggled down to face the floor as they fled away from the room. Then the camera was turned off. It remained off.

Jaz turned to the group, her face drained of blood. She could not speak, although the words formed in her head. She looked hard at the screen again, rewinding the image to the point that showed the figure's face, a pulse jumping in her temple and neck. She hit pause, forcing herself to look closely.

'Are you going to be alright, Ms Freeman?' asked Father O'Malley.

But her eyes were locked to the image on the screen.

'A demon,' said the priest.

Jaz turned to O'Malley. His face showed that he really believed he'd seen a demon. Jaz was still processing the image, still processing the fact that there were people being held against their will in cells somewhere on McTaggart's property. McTaggart, the rich guy, the wanna-be samurai, the leader of the Dagon's Riders, the jailer. *What the fuck is happening?*

In the room, there were mixed reactions. It was clear that some of them, including Joshua, had not expected to see the *thing* at the end, and having seen it, were convinced it was real. He was whispering urgently with a group of three or four others, their heads close together. By the looks on their faces, they were scared, plain and simple.

Others, like Charlie, were less convinced of the video's veracity. She looked confused more than anything. But certainly not particularly shaken. A clever mask, or some makeup combined with editing could produce a film like that. What was clear was that Eric had entered McTaggart's private land, probably on some kind of dare, had broken in and filmed a party. That part at least seemed real. Then the video had stopped and the next thing, he and his female accomplice were in an underground area and the film took a dark turn. There was no continuity in the film and therefore, no proof that the underground area was on McTaggart's land at all.

But if Eric was playing a trick on his friends, it was a good one. Perhaps Eric had paid the girls in the cells, and they were actors. Maybe they were in on the prank. But Eric was dead, she reminded herself. Seven years ago, he was found far from the town, out by a railway line, killed.

Jaz went to the window, opened it and breathed in some clean, cold night air. She felt uneasy more than outright scared. She took some deep breaths and the feeling slowly receded. If she hadn't seen the video and had been simply told what was on it, she would not have believed it, not that last part.

Eric had been murdered for this film, or for making it. He was dead because he had seen the place he was not supposed to see. Maybe he had gone to the cops, and maybe that sealed his fate.

The other priest came over to her – the pretend priest, as she thought of him. 'What the fuck was that thing? What do you think?'

Jaz blinked at his colourful language. 'I don't know.' She slowly shook her head. 'It looked real.'

'Yeah.' He nodded. 'What do you think I should do?'

Jaz thought this a strange question. It was clear now that this guy was no priest, and her instincts told her he was not to be trusted. 'Why don't you go and pray,' said Jaz, searching his face.

The pretend priest looked like he wanted to say something more but in the end, he shrugged, then walked away, glancing back at her once before slipping through a side door.

Looking out at the stars beyond the window, she considered what she had just witnessed. They were the same stars, but the world wasn't the same anymore.

She opened her phone and looked for the list of contacts. Her hands had a slight tremor. She scrolled to *Harvey* and pressed call.

CHAPTER 27

There were no bars on the cell phone. Jaz walked to another area of the loft, holding her phone up as if to catch an elusive signal. She needed just one or two bars but got nothing, not a God-damn thing.

'Anyone else having trouble getting a signal?' she asked as the priest's inner circle milled around, still debating amongst themselves about what they had seen on the video.

Charlie J, the disk jockey, flipped out her phone from within her jacket and her eyes narrowed. 'No signal. They're doing it again.'

'Doing what?' asked Jaz.

'Blocking us from calling out of town, or within town for that matter.'

Jaz stared. 'You're kidding, right?'

Charlie smiled. 'This has happened before. It's when *they* are in a lockdown. They close everything from the outside world. No email, no calls, nothing.'

'How can they do that?' asked Jaz. But deep down, she knew that with only a little well-placed tech, many things were possible. If the local police were complicit, then it was very possible.

'They would have blocked the roads too,' said O'Malley, having suddenly reappeared near them. 'We are, for the time being, cut off from the outside world.'

'Roadblocks?' asked Jaz.

'They do that around here,' said Joshua.

'Until when?' asked Jaz.

'Until they locate the person or persons they are looking for,' said Charlie. 'But they can't block my radio transmissions. Not yet anyway.'

'Can you get a message out?' asked Jaz.

'Yeah, to whom?' asked Charlie.

'There is a guy called Seb Straeker. He seems to be missing. It might be him that the cops are after,' said Jaz.

'Seb Straeker,' repeated Charlie. 'What do you want us to say?' said Charlie.

'Tell him… tell him to come here, to the church,' said Jaz.

O'Malley was listening. 'Go and do a segment, get the word out.' The priest made a sign of the cross over Charlie. 'Please be careful.'

'I will,' said Charlie, rising from her seat. She glanced at Jaz and walked away.

'I'll let you out,' said O'Malley, and he left with Charlie via the door they had entered, back onto the balcony above the nave.

Jaz remained at the table, staring at her phone and the loss of signal. She really needed to talk to Harvey. This wasn't something she had anticipated. Nothing tonight was quite what she had anticipated.

Joshua lay a hand on hers. 'Thank you.'

'For what?' she said.

'Coming here, to the Cove, following your hunch.'

'It's what I do, Joshua. But this…' she said, holding her phone, 'this I did not see coming.'

Joshua smiled, his blue eyes glittering. 'They have kept this going for years. They are very organised, Jaz.'

Jaz nodded.

'You thought that maybe I was wrong. But now you know I'm right.'

'Yeah, now I know. The question is, what I can do about it?' said Jaz. Stuck in a church, outgunned and cut off, she had to think hard about what to do next. The wrong move could get her killed.

*

184

Seb had earlier driven into the outskirts of town, manoeuvring the hatchback off a street, into a field amongst overgrown shrubs, then beneath a low-hanging tree. He stayed in the shrouded car, the smell of used food wrappers unpleasant but the space warm.

Waiting for nightfall, he used the time to consider his options. There weren't many. Without intel, his ass was blowing in the wind, waiting to get shot off, as his old Colonel used to say. He couldn't move on anyone without first knowing where they were. He was outnumbered and any confrontation now was going to be deadly.

Would Krystal give his description to the cops? Would the local cops come after him before the gang could locate him? He thought about Krystal, about how her eyes had momentarily changed, becoming serpent-like. But he also thought that the dead stoner boys had hitched a ride back to town in the rear seat. Lacking sleep, short of blood, he suspected that his mind was playing tricks.

As night approached, feeling cold, he left the hatchback and walked back into the middle of town, looking to locate a drugstore. It did not take long. Watching from across the street, hidden in an alleyway, he waited for the store to close.

An hour after dark, he watched the lights go dim. But it was another full hour after when three employees left in cars that must have been parked around the back. Satisfied the store was now vacated, he crossed the street, went up the side driveway to the rear car park, found a window and broke in.

Ten minutes later, he emerged with antibiotics, bandages and a few bottles of electrolytes. Worried that he'd probably tripped a silent alarm, he re-crossed the street to the dark alleyway. Retreating to a point at the far end, he crouched behind discarded boxes and some trash cans where he swallowed the electrolyte drink with four antibiotic pills.

Shrugging out of his shirt and peeling off the bloodied bandages on his shoulder, he winced but kept going. Shivering as he fitted the new adhesive bandages, he quickly put the shirt back on.

A Chinese food smell triggered his stomach to growl. Placing the bloodied bandages in the trash, he went looking for the restaurant that must be close by.

Along the sidewalk, only twenty yards away, around a bend in the road, he came to the Lucky Red Cat Café. It was a narrow shop front set in a red-brick two-storey building. He walked in and noted that there was a group of teens occupying a table to his left. They glanced at him and then stared openly. Seb realised he must look like a beaten-up homeless guy.

Seb sat down. Producing his wallet to show he could pay, he waited. Within moments, a Chinese woman appeared holding a menu. She nodded and smiled while handing him the menu. Seb pointed – 'I'll have this.'

His eyes were drawn to a TV set above the counter. It was a black-and-white TV series called *Kung Fu*, which he recognised from his childhood, about a guy who was always getting into trouble defending people despite his best efforts at peace. Perhaps the owners wanted to add a certain retro ambience to their restaurant, or maybe it just happened to be playing. Either way, David Carradine was doing his best impression of a Shaolin monk as he beat up cowboys in a bar-room brawl.

The kids at the other table were staring at him every now and then, and Seb heard a comment or two which brought giggles. He watched the door, hoping that he would be left to eat in peace. The teens were now annoyed about something. Holding their phones, they moved them around like they were trying to catch a signal. Seb took his cell from his pocket. He too had no signal. He put the phone back. He didn't have anyone to call anyway.

The food arrived and he ate it a little faster than he should have, taking a handful of painkillers whilst guzzling water. He dropped a few notes on the table to cover the meal and exited. Having only taken a few strides down the sidewalk, he turned around and went back to the restaurant, going directly to the table of kids. One, a teenage boy who was pretty big for his age, looked up at Seb, eyes large. The kid was dressed Goth, face white, hair black, a long black coat.

Seb produced his wallet and took out two fifty-dollar bills. 'I really like your coat.'

'Here, take it, man.' The Goth kid took the cash, shrugged out of the coat and handed it to Seb.

'Thanks. You never saw me, okay?'

'We never saw you.'

Seb left for the second time and a few strides down the street, put on the black coat. To his surprise, he found that the coat had a hood. He pulled the hood up to cover his face in shadow and kept walking, just another Goth in the neighbourhood. He looked at his watch, noting that it was close to midnight.

*

Officer Benson was cruising. At midnight, technically her shift ended. She would return to the station and tidy up before going home. The phones were programmed to switch directly to her cell if a call came in. As she approached a stop sign, she checked her cell and found that there was no signal. That was strange, but not unheard of in a country area.

She turned onto Maple Street, then cruised to where it crossed onto the High Street. It was a beautiful night, and so she coasted slowly downhill toward the docks where she could catch a whiff of salt air. She passed a guy with a long black coat, hood pulled up so she couldn't see his face. Some of the local kids were into that stuff. Guyatt might have pulled over and hassled the kid but she wasn't Guyatt.

Benson parked near the docks, where the jetty struck out over the waves. She allowed the wind through the open windows and sat in the cruiser, simply taking the air. The shops nearby were still open despite the late hour. The Crab Shack was nearly always open, and she could see people standing outside it, smoking, leaning against the wall. She wondered what it was like to have a night out. Being a cop, she had not taken the time to do much of that. That made her think of Seb Straeker once again, and she wondered where he was.

The closest bar to where she now was locally known as Jack's. It was a whiskey bar, one that the older folks around town liked for its high-end liquor, laid-back vibe and chef-prepared meals.

She tuned the police radio to the channel they officially used in the Cove, but it was silent. Either nothing was happening or they were using another frequency. She turned on Bay radio and it came through the speakers, loud and clear. Sunday nights they played some golden oldies tunes, and right now it was Dean Martin singing *Ain't That a Kick in the Head*.

Benson settled in and considered for the first time lighting a cigarette in the car, despite it being against regulations. She put her feet up through the open window, crossing them at the ankles. The guy in the black coat walked into Jack's Whiskey Bar, and Benson suddenly sat forward. Just before he walked in, he took back the hood on the coat, and Benson could have sworn that it was Seb Straeker. Exiting the police car, she strode across the docks toward Jack's.

CHAPTER 28

Astrange figure walked between the two houses, across the lawns, enjoying the air, his garish red robes flapping in the wind. Although he had built the new house with glass and steel, and embellished it with Japanese features, he often found himself drawn to the other, older house, the one perched precariously on the cliff's edge.

McTaggart both frightened and intrigued the people who worked for him. He would strut about proudly in a Japanese robe, often carrying a katana, humming tunes to himself that no one really understood. Although he was not Japanese, he was obsessed with their culture, and in particular the Samurai.

Aware that he was obsessed and eccentric in the extreme, he embraced these as qualities and cultivated them. Deliberately unpredictable, purposefully enigmatic, McTaggart derived perverse pleasure in keeping everyone around him either confused or at least unsure.

If he thought someone expected him to do a thing, he would do the opposite, merely to keep people off-balance.

Much older than he looked, in fact, a good deal older than even the rumours had him, McTaggart had discovered the secret of a long life. A brilliant biochemist, his operation relied on secrecy, a constant supply of certain key ingredients and a good deal of money.

Although he was only one part of an elaborate machine, he was perhaps the key piece. And now it was being threatened, just as it had been seven years before, when a stupid child had stumbled into his den.

Guards saluted as he entered the old house and ascended the stairs. At the end of a corridor, he came to a room, secluded behind a heavy door with an electronic lock. It was one of the only modern features in the otherwise old house. He punched in a code and entered a small room.

His young team of techs were talking quietly amongst themselves. They were wide awake, amped on coffee and the thrill of a pursuit in which they played no direct part.

McTaggart watched as the three young men and one woman, each fitted with headsets, operated their workstations, outfitted with the latest high-tech gear.

'Tell me what's happening,' demanded McTaggart.

'Nothing at the roadblock,' said the woman. She refused to look at McTaggart, who assumed that she was simply overawed by his presence.

Earlier, upon his command, they had interrupted the local telecommunications in the town. McTaggart did not own the local phone companies, but he may as well have. It was, with the right people, easy enough to cut the Cove off from the world outside.

'Tell me – have you heard anything in Ms Freeman's flat?'

A male tech with a beard turned and reluctantly looked up. 'No, sir... Mr McTaggart. She isn't there.'

'Then where is she? I need to know if she is with them or not.'

The tech swallowed and averted his gaze. 'I'll keep looking.'

McTaggart considered that twenty-seven homes were being actively monitored with phone taps. Surely someone in one of these homes had mentioned something.

They kept a list of people that could not be trusted. Every day, the recordings were played and special software would listen for certain keywords – *McTaggart, conspiracy, Dagon's Riders, gang, Eric Winters* and over one hundred and forty other words. If a hit occurred, the whole phone conversation would be reviewed.

Donna O'Brien, the police chief, entered the room. She remained in the corner, her walkie-talkie to her ear. She wasn't in uniform, which was a pity. He preferred it when she was. Without it, she looked dumpy and old. McTaggart did not like her very much, but the woman kept her side of the bargain and the local police did what she wanted them to. She was in the midst of a conversation. 'Go ahead, I'm listening, Webster. Uh-hah, okay, yep.'

McTaggart hated such half-formed words and resisted the urge to slap the woman. He paid her well, he reflected. Large sums of money were regularly transferred to her offshore account. One day, he may decide she was no longer relevant. Perhaps that was why she was carrying a pistol concealed under her puffer jacket. She may not have been as stupid as she looked. Wearing a side-arm in his presence was against the rules. Rules were all they had when they needed to be this organised. He turned his eyes on her, and she swallowed.

McTaggart began asking, 'The policeman that followed Leo's crew...'

'Is dead,' confirmed O'Brien, glancing at the technicians, who were seated in front of screens, talking quietly. 'He was a sheriff from a county to the south. He was tracking Leo from the last pick-up point. I think he was lucky to find their trail.'

'Or unlucky,' suggested McTaggart. 'His car?'

'It's being towed away. There will be little left to find,' confirmed O'Brien.

'His phone?'

'Destroyed,' said O'Brien. 'Relax. We're doing the usual clean-up.'

He hated being told to relax, especially by this toad. 'This time, we shouldn't provide a body to his family. He just *disappeared* – understand?'

O'Brien nodded and hastened out.

'Situation report,' McTaggart said in his louder voice.

One of the techs swivelled. 'Phone lines are still down. They have someone onsite but they haven't worked out how to fix the issue.'

McTaggart nodded. 'And our missing friends?'

'The one who calls himself "Miller" is still nowhere to be found. He could be on foot or lying low. The other one – the one Krystal said was looking for his sister – Sebastian Straeker, hasn't surfaced yet either.'

McTaggart took a deep breath. From the windows, he looked out onto a stunning night ocean vista, waves crashing hard against the jagged rocks just below. Miller and Straeker did not appear to know each other at all. Without turning, he asked, 'Is he really Angel's brother?'

'It seems likely, Mr McTaggart,' said the female tech.

'How did he locate her?'

No one answered.

'Where is Krystal?'

'Still looking for Straeker. She refuses to come in.'

McTaggart should have been angry, but he liked Krystal. She was precisely his kind of woman. She possessed a natural aggression that was difficult to cultivate in an individual. But now she brought some risk to his operation. He couldn't have her disobeying orders. Once that began, others might follow suit.

'Leo's crew are approaching now,' said a tech. 'I have them at the gate.'

McTaggart glanced at the monitor. The bikes coasted in at a low speed. He left the control room, heading downstairs.

*

Angel's campervan approached tall, wrought-iron gates topped by sharpened spikes which opened automatically on quiet hinges. A single security camera was set on a post above the left-side gate post. The walls on either side were tall, around ten feet high, constructed of old stone, topped with razor wire.

The motorcycles cruised on ahead along a driveway. The

campervan stopped on the manicured lawn between the old mansion on the sea cliff and the ultra-modern house on the edge of the forest. Leo led the two captives from the campervan, their hands bound before them. Three black-clad security guards, sub-machine guns slung across their backs, took possession of the women and kept them moving toward the old house.

Belle was openly sobbing. Matti stumbled, an unfocused look in her eyes. Angel averted her gaze, instead focusing on the old mansion. A few lights shone from within, mainly from windows on the top floor.

Angel was feeling twitchy, like a drug addict before that next big hit. The others in the crew were probably worse. Although they said nothing, she could tell by the pensive looks and cold sweaty sideways glances, they were needing it. Needing it bad. They had been affected longer than her. Little Bear and Screamer were almost veterans in this crew. Despite their apparent ages, they were in fact much older. The drug had many side effects, and the first of them was that you barely aged. It was like hitting the pause button. She didn't mind the idea of that part so much. But Little Bear was always just one step from going ballistic. He would have been approaching his twenties, she realised, but he still looked like a pubescent boy.

Inside the house, the ground floor was dimly lit. McTaggart was standing at the dinner table, arrayed in silk robes of bright red, with matching slippers. Although clearly a genius, Angel believed that perhaps he was a high-functioning psychopath. She was always careful to avoid meeting his eyes, just in case he saw the truth hidden there.

Instead of food, the table was simply laid out with six large syringes filled with a luminescent blue liquid. Microscopic floaters seemed to move around within the vials. Little more than specs, Angel wondered what they were and where they came from.

'Only six?' said Leo.

'The two women you brought in – they won't be converted,' said McTaggart.

'I like the cowgirl, Belle,' said Angel, hoping she might be able to save one of them.

'Well, I don't,' snapped Leo, rounding on her.

'It's impossible anyway. We have six. That's all,' said McTaggart.

Angel wondered how much of the elixir McTaggart had ever used. It was rumoured that he took small amounts, enough to stave off age and sickness.

Angel observed the serum's other properties too. The side effects were no less extreme than the anti-aging properties. It was addictive, but not like heroin or other drugs precisely. You could go for a while without it, but after about a month, the feeling that you were dying became exponential with each passing day. Angel knew that as twitchy and uncomfortable as they were today, tomorrow they would be feeling twice the sensation. The day after – they would be craving it without a thought for anything else. The day after that… well, she had no idea what that would be like. For her crew, it had never come to that.

The third side-effect was a strong aversion to sunlight. It hurt their eyes, and the sensation of natural light on their skin was like small needles. Angel had found that while they had avoided daylight, her vision at night had improved significantly. Whether that was the drug or simply her eyes becoming accustomed to the darkness, she wasn't sure.

Taken in small quantities the anti-aging effects were said to be incredible. Taken in larger doses by syringe, the primary or desired effect of the drug was seismic. After a shot, immediately following, you were what Angel thought of as *super*. Strength was heightened, fear lowered, sex drive increased, wounds healed quickly, mental agility, and even a person's sense of smell and taste went *through the roof*.

Then, over the next thirty days, the effects would slowly dissipate. By the last few days, the subject would return to normal, except for the feeling that you just had to have that the next dose.

The first and only time Angel had been given the serum, she had no idea what it was. On that occasion, she had been given some in a cocktail, the taste masked by many other flavours. Even so, she had felt ill at first, and then later, despite it being a weak dose, she was high on the ecstasy of it.

She glanced at Little Bear and Screamer. They were literally shifting from foot to foot. Screamer's mouth was working silently, licking his lips and drooling. Angel was reminded of a feral German Shepherd she had once seen that had rabies.

'I think you will find it improved over the last batch,' said McTaggart. Hands on hips, legs apart, head high, he smiled with perfect white teeth. If the old guy only knew how bad they needed this now, he would step aside. But he looked at them like they were his children and he, the proud father.

Angel suspected that he would only start taking the full dose himself once he was certain that they had perfected it. *He must be close*, she thought because he was here in person, and he looked pleased. This serum was *everything*, the reason for all that they had taken, all the lives ruined, for the hundreds of miles covered in their endless quest. In a moment of clarity, Angel saw the truth. There would be no end to the torment.

Leo had gone very still. He had not blinked for a full minute, his face remaining expressionless, though a single droplet of sweat began slowly snaking down the side of his face.

Until tonight, until this very moment, Angel harboured secret thoughts that she could still leave. The last true test would come very soon – to make her first kill. The door to the outside world would then be closed forever.

'Take it,' said McTaggart.

And like Dobermans trained to await a command word, the crew snatched up a needle each and were already plunging them into their flesh. Although Angel had not recalled doing so, she found herself holding one, the needle poised above her arm. After a moment, she put the needle down on the table, and watched as the others fell onto chairs or collapsed to their knees, feeling a rush of liquid fire, a wild exaltation, the waking of a beast within them. Angel wanted to partake, for the drug was also in her system and was wearing off rapidly. But watching the others in the crew, she guessed that once she took a full dose, she would never leave.

McTaggart stood back, watching with glazed eyes, enraptured. Angel walked from the room, hearing Leo and one or two others howling at the top of their lungs, between pain and joy, fire and ice, their veins in overdrive.

She exited through French doors at the rear of the mansion, not wanting to be anywhere near the freshly charged crew. Walking down wide steps onto a stone balcony that overlooked the ocean, she leant on a railing. Some fifty feet below her, surf smashed against the cliff face, a fine spray misting into the air. Looking out to sea, white caps formed on large swells. She stood there for a long time, wondering whether to hurl herself from the cliff, freeing herself from all that she had done and all that she might yet do. Time was running out. It was the second time she had walked away from a syringe. They needed her to become one of them and complete what she had started.

A hand touched her shoulder, and she recoiled. When she turned, McTaggart was standing there in his ridiculous red robes. He was smiling at her with an expression that was at least an imitation of empathy. Beneath it, Angel could almost smell his sexual desire for her.

'What do you want?' she asked, though she already suspected.

'I have news for you, Angel.' Here he paused as if his words were somehow magical, like she would swoon or something. A smile was frozen on his face.

'What is it?' she said, not attempting to reciprocate a smile.

His face hardened slightly. 'Your brother has come looking for you. Do you know why that would be?'

Angel's eyes widened. Could it be? A smile now crossed her face. It came unbidden and she wished she could have hidden it.

Four security men appeared from the house, black-clad, in military vests. They advanced, looking down their gunsights. The red-dot laser pointers were marking her chest and face. She had nowhere to run and time had run out after all. She glanced at the ocean, the idea of leaping to her death lingering in her heart.

'You didn't take the elixir,' said McTaggart.

'It's poison,' she said flatly.

'It's the future,' he countered. 'Take her.'

Angel didn't resist. They pushed her down onto her face, dragged her arms behind her and secured handcuffs. She was hauled up, marched away, knowing that soon she would find out exactly what they did with the ones they kidnapped.

With every step, she felt a weight lift from her. A slow smile spread across her face, because she had not surrendered to him. Angel was willing to pay the price. The decision was made.

It was done.

CHAPTER 29

No sooner had Seb taken a seat at the bar, ordered a whiskey and taken in the room than a familiar face appeared.

Benson, in uniform, mirror sunglasses tucked neatly in her breast pocket, was coming toward him. Seb slammed back the whisky, turned on the stool and watched as she approached. Her hand did not stray to her holster, and she wasn't calling anything in on her radio. Her face showed concern rather than tension. Seb realised that he was not a 'wanted' man after all – at least not yet.

'We've been looking all over for you. Are you okay?'

He nodded, signalling the barman for another drink. An older guy, handle-bar moustache neatly brushed, approached the pair. 'Do you want something? Or are you on duty?'

Benson hesitated. 'Yeah, I want a drink. I'll have what he's having.'

Something had shifted in Benson because she would never have drunk anything whilst on duty. Seb wondered what it was. Two more whiskies were poured. They sat, sipping for a few moments. The silence stretched, with Benson hoping Seb would spill on where he'd been. But Seb was waiting to see how much Benson knew about recent events.

'So, you've been looking for me,' Seb said at last.

'Your place has been broken into and ransacked. You know that – right?'

'I'm aware,' he said. 'Say, you haven't seen my dog?'

'No. What's going on, Seb? Was it the gang?'

He nodded. 'They tried to kill me.'

Benson's eyes widened. 'They tried to kill you?'

Seb knocked back more whiskey.

'My... colleagues are out looking around town for someone. They've left me way out of the loop, which means...'

'They have no intention of bringing in the person they are looking for alive,' said Seb, finishing her thought.

'You don't know that,' said Benson.

'Are you really off duty now?' asked Seb, leaning back in his seat, eyeing her.

She hesitated, aware that she still wore the uniform. 'I am.'

'It may not be me that your fellow officers are after tonight. There is another person they are interested in. A guy called Miller.'

Benson tensed. Noticing, he asked, 'You know him?'

'Yeah, he was questioned and released.'

Sipping his whiskey, he said, 'I doubt he was released, not on purpose.'

'Why do you say that?'

'I was privy to a conversation, a phone call I wasn't supposed to hear. Your colleagues are in cahoots with the Dagon's Riders gang.'

Benson reached for her glass, drank some more whiskey, her face screwing up as the amber liquid burnt down her throat. Seb didn't know if it was the whiskey, drunk neat, or the idea that her police force was corrupt. 'I don't know that at all, Seb.'

'Come on, you must at least suspect it.'

Benson sniffed and shook her head. Dropping her eyes to the glass, she said, 'You need to come in, make a formal report.'

'I won't.'

'The hell you won't.'

Seb pulled out his phone, pretending to be more interested in it than Benson. 'Do you have a signal?'

Benson wondered why he changed the subject. She took her personal cell from her pocket and looked at it. 'No signal.'

'Don't you think that's off somehow?' He slipped the phone back into his pocket and finished the second whiskey.

Benson shook her head.

'Try the pay phone,' he suggested.

Benson put down her glass and walked over to the payphone near the bar. She picked up the receiver, listened, tapped at the cradle a couple of times, and put it back.

When she sat down again on the stool beside him, she said, 'It's not working. But that doesn't mean anything.'

'It may not mean anything, but I reckon it does.'

Benson studied him. 'What else is going on, Seb? You've clearly been through some heavy shit today.'

'Okay, I'm going to level with you about a couple of things. But I need you to understand that I'm telling you these things out of respect for you, out of respect for the fact that you seem to be the only straight cop around here.'

He waited for her to nod. 'I came here looking for my sister, Angel, who I know was in this town at some point. She was running with the Dagon's Riders gang. I came looking for any signs of her. I provoked the gang. I admit, it was kind of deliberate. At some point, they drew the conclusion that I was more dangerous to them than they thought. They came after me – hard.'

'They thought you were Miller,' guessed Benson, her eyes now far off. Seb could see her drawing the lines between the dots.

'Yeah, whoever Miller is, they want him bad.'

'You think your sister... Angel is with them?'

'She's with them alright.'

Benson glanced down, becoming aware that Seb was wearing clothes that did not quite fit. Bloodied patches marked his neck and shoulder. 'You've been injured.'

'I've been bitten, punched, kicked and shot.'

Her eyes softened. 'We've got to get you some medical attention.'

'That's the cop speaking. I thought you were off duty.'

'I am. Look, I'm just looking out for you Seb.'

He took her hand, turning in his seat. 'I need you to tell me where I can find the gang. You must know where they are.'

Benson tensed, then slowly shook her head. 'How would I know?'

'I bet your colleagues know where to find them.'

She thought for a moment. 'Maybe. If they do, I'm not in the loop.'

'Who's this Miller guy?' asked Seb

Benson shrugged. She now felt like their roles had reversed, and he was questioning her. 'An asshole. Just some guy.'

'Come on, Benson. If he was *some guy*, why was he picked up? Why would your people be so hot to find him? He knows something important. He turns up in town, out of the blue. He's here to do something... probably has a mission. The cops – your buddies pick him up, and then let him go...' He sipped again. 'Nah, he got away from them somehow. Ask yourself – what was he doing here? Then ask yourself – who brought him here?'

Benson thought for a moment. 'He had a Boston accent. He was built like a cage fighter. Miller was a nasty piece of work, I'm sure of that. The day we found him, down by the docks, sleeping in his car, Guyatt seemed to know he was in town before we even picked him up.'

Seb nodded thoughtfully. He looked at the mirror, past the array of spirits behind the bar, making eye contact with Benson only in that surface. He spoke quietly. 'Look, Benson...'

'Rebecca,' she cut in.

Dropping his voice to almost a whisper, he said, 'Okay, Rebecca... I have more to say, because I need your help.'

'I'll help you if I can,' she promised.

'If I tell you, it could place you in danger.'

'If I'm the only straight cop, then maybe I'm in danger already.'

He nodded slowly. 'I killed someone last night.'

Benson was holding her breath.

He continued quietly, 'In self-defence.' Seb thought about the bikers in the woods that he'd shot but was not about to mention them at this point. One homicide could be self-defence, two sounded bad and three was a spree. The cabin was full of his prints. If he was going to have that put on him, he might as well get out in front of it.

Benson had become very still as she processed his words. Her hand had strayed to her gun.

'You said you'd help me,' he reminded her. 'They were trying to kill me, and if I hadn't defended myself, I would be the one lying in a pool of blood in that cabin.'

'Goddamit, Seb!' she said, letting out a breath. The barman looked across at the pair seated at the bar. Benson's voice had travelled to the ears of more than a few people.

'Has anyone called in a homicide today?' asked Seb quietly.

'No.'

'That's funny because I called 9-1-1 and left the phone off the hook. That was at dawn this morning.'

Benson was still processing. Her face was turned down, looking at the glass, cradled in her fingers. 'No calls. Nothing that I have been privy to. What happened?'

'Like I said, they came at me. There was some collateral damage. I hate using a military term, but that's what they were. The gang killed a couple of teens in a cabin out on a lake in the forest. I was hiding there, after being tracked all day from my place. But yeah... I killed one of the gang. It was me or him.'

'You really did call 9-1-1?' she asked.

'I did. I left the phone off the hook,' repeated Seb, 'and left the scene. It was something I was not sure about. But now, knowing that you were not told anything, I think maybe it was the right play.'

'What the hell is going on?' she breathed.

'You would have been told, right?'

'Are you sure they were dead?'

Seb grinned. 'I'm pretty damned sure.'

'Well, we have a dilemma, don't we?' she said.

'Do we? No offence, Rebecca, but I'm going after them. If they have my sister, I won't stop.'

'What if I said you were under arrest?' she asked.

'You would be disappointed, I think. I won't be stopped, by *anyone*.'

'How many bodies will they find in that cabin, Seb?'

'Three. Two guys that they murdered and one that is on me.'

'Anything else? Just three bodies in the cabin? Jeezuz!'

'Maybe another one or two in the woods.'

Benson just stared at him.

'How much do you want to know?' Seb tilted his head back to drain the glass.

'I really don't want to know. Not now, not tonight.'

'You're going to have to open your eyes, Rebecca, or they'll open them for you.'

*

Angel was escorted down narrow stairs that had been hewn into the living rock. The sounds of crashing waves receded as they descended. Then she was shoved through a door into a long corridor. The stairs continued further down, at least a couple more levels, disappearing into utter blackness. What was down there?

The corridor was like a converted wine cellar, though the doors all had bars over windows. It was cold. Water dripped. She could hear the sound of the guards breathing behind her. Escape was impossible. They followed close, guns trained on her. At the end of the corridor, they used a swipe card, then shoved her through a door with no window. It was steel, the kind of door you might find in a bank vault. Angel wondered what this was. The chamber was dark, but her eyes could make out dim humanoid shapes. The cuffs were removed and the door slammed behind her. It sounded like a vacuum seal was engaged. Her eyes grew even more accustomed to the dark and she could see three women approach her.

Belle, Matti and Codi were staring at her.

'It's her, she's one of them,' said Belle.

'Why am I in here with you if I'm one of them?' asked Angel.

'Come on in,' said Codi. She was calm, like she had accepted her fate. 'But don't walk over there.' Angel could see her pointing and she followed her extended finger.

In the centre of the room, there was a round hole, roughly ten feet across, like a large well opening. Angel walked directly to the edge of it, her eyes already adjusted to the darkness.

'Be careful!' said Codi.

'It's okay, I can see it.' Angel suspected that the three women could barely see anything, let alone beyond the utter blackness of the well.

Turning to the hole, Angel crouched beside the opening and leant out, over the edge. Despite her heightened vision, the chamber below was insubstantial. It was a good twenty or thirty feet to the chamber below where a mist clung to the floor. She stared, could almost feel something was in there. She listened but could hear nothing. Angel lay down, allowing her upper body to protrude out and over the ledge hem. Still nothing. Her eyes adjusted maybe a little more. Something moved down there, something beneath the layer of mist.

Angel backed up and turned but remained seated. What was this place?

'Can you see down there?' asked Belle.

'No. But...'

'But what?'

'Just stay away from that opening,' instructed Angel

'Why is there a hole in the floor?'

'I've never been in this place. I don't know.'

'But you were with them!'

'Lower your voice,' hissed Angel.

'Are they going to kill us?'

Angel nodded. Judging by the vacant looks on their faces, they must have been practically blind in here. 'There are worse things than dying. But yeah, I would say we are all as good as dead.'

CHAPTER 30

t was nearly nine a.m. when Seb rolled over, feeling the makeshift stitches pulling tight. His shoulder hurt, a lot, for the painkillers and alcohol had worn off sometime in the early hours before dawn. Groggy with a slight hangover, he had to think about where he was. Benson's house was a low-set place on a quiet backstreet about four blocks from the centre of town. It was a rental that came already furnished with 1950s décor. The only modern thing about the place was the wide-screen television that Benson must have brought with her.

Rebecca walked into her living room, wearing nothing but a white T-shirt, which barely reached her legs. Out of uniform, her hair down, there was no trace of the cop. He stared. It was hard not to.

Hands on her hips, she said, 'You're awake. How did you sleep?'

'Okay.' His body ached, pretty much everywhere. He probably had bloodshot eyes, judging by how much they stung – but more than anything, he needed caffeine. Right then, he would have killed to have someone put a black coffee right into his hand. He rolled to the side and put his bare feet down on the carpet. 'Where did I leave my pants?'

'They're beside my bed.' She looked amused. 'Don't you remember?'

'How could I forget?' He scratched his head and yawned, trying to keep that cat-that-swallowed-the-canary look off his face.

'If I run your name, what will I find?' she asked, smiling, though this time it didn't quite reach her eyes.

He hadn't seen that coming. 'I have no criminal record.'

'Good to know.' Frowning, she said, 'I sense there is a "but" in there somewhere.'

'I'm technically AWOL from the army.'

'You can just tell them that you came looking for your sister.'

'The army doesn't care about missing sisters. I'll be in trouble when they catch up with me... eventually.'

Rebecca nodded. 'I have to go to work. I shouldn't have had so much to drink. Today is going to be hard and I'm late already.' She headed back to her bedroom. Over her shoulder, she called to him. 'There's food in the refrigerator. I wouldn't go anywhere today, at least until I can...'

Rebecca came back into the room, her uniform in place. She was tucking in her shirt. 'Until I can find out what is happening.'

'I'd prefer you didn't even say my name today.'

She paused, buckling on her gun belt, then walked to the door. 'I'm not an idiot. Stay here. Wait for me. Whatever happens next, we need to face it together. I can help you find Angel. Okay?'

The door closed and she was gone. Seb heard her drive away. He'd already decided there was no way in hell he'd expose Rebecca to any more danger than necessary. She already had her hands full working with a bunch dirty cops.

Checking the lock on the front door, he returned to the sofa. Bending and looking beneath it, he retrieved his Beretta and Krystal's Scorpion machine pistol. Examining the Scorpion, then thinking about that blonde psycho-bitch, he considered if perhaps he should have stashed Krystal somewhere and leant on her until she cracked. Could he have tortured the information from her? That was a slippery slope, and a path he had never trodden.

He lifted back the curtain, looking out on an overcast day. At the front door, he tucked the two guns in under his shirt.

CHAPTER 31

When Benson arrived at the police station, she found only Webster waiting there. He looked down at her with suspicion when she came in. 'Big night?'

'Sorry I'm late,' she said, moving toward her desk.

'Chief says you're here today. I have to go now that you bothered to show up,' he said.

She forced a smile. The old, ignorant Benson liked Webster, and she needed to at least give that impression. Never before had she felt intimidated by him, but now she felt like she needed to take care with how she spoke to him.

'I hope he was worth it,' said Webster, picking up his car keys.

'How did you know?' said Benson.

Webster tapped the side of his nose. 'I have ways, Benson. You know you should be careful picking up strange guys. Who was he, anyway?'

'Just a guy – you wouldn't know him.'

Webster frowned and then changed the subject. 'Listen, Rebecca, we have some roadblocks in place. All exits from the Cove are being monitored. We're now looking to apprehend Miller… again.'

'Why? Didn't we cut him loose?'

'Chief says there is some new evidence in two homicides. She thinks Miller could be our guy.'

'What homicides, Webster?' Benson tried to project surprise.

'We have two deceased persons in a cabin, out by Silver Lake. Two males aged in their early twenties.' Webster stopped near her desk, looming over her, one hand casually resting on the handle of the pistol. 'It was an anonymous tip-off. We think Miller came to town looking to fulfil a contract. He may be a hitman and well... we think the two victims were his targets.'

'We had him here,' said Benson.

'It's not your fault, or mine,' said Webster.

'I hope we get him,' said Benson.

'Yeah, we think it was a drug thing,' said Webster as he headed out the door.

'Okay, well... I'll be here,' she called.

Benson watched as Webster drove out of the car park. She went to call Seb but realised the cell phone still had no service.

Nothing made sense, or rather, it all made too much sense. She just didn't want to think about the implications. They had set roadblocks and she hadn't known a damned thing about that either.

*

Gunther's sudden appearance surprised the techs in the control room.

'Show me cell three,' he commanded, leaning over the female tech, whose neck immediately reddened.

On the monitor, cell three appeared, low light cameras showing four women huddled close in near complete darkness.

'Give the order that the guards should enter the cell and remove Angel and the other woman – the one identifying as Codi Stevens.'

'The one with the beret?' asked the female tech.

'Yes, that one. Move them to cell one.'

The female tech relayed Gunther's instructions into a microphone. On the monitor, six security guards suddenly entered the room, night-vision goggles in place, sub-machine guns aimed at the captives. They removed Angel and Codi from the cell at gun point. The remaining two women clung to each other, crouched low to the stone floor.

'Good,' said Gunther.

'I love this part,' said one of the male techs. In the green-tinged light from the monitor, he watched the screen with a morbid curiosity.

'Now move the other two below,' commended Gunther.

'On it,' said the female tech. Speaking into her microphone, she said, 'Move the remaining captives into the hole.'

'What's down there, anyway?' asked one of the techs.

'If you don't know, then you can't tell anyone,' said Gunther. 'Your curiosity could get you killed.'

'Forget I asked.'

The guards came back into cell three and although they couldn't hear the words, they could tell that the two women were being told to jump down into the well or risk being shot. The techs watched with fascination.

There were no cameras in the well-chamber below the women. For some reason, that area remained off-limits to just about everyone. Although curious, the techs remained silent. Gunther watched and waited. Only one of the women, the older one, jumped down into the hole. The other, Belle, struggling and kicking, was at the last, shoved, screaming. She fell from view.

'Wow, that was cool,' said the female tech. 'Whatever you have down there, it needs to feed.'

Gunther nodded. 'That is all you should know. That, and the well is precisely twenty feet deep. The... is not capable of making it up that kind of height to escape.'

'Why not just take them through a door?' said the tech with the glasses. He pushed them back up his nose. Gunther didn't know his name, and he didn't care to learn it.

'The last room we kept him in had a door. He nearly escaped – several times. We feed him through the opening at the top, and...' Gunther stopped, realising he had said more than he had intended.

The four techs sat quietly, digesting the new information, hoping that Gunther might divulge something more. When Gunther left the control room, he could hear them whispering excitedly amongst themselves. They had no idea that McTaggart had new techs brought in every six months and had no use for the previous ones.

*

Benson picked up the radio, tuned it to the usual police band, but heard nothing but static. She tuned in to the backup frequency, but again, heard nothing. *They must have another frequency open*, she thought. Cops at roadblocks were always chatting. They would be talking to the State Troopers too. And yet, they had kept her out of the loop.

She got off her chair and went to the weapons storage room. To a casual observer, it could have been a closet for the cleaner to store mops and hoovers. She produced a key and opened the armoury. Although most of the police cruisers were fitted with shotguns inside their trunk compartments, the Cove police had a few extra weapons stowed in case of an emergency. Benson took a M4 carbine out of a case and placed it on the ground. It was the only one the station had. It was for 'dire' emergencies only. The weapon had a 30-round magazine and a sight. She found five spare magazines to go with the weapon. Closing the armoury, she took the weapon straight to her cruiser and placed it in the trunk. She had no idea what she might need it for, or if she would need it at all. Somehow, she just felt like if an edge were needed, she would have it.

Returning to the station, she found Mr Crossly and his friend, Mr Jackson, at the front counter. Both guys were old, well into their seventies, with frizzy grey hair and outfits that included bell-bottom jeans from their youth. She walked past them and in behind the counter and said, 'Can I help you two?'

'You're packing some heat today, missy,' said Mr Crossly.

'Goddam right I am,' she said back and winked.

The old codgers chuckled. 'Why do police need a gun like that anyway?' said Mr Jackson.

'You spied on me taking that gun to my car?'

'Uh-ha,' they said in unison.

'I have some target practice later,' lied Benson.

'Uh-ha… okay,' said Mr Jackson.

'Why are you silver foxes here?' asked Benson.

'I wanted to make a complaint,' said Crossly.

'Me too,' said Jackson.

'What about?'

'The phones are still down,' said Crossly.

'I know that. But what do you want me to do about that?'

'Can't you do something?'

'I would call the phone company, but I don't have a working phone either, Mr Crossly.'

'Well, what the hell is happening?' said Crossly.

'Honestly, have no idea,' she said.

The old guys gave her a long withering look, then sauntered off, grumbling. Benson went back to her desk, feeling tense, knowing that things were definitely off and not quite knowing what she should do. The easiest thing was to keep her head down, pretend everything was fine. But she had never been that kind of person. She was always the kid in school who protected the weaker kids from the bullies. It was in her DNA.

*

Walking along the sidewalk, Seb angled for the centre of town, feeling the cold wind biting at his back. The day was bleak, and it matched his mood perfectly.

By the time he arrived at a small discount clothing store – *Wiles New and Used Fashion* – he looked even more dishevelled, hair blown all about, unshaved, chilled to the bone. As the door opened, a small bell jingled.

It was an old place, with wooden floors that had been there

perhaps a hundred years and creaked underfoot as he walked between racks of clothing. Some music he didn't recognise was playing on a radio. Glancing back out the front to the street, he noted that the view from the street into the shop was obscured by a number of mannequins, each dressed in different outfits.

Conscious of how he looked, he went forward to the counter and waited. A second later a short teenager appeared from behind a curtain, purple hair, shaved close on the left side of her head. A nose ring and dark eyeliner completed her look. Both Seb and the store assistant regarded each other for a long moment before Seb took out a wallet and placed his remaining cash on the countertop.

'I have thirty-nine dollars and some loose change. I need one set of new clothes, including a coat, shoes and socks. Will I get that with the thirty-nine dollars?'

'Most folks help themselves around here. But you look like something the cat threw up, and maybe feel worse than that. Go to the change room and I'll bring you some stuff.' She looked at him with suspicion, pushing the crumpled notes Seb had provided into the cash drawer.

'Thanks.' Seb found two change rooms. He entered one and sat himself down on a chair. Then carefully, he pulled the Scorpion machine pistol out and laid it on the carpet, followed by his Beretta.

'Our new clothing here is crap,' called the assistant. 'I'll bring you some second-hand stuff which is better quality anyway. Your money will go further too.'

'Appreciate that.'

The teenager appeared and handed a set of clothes through the narrow gap in the curtain. 'You want to keep your old ones, or will I throw them?' Although Seb had showered, the clothes he was forced to wear again were definitely in need of laundering. If you looked at them, you could see blood stains.

'I don't want them,' said Seb.

'Now that's not suspicious. Leave them in there when you get changed.'

'Okay.' He heard her walk away.

Seb heard the tinkle of the bell as another customer came in. He began changing out of his clothes.

'Officer Guyatt, I never expected to see you in here,' said the sales assistant.

'Do you have anyone in the store?' said Guyatt.

Seb recognised the voice. He stopped moving, one leg out of the pants, the other still in.

'No. Why?'

'We're looking for someone. He's dangerous,' said Guyatt.

'Oh, really? Is that why you have the roadblocks? What does this guy look like?' she asked.

'Six three, heavy set. He has a tattoo on his neck. He killed someone.'

'Like I said, no one here. I'll be sure to let you know if I see him.'

Seb heard the front door open and close. A minute later, the assistant came back to the change room and spoke through the curtain. 'You don't have a neck tattoo, do you?'

Seb chuckled, continuing to change into the clothes, which seemed a good fit. He sat on the chair and put on the joggers. They were spot on too.

'No tattoos.'

She handed him a jacket through a gap in the curtain. This one is second-hand too, but it has hardly been worn. Seb took the jacket. It showed signs of wear, but when he tried it on, it fitted him perfectly. He slipped the Scorpion into his belt at the back and the Beretta into his front belt. The spare clips he shoved into the jacket pockets. Zipping up the jacket, the weapons were concealed. He regarded himself in the mirror, noting a couple of bruises that had come out on his face.

Opening the curtain, she said, 'Were they looking for you?'

'No.'

She tilted her head. 'The clothes fit.'

'Yep.'

'This sure is a strange day. Roadblocks, a killer on the loose and all the phones are still down.'

'Did I have enough money?'

'Let's call it even. Were they looking for you?'

'No.'

'But you know *something*.'

'Yeah, I know something. Don't trust the cops around here... unless it's Benson.'

She thought for a moment. 'I know her. She seems okay.'

Seb nodded and headed for the door.

CHAPTER 32

After an hour, Angel and Codi were returned to cell three, finding the other two women gone. There was no sound, except a constant dripping of water somewhere. The captives, Belle and Matti were gone. And if they weren't there, there was only one place they could be. Angel stared into the well. She did not share her thoughts with Codi, who was trying to be brave, and doing okay for someone so young.

They were given water and some food, shoved through a hatch in the door. Angel ate ravenously while Codi picked at her plate.

'Where did they take them?'

'I don't know,' lied Angel.

'Oh God,' said Codi. She wailed, long and piteously. 'They went down the hole, didn't they?'

Angel went to Codi and wrapped her arms around the youth. 'You're too young to be here. I'm sorry this has happened to you.'

'They killed my brother,' she whispered.

'I'm sorry.'

'Were you with them? Matti and Belle, they said you were with *them.*'

'I was… for a while. But not anymore. I wanted to be in their gang. Then when I knew what it was that they were doing… it was too late.'

'Why? I want to understand. Please, it's important. I need to know who you are.'

Angel sighed. After a few moments, in a tired voice, she said,

'Okay... I met Leo in a nightclub. He was... *extraordinary*, and I was drawn to him. He seemed to know what I wanted to hear.'

'Was he the leader?'

'He leads one of the night crews, yeah.' Angel stroked Codi's hair. 'There's something you have to understand about me, Codi – I've never been a good person. I can't help but fuck everything up. These people... they were like me. I could sense they had each other, and they didn't care where I came from... what I was. They just flew through life, free as birds, doing whatever the fuck they wanted. It was exactly what I wanted too.'

'Then you found out.'

Angel nodded. 'One night, we were robbing a store. They killed the night clerk. He was just a kid like you. They hooked him to some rope and dragged him along the road until his face and arms peeled right off him. I tried to leave that night. It was then that two of them tried to rape me. Leo stopped them. They were *so* strong. I was given a choice – to either run with them, or he would let them finish what they'd started and then I would get dumped in a hole somewhere on the roadside. They took my phone and my wallet that night. The honeymoon was over.'

Codi was silent, absorbing Angel's words. Then she said, 'I was with my boyfriend and my brother. We were trespassing in this cabin out by Silver Lake, just taking a nap, staying dry from the rain. The next thing I know, these people are there. They killed my boyfriend and my brother. I thought I was going to die too, but Gunther brought me here instead.'

'That's not how they usually operate,' said Angel. 'They hunt far from the Cove, to avoid suspicion.'

'They were looking for some guy in the woods. He met up with us earlier. Then they came, and they must have tracked him or something. It was a mix-up. I know that. We were not meant to be there. It was all a big mistake.'

'Who was he – the guy they were after?'

'I dunno.'

'What did he look like?'

'He was kinda blond, with intense eyes.'

Angel wondered if this was Seb. He was both of those things. Perhaps he was close. The thought excited her for only a moment. As the reality of her situation hit, she hoped that if it really was Seb, he would just run. No one else needed to die because of her.

After a while, the girl asked, 'What time do you think it is?'

'I would say… around midday. Why?'

'My folks will be wondering where I am. I should be at school. Maybe they'll go to the police and…'

'Yeah, maybe,' said Angel, trying to sound convincing. But the police were not looking for her and when Codi's parents did show up, they would listen and nod, and write down a few details. But that would be all.

A few hours passed. Angel left Codi and crawled on her knees to the edge of the well. The smell emanating up from within the hole was putrid. Those two women were definitely down there.

'Don't get too close,' said Codi in a small voice.

'I won't,' said Angel.

'What can you see?'

Angel strained her eyes, but she couldn't see any more than before.

'I can't see anything.'

There was movement, a shifting in the mist, and a hand reached up and out of the murk, the arm of a corpse, which flopped over. Angel's breath caught in her throat, and she slid back away from the hole.

'What did you see?' asked Codi.

'Nothing.'

'Don't lie to me, don't you dare do that,' said Codi.

Angel remained quiet. There was no need to frighten the girl more than she already was. They sat, leaning against each other for warmth and comfort. After a long while, Angel became aware of Codi's steady breathing, and she knew the teen had at last fallen into a deep, exhausted sleep.

'Hello?' Even though Angel was also drifting toward sleep, she heard a faint voice.

'Hello?' The voice was coming from down below, faint and possibly male.

'I'm stuck in here, help me,' it pleaded.

Angel allowed Codi to tip onto her side, while she slid out and away from her. Angel crawled to the lip of the hole. When she peered over the edge, she could just make out a roughly humanoid shape in the mist. It was so dark that she could see very little of it, but it seemed to be looking up in her direction.

'Hello?' said Angel. 'Is there someone down there?'

'Yes, I'm stuck in here.' The voice was low, and it barely carried.

'How did you get in there?' asked Angel.

'They keep me in here.'

'I'm captive too,' admitted Angel.

'It's *so* cold down here. So very cold.'

'I wish I could help you,' said Angel.

The voice from below remained silent, and so Angel said, 'Is there anyone else down there with you?'

'No, I think they... found a way to escape,' said the voice.

Angel was suddenly very frightened, but she held herself near the opening. It was lying, of course.

'You are very beautiful,' said the voice. 'I like your long hair.'

'You can see me?' asked Angel.

'I can see well in the dark. I can see everything,' said the figure.

'They're dead, aren't they?' said Angel.

'Yes, but I would rather talk to you than... anything else,' he said.

Angel backed away from the hole and sat with her face in her hands. She didn't want it to see her.

'I know you are there; I can smell you.'

'I'm here,' said Angel.

'I've been down here for years. Did you know that?'
'No.'
Angel crawled back to the lip of the hole. 'Let me see you.'
There was no reply.

CHAPTER 33

The belltower in Saint Anthony's was the highest point in the town. At the very top of the winding stair, Jaz and Father O'Malley emerged into a small chamber with a wooden stool. It had four small open-air windows, facing each direction of the compass.

A telescope had been set up to face the streets downhill, towards the docks. Through one of the open windows, which tilted on a central hinge, the long lens protruded through the opening.

'Three years ago, I converted this place. It used to house a bell. I felt this would be more appropriate, at least for this town,' said O'Malley.

Jaz took a seat and put her eye to the telescope. 'Not bad, not bad at all. You can see a lot!'

'This telescope cost a pretty penny. You can zoom in and out with a button on the side,' said O'Malley.

'But the angles are limited by the window, unfortunately,' said Jaz. 'Have you seen anything using this thing?'

'Not as much as you might think. Trees can obscure the view. But at maximum magnification, you can see right down to the docks area and out onto the bay beyond.'

'Have you seen anything useful though?'

'I allow myself some time nearly every day to come up here, and although I've seen things, I have never really seen anything you would call useful,' admitted O'Malley. 'The view is particularly beautiful at night-time. When the mood takes me, I have looked to the stars.'

'So, why did you want me to see this?' asked Jaz.

'Today, I thought it *might* show us something useful.'

'Yeah, you may be right about that.' Jaz looked through the eyepiece and swung the telescope a few degrees to her left. She tilted the telescope down a little and then had a clear view of the streets around the docks. 'I don't know what I'm looking for though.'

'On a day like today, with the weather the way it is, you won't find many people walking around town. Maybe look to see *who is* walking about on such a bleak day,' suggested the priest.

'You think Seb might be around? If I were him, I would have left town already.'

'He came looking for his sister. If he's the kind of person I think he is, he's still here, somewhere,' said O'Malley.

Jaz moved the telescope, scanning the streets. 'I see three local police cars moving around.' She gave a low whistle through her teeth. 'And two state-trooper vehicles too. Just cruising.' She sat back and looked at O'Malley. 'Think about that for a moment. You have all the road blocks – at least two we know of – with police at each. And you have five more cars cruising in the town.'

O'Malley nodded. 'They are looking for someone.'

'You think it's Seb?'

The priest looked away. 'Perhaps.'

Jaz suspected the priest was hiding something from her.

She looked back through the telescope. Scanning, she discovered that the priest was right. Not many people were out and about on such a miserably chilly day. She watched a couple of kids, hoods pulled up, riding bicycles down a hill. Each had a backpack. They turned up a side street and she lost sight of them. But that was all so far. The usual foot traffic was not there.

'I will come back later and bring you something to eat and a thermos of coffee. It gets cold up here,' said the priest.

Jaz nodded. She discovered she wanted to spend some time in this eagle's nest to try and see where the police cars were looking.

The priest disappeared back down the spiral staircase, and Jaz took out her phone. The signal was still down. She wondered if Harvey would send back up once he realised he couldn't reach her. But knowing her boss, Jaz felt that he would check the area of the Cove and simply discover that all lines were down. He would see it as a maintenance issue, a broken server or something. No immediate help would not be coming from that direction, thought Jaz.

An hour passed, and Jaz spent the time with her eye to the telescope, moving it and following the police cruisers as they did slow laps of the grids of streets. There was some light town traffic too, with small trucks and vans stopping at the various shops, cafes and other small businesses around the town.

The priest appeared, holding a thermos and a plate of sandwiches. 'I'm sorry, this is the best Mrs Blackwell could muster.'

'I'm starving,' admitted Jaz, her hand taking a sandwich off the plate. 'And a coffee would be nice too.'

'Seen much?'

'No – not really. The cops are buzzing. Doing some slow circuits... looking hard.'

O'Malley smiled. 'It's good to have you here.'

'Can I ask you something?' said Jaz.

'Go ahead.'

'The other priest – what can you tell me about him?'

The question almost caught O'Malley off-guard, thought Jaz.

'I can tell you that he isn't a real priest,' allowed O'Malley.

'Why is he here?' questioned Jaz. She sipped her coffee.

'I wondered if I could hide him here, but he just doesn't look the part, does he?' O'Malley shook his head. 'I took his confession the night he came in. There is nothing I can tell you that wouldn't somehow breach the sanctity of the confessional.'

'That's some bullshit right there!'

'I don't care what you think it is,' said O'Malley. 'He confessed his sins, and he had many. He is now on a new path.'

'A new path? Listen to me, O'Malley, I don't know what or who that guy is, but I've seen his *type* many times. You may think you have a new pet Rottweiler, but I guarantee he hasn't changed.'

'He has much to make up for. I think he will find God through his absolution.'

'And what is his absolution?' asked Jaz.

'If I were to tell you that, perhaps you would try to interfere. No, Ms Freeman, you are best not knowing.'

'You want to know what I think?' asked Jaz.

O'Malley simply looked at her.

'I think you're hiding him. I think you brought him here, to Crabtree Cove, for a specific reason. But he got made, and he ran, and now he's here. And those people out there, they're locking everything down until they have him. Catching him means they get a chance to question him, and that could lead back to you and your... flock.'

'You are a perceptive person.'

'I had a chance to think, sitting up here.'

CHAPTER 34

Litter and leaves blew along the street, swirling, caught in dust devil winds. Seb ducked into Lucille's diner and seated himself in the same booth he had used once before.

Deliberately putting himself out in the open, he was hoping to meet with the gang, maybe even have a conversation with them in a public place where they would be less likely to pull a gun or try and otherwise start a fight. If he couldn't find them, he would have to let them come to him. It was a bad plan, maybe not even a real plan, and he knew it. But to get to Angel, he would do anything, even dammed stupid things like this. Perhaps he might even find Miller, and Miller might know where to look for her.

Grace and Lola were looking after the diner in Lucille's absence. Grace sauntered over, adjusting her top. She smiled and Seb smelt cherry-flavoured lipstick. 'Hey, what are you doing in here?' She slid into the booth opposite him. 'You know, some folks were looking for you the other night. So was the FBI.'

'The who?' asked Seb, his eyebrows going up.

'Jaz Freeman. She's with the FBI,' said Grace.

'Jesus Christ,' he blurted. 'She's FBI?'

'They were out half the night in that rain, looking all over the place for you.'

He sat staring at the girl, who gave an embarrassed smile. Grace continued, 'Lucille has your dog, Ripley, by the way, at their house. Gab and Kelt brought her.'

Seb let out his breath and said, 'I was hoping they made it out.'

'I met your sister, too.'

'Angel?'

'Yeah, months ago,' she said brightly. 'She handed me the letter, the one she sent to you.'

He was stunned. He fumbled the letter from his wallet and showed it to her with shaking hands. At last, he met her eyes. 'This letter?'

Grace took it from him and read it. 'I never read it.' She handed it back. 'None of my business.'

'Thank you, Grace.'

'You're welcome, Seb.' She smiled, and then slid out of the booth, heading back to talk to Lola, completely unaware of the gravity of the information she had just imparted.

A state trooper's car went by, the cop inside looking right at Seb, making eye contact. But he just kept going on down the street. *They're looking for Miller.*

Seb's head was suddenly spinning. He had just met the person who had posted the letter for Angel, which meant that she could tell him where she was when she handed it over. And Jaz was FBI... in the same town, asking questions... *a lot* of questions. 'Hey, Grace!' he began.

The girl turned, a smile on her face. 'Yeah?'

At that moment a campervan was cruising by, and as it headed downhill, it caught Seb's eye. The driver was just some bearded guy, but the woman in the passenger seat was Krystal. Her short-cropped, blonde hair and heavy makeup were unmistakable. She glanced in his direction, her eyes widening.

The van had gone maybe fifty feet past the diner when it jammed on its breaks with a screech and a cloud of blue smoke.

'Do you have a back door out of here?' he called to Grace.

Seb could hear the whine of the van's motor as it reversed. Grace and Lola stared at him.

'You need to go!' he barked.

They hadn't moved. They looked at him like he was crazy. The reversing van stopped in the middle of the street, just outside. Seb moved out of the booth, dropping low instinctively, his hand already going under his coat.

The van's front doors opened, with Krystal and the driver leaping out. Krystal moved like a dancer – fast and fluid, long leather jacket billowing around her as she brought up a shotgun. *Boom*. The rapport registered as the glass window in front of him imploded. Seb had ducked lower. Grace screamed, hurled backward, peppered with pellets and shards of glass.

Then the van's side door slid open and four more guys exited the vehicle. They spread out around the diner, a variety of guns in hand, firing volleys of shots into the diner. Seb had instinctively reached for the Scorpion machine pistol. From his crouched position, he returned fire, a long sweeping burst above the level of the booths, sprayed in an arc. Two of Krystal's buddies collapsed on the sidewalk, bullet holes in their chests.

It went quiet for about ten seconds.

'Hey, Seb, are you coming outside to play?' called Krystal.

'I don't think so.'

'We can come in whenever we want,' she said.

Judging the direction of her voice, Krystal had already retreated to the van and was peering inside the diner from the edge of the vehicle. Perhaps she had expected to kill him at the outset. Maybe she didn't think he would be well-armed or armed at all. Her courage had evaporated. Now, having lost the initial surprise, it remained to be seen whether she would retreat or save face. It was a personal thing for her. She needed to win, and she wanted him dead. Although Seb wanted to talk to someone in the gang, he knew it could not be Krystal, who was in no mood to talk.

Seb crawled across to Grace. Her eyes, vacant and lifeless, stared at the ceiling. Lola had legged it out the backdoor through the kitchen. Seb went around the counter, behind the old cash register and a coffee machine, giving himself a solid layer of protection. He pulled his second weapon, holding the Beretta in his left hand.

'Hey, Seb!'

'Yeah?'

'We have your sister. She sure is *purdy*... tall... dark... soon to be dead. Oh yeah, we have her, alright. You know, she *was* one of us. But she changed her mind, and well, McTaggart doesn't like that. Once you join us, membership is for life.'

Seb heard a name – *McTaggart*. He wondered who that was.

'If you come out, I can take you to her!'

'You'd do that for me?' called Seb.

'You can join her. Her cell is nice and warm. You can have a reunion before you both die.'

'That sounds interesting, Krystal.' If he thought she would actually reunite him with Angel, maybe he would have surrendered. But Krystal was likely to just gun him down.

*

Benson was cruising near the docks, looking for Seb. He had been down there a few times already and it seemed likely he would return to the vicinity. In her peripheral vision, she noticed flashing lights up a side street, higher up the hill.

She swung the cruiser around in a tight U-turn and approached the scene. A state trooper's car was parked across the street, blocking both lanes, red and blue beacon flashing. At the top of the hill, maybe a mile up the road, another police car – perhaps Guyatt's cruiser, was angled across the street at the top end, effectively blocking off both ends of the road.

She could see a few hundred feet away, cars parked along the street and a van parked in the middle of the road, its doors wide open. It was, she estimated, level with where Lucille's diner was located.

She pulled up near the trooper's car. He was a tall, imposing guy in his thirties. She didn't know him.

'What's going on? Is it a two-eleven?' she asked.

'I think so. Shots were fired.' He was watching the scene, standing behind the car.

'Are police on scene?' asked Benson.

'Stay here,' he said.

'Hey, you don't have jurisdiction here,' she replied.

Benson went to step around the trooper but he placed a hand on her shoulder, holding her back.

Jaz paused for a moment, then went back to her cruiser and entered the vehicle. She picked up the radio. 'I need to know what's going on in Main Street, in the area of Lucille's diner. Respond.'

The radio crackled and Guyatt came on. 'What are you doing here Benson? We have this in hand.'

'What's happening, Guyatt?'

She was answered by the hiss of static. Benson put the radio back in the cradle. She popped the trunk, looked at the M4 for a moment, but then retrieved a pair of binoculars. She went and stood beside the state trooper, noting his name badge – Gibson.

'Gibson, is it? Do you know what the hell is happening over there?' She raised the binoculars and looked at the scene.

Two bodies lay on the sidewalk outside Lucille's. They weren't moving. The window of the diner appeared to have been shot out. Behind a campervan, at either end, a woman and about three other guys were watching the diner. She could see that they were armed, the blonde woman holding a shotgun.

'I need to get up there,' said Benson. Again, she tried to go around the trooper and again he held her arm as she tried to move past. He literally stepped into her path. She stopped and looked at him. 'Stand down, Gibson.'

'No, ma'am.' Stone-faced, the trooper actually put his hand on his gun and unclipped the holster. The weapon could now be pulled in an instant.

Benson froze. If she went further now, there was no going back. She raised her hands. 'Okay.' She backed away, returned to her car, climbed into the driver's seat and waited. *God, she hoped it wasn't Seb in there.*

*

Seb peered out, keeping his head low. They couldn't storm the diner without him killing at least a few of them. Both his guns were close-range weapons and he doubted that the gang was trained in tactical urban warfare. They might come at him but if they did, it would be a clumsy attempt. The doorway was a killing zone – narrow, easy to cover. Coming through the window at the same time would also be difficult. It was a stand-off. Seb wanted to kill these guys; he really did. But now he had a name – *McTaggart.*

The smart thing now was to back off and get to McTaggart. That was the endgame. It wasn't about Krystal at all, and it never would be.

'Give me a minute, Krystal. I just need a minute to think and I'll come out with my hands up. Promise you won't shoot!'

'That's smart, Seb! You lay down your guns in there and you come out slowly, hands above your head. I promise I won't shoot you.'

Seb had already slipped away through the kitchen, out a door into an alleyway at the rear of the diner. He hurried away, his guns up and ready. The car park had a raised wall all around it, with a narrow driveway that led back to the street where the gang was situated. The wall was high, too high to jump. Then he found a large dumpster to the left, hidden in a shadowed corner. He vaulted onto it and then over the wall.

'Seb, are you in there? You come out, like we agreed!' shouted

Krystal. She stood at the edge of the campervan, peeking out at the diner from beyond the large wing mirror.

'I don't think he's in there anymore, Krystal,' said her driver.

She turned and slapped him hard across the face. 'Get in there and check, stupid.'

CHAPTER 35

When Seb left Lucille's, he moved quickly along backstreets. Twice, police cruisers had come close but on each occasion, he had hidden, once in an alleyway choked with garbage cans and empty boxes and again, laying down flat behind a parked car. He had gone only a few blocks when he spied an antiques and second-hand goods store. It was old, two-storey brick, covered in graffiti and seemed deserted.

Smashing a window, he climbed in and crept between old furniture and glass cabinets filled with ornaments. When he found the stairs, they were hidden behind sideboards and stacked chairs. At the top of the stairs, the upper floor opened to a small room with a sofa, a bar fridge, and a few open boxes of second-hand books. Centrefolds showing half-naked women dating back to the 1960s were pinned to the walls. Seb collapsed on a sofa. He tried to gather his thoughts as he peered out the window at the orange glow of a setting sun dulled by spider webs and dust.

A small, old-fashioned radio was plugged in, the antenna extended. Silence gathered around him, pressing in.

He was acutely aware that the bodies were stacking up around him – first the stoner kids at the cabin and now a kid-waitress. If not for him, they would all be alive. His thoughts tumbled, flashing images came unbidden – from Krystal, her angry eyes suddenly morphing into serpent slits, to Grace, blown backwards, in a spray of glass. He closed his eyes to banish the thoughts but this only summoned Angel, his last conversation with her as she walked from the room – *You're leaving, just like Mom and Dad. Don't bother coming back, Seb, I won't be here...*

It was too quiet. He needed distraction. Opening the small fridge, he found a six-pack and someone's left-over lunch. He took a can and popped the beer. If he went back to Benson, he could get her killed too. No – from now on he had to minimise the collateral damage. Jaz might be able to help him though. If she really was FBI, he thought. What did she know? Could he find her again without running into the gang?

Half a can of beer later, he finally began to calm down, his pulse no longer racing, his mind slowing enough to think straight. He turned the radio on and found it tuned to the only station within range – *Bay FM.*

A song was ending and his favourite radio disk jockey's honeyed voice came dripping across the airwaves as a gust of wind rattled the windows. Listening to her, he closed his eyes, allowing her voice to wash over him, anesthetising his wounded soul.

Here we are again, folks. The phones are still down, and the fuzz are still blocking the ways out of town. They don't like me talking to you, but hey... they don't know where to find my little station. She chuckled.

Tonight, I'm gonna be playing some more of your favourite tunes, folks, but let me send out a message... maybe for the fiftieth time... are you listening to me, folks? This is from Jaz, a love song to her friend. You may know her. If you do, this one's for you, Seb.

Seb sat up abruptly, spilling beer down his shirt. 'Jaz?'

David Bowie's *Modern Love* opening riffs were unmistakable.

The track ended and another song immediately began, this time without any introduction from Charlie J.

Seb sat, thinking about what it could mean. Jaz – whom he now knew to be FBI – had sent a message to him via Charlie J, the cryptic radio disk jockey. He had heard her say weird stuff before and thought it was just part of the show. She had been threatened too, on air, he now recalled. He sat, straining to think. He shook

233

his head, hoping maybe something would joggle loose. The lyrics must mean something. He played them over in his head, and a slow smile spread over his face.

*

As darkness fell across the Cove, Jaz Freeman descended from the belltower and found O'Malley in the loft with the pretend priest. The table was set with lit candles and a bible sat there, a red ribbon marking a place. Jaz checked her cell phone again, for the hundredth time, knowing that she would see no signal before she even looked.

Hours earlier, Jaz had heard the blast of the shotgun, the rapport shattering the silence of the Cove, echoing across the sky, unobstructed and clear, all the way to her vantage point. She had trained the telescope in the general direction of the sound, her eyes at first drawn to the police cars that came hurtling along and stopped at either end of the road, forming roadblocks. Then she noted the van parked outside Lucille's diner and witnessed the aftermath of the shooting, except she had not seen who they were shooting at inside the diner. The view was clear once she had the lens correctly adjusted. The campervan rolled on down the road, away from the scene and up to a police car.

The group chatted with the cop and the van was allowed to move through the blockade. It was the most damning thing Jaz had seen and clear proof that a gang was operating without limitation in the town – probably with active assistance from local law enforcement.

Then the police car from the other end of the street, closest to Jaz, coasted down to the scene. Jaz watched as Guyatt stepped around two bodies on the sidewalk, then went inside. Ten minutes later, an ambulance came to the diner. Jaz noted that the paramedics arrived quietly, without lights or a siren. The lack of urgency meant that whoever they had come for was dead. She was zoomed in when they brought out Grace's body on a gurney.

Sitting across from O'Malley and Clyde, Jaz described the scene she had witnessed.

'This is escalating,' said O'Malley.

'You need to let me get on with my job,' said Clyde.

'And what would that be?' asked Jaz.

'Retribution,' said O'Malley.

'You think that's your job?'

'McTaggart has brought evil to the town.'

'You seem to have it all worked out,' said Jaz.

'McTaggart's operation must be stopped. The Dagon's Riders will be diminished without him. They will no longer feed the beast. The trade in lost souls will cease.'

'Lost souls... yes, I suppose they are,' said Jaz, thinking of the faces of the victims she had identified in her investigation. 'You honestly think he's feeding that thing? For what purpose?'

O'Malley sat, his fingers arched, chin resting atop them. 'Consider everything together. Thanks to Eric, we know a great deal. Forget the image of the creature, whatever it may be. Instead, focus your thoughts on what else the film showed us.'

Her brow furrowed. 'The party.'

O'Malley nodded, a slow smile forming. 'Indeed, the party. If I had access to your resources, Ms Freeman, I would delve into McTaggart's finances, analyse his every transaction, perhaps use facial recognition software and uncover every... single... person on that film. Do that, and you may uncover what his operation is really doing and why.'

'He's a biochemist,' she said, her eyes distant.

They sat in silence for a minute before O'Malley looked at Clyde. 'It's time.'

The hitman nodded.

O'Malley said, 'What prayer did I tell you?'

Clyde looked serious. Jaz could tell he was concentrating when he replied, 'Even though I walk through the valley of the shadow of death, I will fear no evil....'

O'Malley nodded encouragement. 'For...'

Clyde continued, 'For you are with me; your rod and your staff, they comfort me.'

'Yes,' said O'Malley.

Clyde stood and removed the white collar. He placed it in front of O'Malley. The tattoo of a rattlesnake curling around his throat and up the side of his neck, jaws gaping, baring its fangs. With a nod, Clyde left the room.

'So, you brought in a hitman?'

'I did,' said O'Malley. 'I was considering that we should wait until things calm down again... before I sent him to kill McTaggart. But now, given what the town is going through, the potential for innocents being murdered has risen.'

'You could be sending him to his death.'

'The man has found peace with the belief that he can redeem himself.'

'One good act cannot wipe out a lifetime killing,' said Jaz.

'Perhaps... unless in doing this, he saves as many lives as he has taken,' theorised O'Malley.

'Do all priests think like you?' snapped Jaz.

'We all have our place in this universe. Do you think it was a coincidence that you happened to come here when you did? Believe me when I say that there must be a higher power, and you are now part of this,' said O'Malley.

Jaz was about to respond, had opened her mouth, but then closed it and walked to the window. 'Who do you think they were shooting at?'

'If I was to guess, I'd say it was your friend, Sebastian.'

'I agree, but I don't think they got him.' She couldn't disguise her satisfaction.

'On the contrary, I think he got two of them,' said O'Malley. 'Maybe he was also brought here for a purpose.'

'The world is chaos and happenstance, O'Malley. I get that you need it to be something else. But – there is no divine intervention. Just a bunch of us trying to even up the odds, balance the scale.'

'As it has always been,' said O'Malley.

*

Seb turned the radio off and put his jacket back on. Bowie's *Modern Love* had been the song of choice by Charlie J, the track's chorus specifically mentioning a church. It was all he had to go on.

He left the store, stepping into a chill night. Following the shadows of back alleyways, he left the market district. Then shunning the lights from the streets, he slowly crossed the town, keeping his eyes on the steeple of the church, silhouetted against the night sky.

Certain that the streets were unsafe, he then took a direct line for St Anthony's, climbing fences, cutting across lawns and picking through gardens. He ducked under a window where an elderly couple were sitting, eating dinner, distracted by their television.

He went to cross a street but as he was about to move, he heard the distinct hum of motorbikes. He dropped to a prone position, beneath a hedge, watching as three riders coasted past barely ten feet from him. They were looking around, heads swivelling, long jackets billowing slightly.

Climbing to his feet, he crossed the street, jogging along the sidewalk, staying out of the yellow radiance of streetlights. Rounding a corner, he approached the main road. And there it was, the looming monolith of St Anthony's cathedral.

Abandoning caution, he jogged up the sidewalk, ignoring the cars that passed him from both directions. Oncoming lights blinded him as each vehicle swept by. He was only twenty yards from the entrance to the church when a car swung in front of him, stopping alongside the curb. The driver stepped out, but the lights were in his eyes and Seb raised the Beretta, his finger tightening on the trigger.

'Wait – don't shoot!'

'Benson?'

'Jeezuz, I thought you were going to plug me,' she said as she stepped around the door, away from her headlights.

Rebecca wasn't in uniform and she was driving her own vehicle – an old green Jeep. 'Get in, I can get you out of town, right now!'

'I can't, Rebecca.'

'Correct me if I'm wrong, but did they try to kill you again at Lucille's?'

He nodded. Benson reached in and turned off the car's lights. 'Where were you going?'

Seb glanced to his left.

'The church?'

'Come with me. I think I was given a message to come here.'

Rebecca shook her head, but as Seb went striding toward the church, Benson fell in beside him.

'Did your people put out a BOLO on me?' he asked.

'No, they don't want to catch you, Seb, they just want to kill you. An official BOLO would bring a paper trail.'

'Why are you here? Are you leaving town?' he asked her.

'How long do you think I could expect to live if I'm the only cop in town that isn't rotten?'

They passed beneath a polished timber arch and walked into the nave along a red carpet. Their eyes were drawn up to a tall cross, and a figure in black clothing, kneeling in front of the altar. Shadows flickered across a vaulted ceiling cast from rows of candles. The church was very quiet, though their footfalls echoed as they approached the priest.

He turned, smiling and as he stood, he raised a hand in greeting. 'So, here you are.'

'You were expecting us?' asked Seb.

'I was expecting *you*, Sebastian.'

Seb's eyebrows lifted. 'Okay.'

'Who's this?' came a voice. The guy appeared out of nowhere, managing somehow to approach from the side without Seb hearing him.

Seb cleared his Beretta fast, swivelled, his arm extended toward the newcomer. He was all in black, a pistol aimed at Seb. They faced each other, neither man lowering their weapon until Benson stepped between them. 'Miller? What are you doing here?'

CHAPTER 36

McTaggart drifted across the lawn toward the cliffside house, the wind tussling his hair. His silk Japanese robes were now in a silver, gold and red pattern in the shape of a dragon. Armed with the katana, which hung at his side, he felt almost invincible.

He approached the cliffside mansion, hearing waves smashing beneath it, driven onto the rocks by the wind. For a moment the clouds shifted and it was bathed in silvered moonlight.

Every hour that passed, without knowing where Miller was, was another hour that the man could plan his assassination. His first night crew had gone into town, replacing the day crews. And if anyone could get results, it was Gunther.

McTaggart entered the old house, navigating to the second floor, his steps silent, his mind restless. The control room was at the other end of the floor. To his left, a sitting room with a view out over the ocean drew him in.

He found Krystal there, seated on a couch, looking at the sea, red lips pursed and petulant. Seeing him, she visibly stiffened. It was good that she feared him. He was angry with her. She understood the mission, and yet she had failed again. He walked over to her, and her blue eyes regarded him. He could see they were fake – just contacts, as fake as the rest of her. He slapped her across the head with an open hand, as hard as he could. Her head jolted, her small frame twisting sideways. He raised his hand again and she sat, waiting for the second blow to fall, eyes on his long, black-painted fingernails. Slowly, he closed his hand and it fell to his side.

It was another test, to see if she could control herself. He had expected her to become enraged, for she had a hot, lightning-fast temper. Combined with psychopathic tendencies, she was proving to be a liability to his operation. He licked his lips as he looked down at her, seeing that her nose was bleeding. Still, she regarded him, the anger in her eyes held in check.

'Too frightened to report to me,' he said quietly, showing her that he could also control his anger if he wanted to.

'I fucked up,' she whispered.

'You will remain here until I decide your real punishment, Krystal.'

She nodded.

'But you need to be useful. Are you armed?' he asked her.

Krystal lifted back her coat. A pistol was holstered there. 'I also have a knife.'

'Then you will be my bodyguard tonight,' he said.

She nodded eagerly.

'Not that I need one,' McTaggart said, placing his hand on the hilt of the katana. 'Attend me.'

McTaggart left the sitting room, Krystal walking a few steps behind. They came to the wide staircase and descended to the ground floor. On the surface, the old mansion had not changed much since it was built in the 1920s. Even the table lamps were original art-deco pieces of elegant bronze women and greyhound dogs that held up glass-globe lights.

Leo and his crew were reclining in the dining room, messily eating and drinking. The TV they had brought into the room was covered in a layer of food that they had hurled at the screen. They watched McTaggart and Krystal with eyes that could have belonged to hyenas. Their hungry, predatory, gazes followed McTaggart and Krystal as they crossed the room. Even Krystal stiffened when she walked in. They were almost fully charged, having taken the serum only a day or so before.

They wanted to hunt. They were as ready as any wild beast

could be. But he wanted them here tonight, close by, if something unexpected should occur.

Leo stood and approached McTaggart. Krystal tried to stand between them but Leo shoved her aside with stunning ease.

'We're ready to go,' he said.

'I know you are, Leo, I know you are.'

'We're hungry, we need to hunt,' said Leo.

Leo was not talking about food. He needed to release the pent-up energy and fury that was in his veins. McTaggart glanced around. The younger ones – Little Bear and Screamer – were looking particularly amped. Maybe, just maybe he needed to revisit the serum, adjust it down a little. These guys looked as close to the edge as any subject ever given the formula. He would let them loose tonight, maybe a little later, before they did something to each other.

McTaggart started to leave but said over his shoulder 'Stand ready tonight, Leo. I have a feeling I will be sending you and your crew somewhere soon.'

They walked down another corridor, past a kitchen and what had been a parlour. Old books still sat in those oak shelves, covered in dust. McTaggart could almost imagine the men in cravats, smoking cigars, circling the billiard table. They entered the parlour and he went to the bookcase. He glanced once at Krystal, a smile touching his lips, a twinkle in his eyes.

'What, Krystal, was Charles Dickens' most well-known book?'

Krystal looked confused. But her eyes went to the shelves and scanning them, she stepped forward and tried to remove a leather-bound book with the title – *Oliver Twist*. The book barely moved but a click sounded and a section of shelving swivelled. Krystal could see that a stair went down into darkness. She smiled, not at the ingenuity or the perfect engineering that had made such a doorway to another secret area of the complex. No – it was because somehow, McTaggart trusted her enough to show her the secret, one that maybe even Gunther and Leo didn't know about.

At the bottom of the staircase, the corridor bent, following a natural cave wall. Water dripped onto a floor that was slightly damp. As they went forward, lights automatically came on, illuminating the corridor just a few steps in front of them. Krystal could see more doors, on either side of the corridor, suggesting the complex below the house was much larger than she had guessed. On a solid door, at the right side, a sign declared – *Danger – do not proceed past this point.*

Fifty or sixty feet further along, they came to a different type of door, which was more like a metal hatch. Beside it, a keypad.

McTaggart told Krystal to turn around while he entered the pin. Something clicked, and then the door slid sideways, revealing a laboratory. Glass tubes were arrayed along a side wall and several strange pieces of apparatus that Krystal did not recognise sat on a long metal bench in the middle of the room. There were vials of liquid and canisters neatly arranged with unpronounceable labels with more than twenty syllables.

Three people, all old guys in lab coats, turned from what they were doing. One of them, a guy with a white beard, said, 'We don't have the next batch as yet, Stirling.'

'What's the delay?' asked McTaggart.

'He isn't feeding as fast this time,' another scientist said. 'Until he finishes at least another seventy per cent of them, we won't get enough blood from him.'

'We bought him what he likes,' said McTaggart.

The bearded scientist shrugged. 'Look for yourself.'

McTaggart glanced at Krystal. She was totally confused, but she held her tongue. They crossed to the other side of the lab and opened a panel, roughly the size of a large-screen television. Behind the panel, Krystal saw a tempered glass window. The glass was roughly level with the floor of a chamber. Smoke or mist hung close to the stone floor. Krystal couldn't see much, for the room was quite dark. In the corner, Krystal could just see human legs,

243

unmoving. They seemed to be only partly attached to the rest of the woman's body. But it was insubstantial. Krystal was both horrified and intrigued. Then understanding dawned on her face.

'There is a certain level of humidity we need to maintain in the well chamber,' explained McTaggart. 'It must also be kept dark.'

'What's in there,' she said in hush.

McTaggart explained, 'He cannot hear you. And he won't come near the window, because of the lights in here.'

'He?'

'Our donor.' McTaggart smiled. He needed to share his brilliance with someone every now and then. It was a weakness, this need for admiration.

'Where is it?' said Krystal.

'I assure you he's in there. You see, we can't make the serum without his blood. It is the main ingredient. But the more important question is – *what is it?*'

Krystal felt cold despite her coat. She shivered and McTaggart noticed. He laughed at her discomfort.

'This is the well chamber. The cell directly above is where we have Angel and the other girl. As you know, there is a hole in the middle of the floor of that cell.'

'Why?' asked Krystal.

'For obvious reasons, there is direct access between the two chambers. But he likes to smell his next meals days before he eats them,' said McTaggart. 'It whets the appetite, like popping a cork on a good cabernet, the aroma one breathes in.' He smiled, then turned his gaze away from the window into the well chamber and back onto Krystal. 'If you ever fail me, disobey me, in any way, ever again, I could feed you to him,' said McTaggart.

Now she looked frightened, really terrified, and McTaggart was at last satisfied. Krystal realised that she wasn't really playing the part of a bodyguard. She was brought down here so he could scare the crap out of her.

McTaggart looked at the scientists and they all smiled at one another. Then McTaggart turned back to Krystal. 'Now, getting his blood, well, that is a whole process in itself. We won't do that until he's gorged himself on the rest of them in there, and that could be another day.'

Krystal choked back her rising gorge, doubling over, wondering if she was going to throw up. The scientists were chuckling, and McTaggart looked delighted.

CHAPTER 37

Seb and Benson accompanied O'Malley and Miller from the nave, through the door behind the curtain, up into the hidden loft.

Seb stopped before the table where he found Jaz and a group of strangers. As he entered, their sympathetic faces turned to him. If Seb was surprised to find the group sitting in a candle-lit room in the top of a church, he didn't show it.

'Please, sit,' said O'Malley.

But the ranger was too tense. With haunted eyes, he said to Jaz, 'I got your message.'

Jaz nodded.

'Someone we both know told me that you are FBI. Grace mentioned you minutes before she was killed.' His words, spoken quietly, fell upon the room, bringing them to complete silence. 'She also said that you tried to find me when I was being hunted. I should thank you for that.'

Jaz nodded. 'You've been hard to find.'

'I'm alive because of it.' He remained standing, arms folded across his body.

'Seb, we have good news for you. Your sister… Angel…'

'You know where she is?'

'O'Malley knows where the Dagon's Riders are keeping her.'

Seb looked at the priest. 'Tell me.' It wasn't a request.

'Yes, I will, of course. But getting her back may be far more difficult than you realise,' said O'Malley.

Seb looked to Jaz for an explanation. After a moment, O'Malley said, 'It might be easier if I just show you. Then you will understand where your sister is.' He left the loft.

Seb reluctantly slumped into a chair. Benson sat beside him, her hand casually resting on his arm. O'Malley reappeared holding a laptop. He set the thing down, Seb watching, his arms crossed over his chest.

'One moment,' said O'Malley. He opened the screen, clicked on a file and the video once more played, this time with Seb and Benson watching as a teen boy and his girlfriend trespassed onto a sprawling property where a party seemed to be taking place. O'Malley pressed fast forward, making the scene rocket forward. When he reached a certain point, he hit play, allowing the video to return to a normal pace.

Eric stopped in a darkened corridor, and the camera panned to the left. 'There's a door,' said Eric. They held the camera up to a small opening in the door A face appeared and Eric's girlfriend screamed in fright.

'Help me,' said a woman's face pressed close to the bars in the door. 'You have to get me out of here,' she gasped.

A second face appeared at the barred window. It was another young woman. Then a third face pressed close, and it was a young man. They began at once, begging to be freed, talking over each other. 'Get help, get us out, help us,' one voice on top of the other.

O'Malley hit the fast forward again briefly.

'Hey, you in there,' called Eric, his voice pitched, but not too loud. The lens zoomed and the camera adjusted to the low light, and although very grainy, the image of a face turning to the camera was clear enough. The face was not human, the eyes both terrible and sad were animal-like. The irises were vertical slits. When it opened its mouth, it had fangs, that were serpent-like. It hissed, in what might have been despair or warning. As a scream sounded from Eric's girlfriend, the camera turned as they fled away from the room. The screen went black.

O'Malley closed the laptop. Eyebrows furrowed, Seb scratched his head, then looked at Jaz, hoping for an explanation. She just stared back at him. He then looked to Benson.

But Benson shook her head, also confused. 'This is some kind of joke, right?'

'I've seen something like that before,' Seb admitted, the image of Krystal's snakelike eyes flashing into his mind. 'One of the gang… Krystal… she…' But Seb couldn't quite explain it.

'What?' asked Jaz.

'She looked like that – the *eyes*.'

Clyde spoke from the shadows of a corner, 'Whatever that thing is, I don't care.' He struck a match, lit a cigarette and exhaled smoke as he said, 'You and I, we have to go there.'

Seb looked at Clyde. 'They've been looking for you.'

Clyde shrugged. 'They're gonna find me real soon.'

'I don't know you, Miller,' said Seb.

'McTaggart is a guy that I need to kill,' said Clyde, in a way that suggested it was all Seb needed to know. 'I'm coming with you.'

Father O'Malley removed a small thumb drive from the laptop and handed it to Jaz. 'Here is your copy of the video, Agent Freeman, as requested. If you manage to leave town alive, it will be quite useful.'

Jaz slipped it into her jeans pocket. 'I'm getting out, don't worry. Once we get clear of the immediate area, I'm bound to get a phone signal, then I'll make the call.'

Benson said, 'I have a Jeep. Two of us stand a better chance.'

Jaz stared at Benson.

Seeing her hesitation, Seb said, 'Listen, Jaz, you can trust her… I trust her.' Then he approached O'Malley and stood right before him. 'Where is McTaggart?'

O'Malley retrieved a roll of paper from a side table. He spread it on the table before the group. Seb leant closer, discovering that it was a map. He could see that the drawing was old, with stains around the edges. It showed a residence of some kind on the edge of the sea. It was hand-drawn and a note in the corner had a date

– 1921. It showed the outline of a very large house, perched right on the edge of the cliff. Seb could see a name written there – *St Bernard's*. 'He is here.' O'Malley's finger pointed at the house.

'St Bernard's... what is that?' asked Seb.

'A wealthy New York businessman built it. He used it as a vacation house. Back then, the locals often referred to it as the cliff house. Following the Second World War, it became a repatriation home for returned veterans. After that, local records show it falling into disrepair.'

'Where exactly is it?' asked Seb.

'Outside town, to the north. You won't find his complex on any map now. There's a road in, unmarked, through a forest.'

O'Malley grabbed another, much newer map, and it showed the area of coastline he was talking about. Although no road was shown, he had hand-drawn his own road from the coastal road to the complex, where he had put a large red X. 'This is it,' he said, pointing at the mark. 'The coast topography matches up with the old map – do you see?'

Seb studied the maps side by side and nodded. Clyde, Benson and Jaz looked over his shoulder. Then Seb said, 'You said it was a *complex*. What did you mean?'

'Beside the old house – there's a new residence, across a lawned area. McTaggart appears to be living in that house. That was the first house that Eric and his girlfriend entered. The other house... well, that's probably where your sister is being held. From the little we know, there will be security and a lot of it. I suspect that a tunnel may run between the two houses. It is the only thing that makes sense when I look at how easily Eric made it to the basement areas.'

Jaz abruptly stood from the table and took a deep breath. 'Okay... I'm leaving – now! I have what I came for. Thank you, Joshua,' she said and briefly hugged him. 'And thank you, Father.'

O'Malley gave her a solemn nod as Jaz walked to the door.

'Wait!' said Benson. 'I'm coming too. I need to get out, and I can help you explain what's happening.'

Jaz nodded. 'Okay, but we do things *my* way.'

'Benson,' called Seb as the two women reached the door. 'You be careful.'

Benson smiled and nodded. 'You too, Seb.' She looked like she might say something else but then she abruptly left, following closely behind Jaz.

Seb gazed at the closed door and then glanced at his watch. It was after midnight.

The priest came and sat beside Seb. He reached into his pocket and took out a photo. 'This is McTaggart. It is a close-up.'

Seb looked at the photo. The image showed a guy reclining amongst a group of bikini-clad women. He had blond-grey hair that was thinning slightly. He looked at the camera with an arrogant smile. 'I don't care what he looks like. All I care about is finding Angel.'

*

Just after midnight Gunther and his crew entered the Underground nightclub. They hadn't found Miller. It was possible he could be hiding down in the club, and so they went in to search for him.

Located in the basement of an old warehouse, the street entrance quickly descended a steep flight of stairs. Grunge and techno music had the mainly black-clad patrons moving rhythmically. Their bodies twisted and pulsed as Gunther moved through them, a full head above the crowd, his eyes scanning. They parted around him, their pale faces, without expression reminded him of lost souls.

He stood in the middle of the dancefloor, the music hammering at his mind. He watched everyone around him. They stared back, seeming to shimmer and vibrate.

'What are we doing here!' shouted one of his crew. He was looking around, face flushed. 'I can't hear myself think.'

Gunther felt his pulse quicken. The movement on all sides became more than a distraction. Strobing lights flickered across his vision, forcing him to close his eyes for several seconds at a time. It felt to him like a worm was slithering into his brain.

CHAPTER 38

Benson drove the Jeep, and Jaz sat in the passenger seat looking pensive. The town was quiet, with hardly any lights shining from the houses and shops they passed. Jaz noted that Benson had packed only an overnight bag, which sat in the back seat. She also noted that Benson had piled some gear in the trunk space, though it was too dark to see back there.

'Will they know your vehicle?' asked Jaz.

'No, I keep it garaged most of the time and under a sheet. Mostly I drove my police car,' replied Benson.

'I hope you're right,' said Jaz.

Benson had a rough idea where the roadblock might be, and she estimated that they would reach it in around fifteen minutes. They drove in silence, watching the night.

When they arrived at the checkpoint, it was along a section of road where tall pines gathered close on either side. Despite the late hour, there was a queue of three cars in front of them. Although the police cruiser was not blocking the road, two officers were positioned in the middle of the road, one holding a torch, and the other, a shotgun. They were searching within a car, its trunk wide open. The occupants were standing, watching from the verge.

Benson pumped the brakes, slowing the Jeep as they came close. 'I don't like this.'

'*Now* you mention it,' said Jaz.

'I was hoping they'd be state troopers, and they didn't know me. But that car – it's one of ours. A guy called Webster.'

'Could I drive up and you get in the back,' suggested Jaz.

'No – they're going through the cars, shaking everyone down. I have to go back,' said Benson as she pulled off to the side.

The police at the roadblock looked at their Jeep.

'Shit!' hissed Benson. She swung the Jeep around hard and floored it back the way they had come.

'You know they got a great look at us,' said Jaz. 'Your license plate and everything.'

'I know, but what was I supposed to do?' She tramped onto the gas pedal. 'Are they following us?'

'Yep,' said Jaz. She had turned in her seat. 'Slow, but yeah they're coming.'

*

Leo and his crew were playing billiards, drinking, and carousing. Dressed in leather jackets, they could have been a gang of greasers from the fifties.

Earlier, Little Bear wanted to go and talk with Angel, on whom Leo was certain he had a serious crush. But Leo also considered that talking to her would lead to the kid wanting to break her out and it was too late for that now. Angel had set her own course. Such a shame that she would be put to waste.

When the radio intercom buzzed on, they all stopped. *Leo, are you there?*

Leo pressed the intercom button. 'What do you want?'

You guys are up. We have a runner. The control room tech sounded excited.

'Who and where?' said Leo.

Vehicle is a green Jeep. They're trying to make a break for it. It's a cop's car. It belongs to one Rebecca Benson. Not one of ours. Orders are to make sure the occupants don't make it.

'Capture or kill?' asked Leo.

Boss says you have the green light to do what you want. There was a pause, filled with static, then – *we have a transmitter on her vehicle. They're making their way back towards town. Stay on the usual frequency and I'll guide you in close to the target.*

Leo turned to his crew. 'We're up. Let's have some fun.'

*

'Are they still behind us?' said Jaz.

'I don't think so,' said Benson, looking in the rear vision mirror, her eyes wide.

'Can't this heap go faster?' said Jaz.

'My foot is down on the floor.'

Jaz was twisting in her seat. 'I don't see them anymore.'

'That makes no sense,' said Benson. 'Their car should be much faster than ours. They should be close.'

'Well, they're not. Maybe they aren't interested in us.'

'No, they'll be coming,' said Benson.

A minute later, having eased off the gas just a little, Jaz's head turned sharply. 'What was that?'

'What was what?' said Benson.

'Slow down! I saw something.'

Benson slowed. 'What?'

'A road. A track... something.'

Benson was looking at her GPS map. 'Nothing on this.'

'It's not on there, but I know I saw something,' said Jaz. 'If we go that way, you never know where it might go. But at least it's in the direction of the interstate.'

'The way the crow flies, maybe, but you don't know where it would go,' said Benson.

'We should turn around and take it. This is a four-wheel drive, isn't it?'

Benson looked at her. Jaz said, 'If we go back toward town, they may find us. We have to try that track.'

254

Benson slowed, pulled off to the side and swung the car sharply into a U-turn. They headed back about a half mile before they found the track. It looked like the narrow entrance to a private property. It was steep, a one-lane gravel track. There was no post box signifying it as someone's property entrance. 'Was this it?'

'Yeah, let's do it,' said Jaz.

Benson turned off the Coast Road and drove under a canopy of dense trees, heading down a bumpy track that joggled them around. The GPS showed nothing. Benson put her lights to high beam just so they could see twenty feet in front.

*

Leo and his crew were riding fast, leaning hard into the turns. His helmet was fitted with an earpiece and a throat mic.

A voice crackled in his earpiece. *This makes no sense.*

'What makes no sense?' asked Leo, throttling back. His crew also slowed. They rode in a tight pack, keeping pace with him.

GPS tracker puts them in the middle of nowhere. They're not on any road.

'Maybe they found your device and threw it somewhere,' said Leo. He hoped so. It would make the hunt more of a challenge.

Negative. They are moving still. Looking at the topography, they are moving downhill, heading inland, away from the coast. Their progress is slow.

'Tell me where.'

Look for a road, or track, somewhere on your right side, Leo.

'Okay.'

CHAPTER 39

Clyde Miller, dressed in the priest's black, exited St. Anthony's, scanning the street. A heartbeat behind, Seb strode out through the same door. Both men's hands were inside their coats, grasping pistols, ready to pull. Seb watched the street, now entirely deserted, while Clyde walked briskly along the side of the road, looking in each car's driver-side window. He was looking for the right car to steal. Seb scanned the street, waiting to hear the familiar hum of motorcycles, but the only sound came from the wind stirring dead brown leaves along the blacktop.

Seb heard the muted sound of the car window breaking. Clyde was already inside the vehicle he'd selected and within thirty seconds, the car hummed awake. Seb joined him, sliding into the passenger seat. Clyde pulled out abruptly and they followed the main drag out of town. Within a couple of minutes, they were steadily climbing into the hinterland forest.

Clyde put the radio on. Seb wondered why.

A song was playing. Clyde started humming. Seb glanced at him.

'You keep looking at me,' said Clyde.

'I need to think,' said Seb.

Clyde switched the radio off. 'Silence bothers me.'

Cold air was blowing into the cabin through the broken window.

Clyde said, 'This guy McTaggart, he's dangerous...'

'Not my problem.'

Clyde glanced at him and shrugged. 'The video was crazy, right? What was that thing at the end?'

'I don't care, Miller. McTaggart's your problem. I'm going straight for Angel.'

'Okay,' said Clyde. He began humming the song again, though the radio was off. 'Gets into your head, doesn't it?'

'You're crazy, you know that right?'

Clyde smiled. 'Yeah, maybe.' He checked the mirrors. 'We've got a straight run at this. No one is following.'

Seb pulled out the Beretta and checked the gun was clear and ready. He had fifteen rounds in the magazine and another spare. It would either be enough ammo, or he would be dead. There was no scope for a prolonged shootout.

'You a GI or something?' asked Clyde.

Seb nodded. 'I'm something.'

'I like to kill people. Is that why you joined up?'

Seb glanced at Clyde. 'We have nothing in common.'

'I've done some bad things. I have a lot to make up for,' said Clyde. 'O'Malley said some things to me over the last couple of days. He made me realise that there was still some part of me that wasn't bad.'

'You trying to feel good about yourself, Miller?'

Clyde slowly shook his head. 'Nah, but I know I can do something good tonight.'

Seb wondered why Miller wanted to talk. 'O'Malley made you think.'

'Yeah... I guess he did. The guy gets under your skin, you know?'

Seb shrugged.

They drove in silence for a while, both men lost in their thoughts. Seb, who had been thinking about the film that the kid had taken and how it fitted with Krystal's momentary transformation, said, 'They're doing something in that house...' He gave a slight shake of his head. 'Damned if I know what's going on, but I'm getting in and out as fast as I can.'

Clyde said, 'I've been thinking about a plan... the minute I realised you would be with me.'

'Go on,' urged Seb.

Clyde glanced across. 'Okay… here goes. We drive up to the gate. Before we get there, you need to bail, somewhere back down the road. They *will* see me at the gate and meanwhile, you go in the side somewhere.'

Seb considered the plan. It was simple and the simpler the plan in his experience, the less could go wrong. 'You will be a decoy? What do you think they'll do to you when they come out?'

'They won't shoot me, that's for sure,' Clyde said.

'How do you figure that?'

Clyde shrugged. 'They could have killed me last time. They were after information, like who hired me. They want O'Malley. If they kill me tonight, O'Malley will just hire someone else.'

Seb could not get his head around a priest who hired hit men.

Clyde continued, 'When I'm taken, I'll get close to McTaggart. I don't need a gun to kill the sonofabitch.'

'It could work,' allowed Seb. *Could it work though?*

'Do you have a knife or anything?' asked Clyde. 'Maybe a garrot? They are pretty handy when you want to be quiet.'

'I don't have a garrot. Where would I get a Goddam garrot?'

'Personally, I always carry a knife. You can have mine, I guess. Can you use it?'

Seb nodded. 'I've had cause to use a knife before.'

Clyde looked at him as he drove. 'You gotta think like me, tonight, okay? Don't act like a soldier. If you do, they'll kill you. They took your sister, which means they are all fair game. You get that, right?'

'No rules. We kill 'em,' said Seb.

Clyde glanced sideways. 'So… soldier boy, are you a hero? Do you have a bunch of medals?'

'Kill enough people, no one is a hero,' Seb replied, looking out the window. 'Kill enough people, you aren't much of anything anymore.'

'I once let someone off the hook. Five years back, I had a contract on a woman and her kid. They'd seen something they shouldn't have. When I went there, I couldn't do it.'

'What happened?'

'I put them on a bus, and they left.' Clyde pictured the woman, the kid on her lap, a rainy night, the bus pulling out away, destination unknown. It was the only thing he'd ever done that he was truly proud of.

They continued in silence because everything that needed to be said was said. They had a simple plan. Each man would rely on instinct, for both men, in their own way, were natural killers.

'The road should be somewhere close now,' said Seb. And it was. No more than a dirt track, it angled away toward the sea. There was no street sign. 'This has to be it.'

Clyde slowed the car and they pulled into the track, Miller killing the lights. 'The map showed this place maybe a few hundred yards down the track.'

The whole area was densely wooded. They couldn't see the house as yet, but they were certain they'd found the place.

'Let me out here,' said Seb.

The car stopped. Clyde reached down to his trouser leg. When he sat straight, he handed Seb a combat knife, complete with a sheath. Seb took it and jumped out of the car. He jogged off away from the track, angling through the trees, as quietly as he could. The lights of Miller's car as it rolled slowly forward toward the property were barely visible through the woods.

*

In the control room, a security guard suddenly sat forward. He was scanning a bank of monitors, each one showing a different camera's field of view. The camera at the gate showed a car roll up. A guy opened the driver's side door and walked up to the gate, making a show of trying to scale it.

The guard grabbed a radio. 'Intruder at the front gate.'

'Moving,' came a reply.

The guard in the control room watched the camera. The four techs sitting beside him took an interest because no one had ever tried to break into the house before.

The intruder seemed to realise now that he was on camera. He went and sat on the hood of his car and folded his arms. The gate opened, and the techs watched as three security guards approached the intruder, sub-machine guns trained on him.

Clyde just sat there; his hands raised until they took the revolver from his belt and cuffed him. Then they turned him around and marched him through the gate.

*

Seb came along the edge of the bluff, through ancient trees with roots that found purchase deep in the rocky crevices of the coast. He could hear the waves slamming onto rocks somewhere below. Through thick trunks, bent from the constant wind, a large house suddenly came into view. It was built onto the edge of the sea cliffs, around fifty feet above the waterline. He had found it. This was the place once called the cliff house. Lights shone from the upper windows, but Seb couldn't make anyone out. The crashing of waves below and the howling wind that ripped into the tall pines masked his approach. He arrived before a ten-foot-high wall, which seemed to extend in both directions.

Feeling the stone, seeking out cracks with his fingers, he decided that it was too smooth and too high to simply scale. He looked along the wall, seeing one or two trees growing close to the boundary. Holstering his Beretta, he strapped the knife Miller had just given him to his left leg and started up one of the trees. It was hard work, but he managed to get to a lower branch, which was level with the top of the wall. Now he could see over the wall. Open lawns spread out before him, lit in only a few places.

He jumped down, his foot just hooking around razor wire as he fell. He landed awkwardly, rolling forward onto the grass. Backing up, he disentangled his lower leg from the wire. Leaning his weight against the wall, crouching low, he waited to see if he had attracted attention. With no understanding of where any security cameras might be, he drew his Beretta and listened, but no one came.

CHAPTER 40

The images of the goths and punks cavorting flickered rapidly with the lighting – one moment, stark silver, the next green, the next red, each passing moment building pressure in his head.

Gunther could see blood trickling from the noses of two members of his crew. It was a strange sight and he didn't understand why it was happening. He searched amongst the crowd, from the seething dancefloor to booths, hidden behind curtains, but there was no sign of Miller anywhere.

Five of his six crew were down in the nightclub, while Preston waited near the entrance to the club, watching the street.

A goth punk spied his girlfriend trying to dance with Victor. The punk obviously said something stupid to Victor. Gunther couldn't hear them, for the music drowned out their words. The punk kid threw a punch. It was weak, ill conceived, and Victor easily blocked it.

But then Victor hit the kid in the face so hard he broke his neck. The kid collapsed, choking blood, his neck jutting at an impossible angle. Clubbers began screaming, and some made a run for the stairs. A switch had been flipped. Perhaps it was a cocktail of noise and sudden movement, but the night crew's mood shifted.

Another of his crew, Jake, leapt on a fleeing woman, bore her down and started clawing at her throat with his hands. His long nails sliced into her and she was bleeding out in seconds. Millie was only watching when the scent of blood reached her nose. She grabbed a random guy, ripping out his nose ring, then began biting his face. She ended up on top of him, right in the middle of the

262

dancefloor, astride his chest, furiously hammering her fists into his skull. The guy's face literally caved.

The screams grew louder. People were running for the narrow stairs, their only possible escape, the street above. But Preston was blocking the way. He'd caught the scent too, and he came down the stairs, driving them back. Bodies piled up on the stairs as people crushed each other.

Gunther grabbed a woman by the arm and swung her around, before wrenching it from its socket. He stood on her with his boots, pinning her, and kept pulling until he heard a wet pop, and then the arm tore loose completely from her body. Blood sprayed everywhere, landing in warm droplets on Gunther's face.

Gunther regained control only slowly, realising that no one was left to kill. With a pounding heart, he tilted his head back, forcing himself to breathe normally. Dropped the arm he had pulled from the woman at his feet, he looked around with confusion.

The crew had never completely lost themselves like that before. This time the pack mentality had taken over. Gunther licked his lips and savoured the taste of blood. Revulsion and ecstasy fought for control.

Looking around at the carnage, one thing became crystal clear: they needed to leave – immediately. None of this should have happened. Gunther strode toward the stairs, his crew falling into file behind him. Bodies were jammed along the narrow staircase and they walked over them, ignoring the moans of the dying.

When he reached the top of the stairs, Gunther felt like he was back in complete control. He called the orders – 'Burn everything. Make sure nothing can be salvaged.'

Striding to his Harley, he sat waiting, the familiar feel of the bike between his legs a comfort. He revved the machine, waiting for the crew to set the fire. Was this a new side effect? Was it a natural progression from having had so many doses? He didn't much like either choice. How had it happened? It shouldn't have happened. They were two weeks after the last dose of the serum and two weeks away from the next.

He steadied his mind, sucking in cool, clean air, preparing to leave, to get on their bikes and go home. Did that son-of-a bitch McTaggart know this could happen?

'Are we all here?' he called.

*

Despite its four-wheel drive capabilities, the Jeep struggled to reach any kind of speed greater than a jog. The track, which had started as a single gravel lane, soon became a muddy, two-wheel-rut, off-road nightmare. Under the trees, moonlight was fleeting and Benson relied heavily on the high beam to see anything.

It took them close to an hour before they drove off the steep track and into moonlight once more. Jaz was relieved to see that the track joined a more conventional dirt road. Though it was old and in need of repairs, it would at least allow them to drive faster.

Benson paused to get her bearings. Jaz looked at her, then at the landscape before them. They had emerged from the woods onto a section of barren hills. Benson shifted gears and they pushed to the right, continuing downhill, building speed. Stunted trees and coarse grass dotted the hills. They passed old shacks, the remains of broken fences, where people had given up and abandoned the land.

'This is a sad and lonely place,' said Jaz, looking from the window.

They gathered speed, the Jeep slewing a little from side to side on the gravel, with Benson having to make constant steering adjustments. Jaz faced backwards in her seat, peering back at the direction they had come.

'Try to relax, you're making me tense,' said Benson.

'I thought I saw something.'

'What?'

'I don't know,' admitted Jaz. She strained her eyes. 'There's something moving behind us, but I can't tell what.'

Benson stared into her side mirrors, frowning. 'I can't see anything.'

*

Only five of the six motorbikes had riders in Gunther's crew.

'Where's that bitch, Millie?' asked Gunther.

'She never came up. She's still in there,' said Victor, wiping gore from his face with the back of his coat.

The fire had just been lit, but it wouldn't take long to get hold of the whole place. Gunther dismounted from the Harley and ran back through the entrance. He leapt down the stairs. Halfway down, his face slapped into a wave of heat. In the basement, flames were spreading everywhere – over bodies, up the walls and across furnishings. In the middle of the dancefloor, Millie crouched, oblivious to the fire, her head bent forward over a corpse.

'Millie!' screamed Gunther.

Her head came up, displaying a mouth and chin covered with blood. Her eyes were now elongated slits, a sickly green colour that glowed slightly. She hissed, her tongue darting out and back. Through teeth like razor blades, a vaguely human, piteous moan escaped.

Gunther backed away from the scene. Millie finally stood, now aware of the imminent danger.

'This way!' he shouted.

Gunther didn't think she could make it, but she had to try. He backed up the stairs, waving to her, as the flames spread, almost blocking the path between them. He smelt fuel on the stairs under his feet. Millie darted, heading across the floor toward him, avoiding pockets of fire. Gunther was nearly at the top, staring down when she appeared, flames licking up her legs. Millie crawled halfway to the top before the flames engulfed her entirely. She screamed, a sound that was not entirely human.

Sprawling from the doorway into the street, flames billowed out past him. He sheltered momentarily under his leather coat, patches of fire clinging to his back. Rolling across the ground, his coat finally extinguished. Back on his feet, smoking and singed, he peered inside, into nothing but leaping flames and thick, billowing smoke.

'What happened?' asked Victor.

'She didn't make it,' said Gunther, his voice flat. He said nothing more. The crew didn't need to know that Millie had rapidly undergone a change, becoming something very like the creature McTaggart kept imprisoned. What had caused her to transform? And… if they all did, would they too end up being McTaggart's prisoners?

They climbed on their bikes and rode, gathering speed, putting distance between themselves and the fire. Gunther was frightened, for the first time in years, he wondered if any of them had a future at all.

CHAPTER 41

Clyde walked between the trio of guards, his hands cuffed behind his back. They stopped near a large swimming pool surrounded by fragrant flower beds. Adjacent to the landscaped Japanese gardens, against the backdrop of the shadowy forest, was a modern mansion of glass and golden light.

Clyde did not see where precisely McTaggart had emerged from the house, striding purposefully toward them, dressed in a kimono of red, silver and gold silk. He wore a katana across his body, the weapon sheathed in an ornate scabbard. Beside him, a short blonde woman dressed in figure-hugging leather walked with the same self-assured stride, though she struggled to keep up. At her side, a pistol was drawn, ready. One of the guards handed Clyde's Colt Python to McTaggart who examined the weapon, turning it this way and that before handing it back to the guard.

'Are you the one?'

'I came here looking for you, Mr McTaggart,' said Clyde.

'You show respect, I like that,' said McTaggart.

'I know a superior when I see one,' said Clyde.

McTaggart smiled. 'Are you the one they sent to kill me?'

'I am. But I have a better idea... if you care to hear it.'

'I could have you killed right now. In fact, I could just do it myself,' he said, his hand curling around the katana's handle.

Clyde knew this kind of guy. He had even worked for guys like him before. 'No doubt. But maybe we can come to a deal?'

'Why? What can you offer?'

'I can tell you who sent me.'

'And why is that important to me?'

Clyde smiled. 'You know why. If you kill me, you'll never know, and they'll just keep coming, one after the other, until one of them maybe gets lucky.' He settled back on his heels, feeling relaxed.

McTaggart made a show of thinking. Clyde could see that the guy made a show of everything he did. He paced, back and forward, then stopped, and turned. 'What do you get out of it?'

'I get paid, of course. You have the whole local police force and half the state police on your payroll already. I can't see you paying me being a problem. And then, you employ me. I am a good fit for your organisation.'

'You want to come work for me? You have shown a complete lack of loyalty to your current employer,' said McTaggart.

Aware he was arguing for his life, he said, 'No offence to them, but they don't pay so well.'

'We don't need him,' said Krystal. Her eyes flashed toward Clyde.

McTaggart raised a hand and she stepped back, closing her mouth. Clyde almost had him. The guy was halfway convinced.

'Tell me who sent you.'

'Not yet. I need assurances you won't just kill me. I need terms.'

'I could have you tortured. Everyone has their limits to what they can take. I could have the name from you, given time.'

'I won't break. I never do. And you don't need to waste time.'

McTaggart focused on Clyde, noticing his neck tattoo. 'What is that?'

'It's a serpent,' said Clyde.

McTaggart was gazing at the tattoo. 'Do you believe in signs? Portents?'

'I don't know what that means,' admitted Clyde.

McTaggart seemed lost in thought. Then he said, 'So, you think you are worthy of serving me.'

'I know I am. Let me prove myself.'

McTaggart looked up at the night sky, and back at Miller, then at

Krystal. He smiled. He did like a contest. It made for a wonderful sport.

Now Clyde knew he had him, if not his trust, then the next best thing – his interest. The guy was intrigued. He had not considered that his would-be assassin might change sides.

*

Sebastian watched Clyde being escorted across the lawn, flanked by guards. He edged around the wall, staying low, hugging night-shadows. He could see the new house, the area around it simply too bright to try and sneak into. Besides, O'Malley had told him that Angel would be in the original house.

He followed the boundary wall, and as he neared it, the cliff house called to him, pulling him toward it like an undertow. He could see that it was mainly dark with only a couple of lights shining from the windows on the second floor. There weren't any balconies up there either. On the ocean side, he could make out a platform above the cliffs. Possibly there would be an entrance from that area into the house.

Seb stared at the windows facing him, looking for movement. The minute stretched to two, then seeing nothing, he darted forward away from the shadows of the boundary wall.

Crouched under a window ledge on the ground floor, he waited only a heartbeat before sticking his head over the window frame to peer inside. Nothing. Just a large room, dimly by a few antique lamps. There was a lounge and rugs, and a set of wide stairs ascending to the second level. Other rooms could be glimpsed beyond.

He crawled past the window, up to the edge of the house closest to the cliffs, his movements concealed by the pounding waves. He chanced a look around the corner and discovered a paved balcony with a balustrade and a security guard standing there, rock still, with what looked like a sub-machine gun casually cradled in the crook of his right arm. Seb smiled at the guy's attempt to light the cigarette. The guard was looking out at the sea, but the wind was blowing hard and he couldn't manage to get the lighter working. On the wall of the house, there was movement, a small red blinking light that gave away the position of a camera. It was mounted above the French doors leading from the house to the balcony. Seb backed away and returned to the window he had just looked through.

He slipped the knife from its ankle sheath and used it to lever up the window from its resting position. With the window open, he climbed through, returning the knife to its sheath. He left the window open and advanced into the living area, his Beretta up, the safety off.

*

In the new house, Clyde was taken to a dojo on the second floor. It had a timber floor and mirrors on all four sides. When they entered, he saw four reflected images of himself, McTaggart, the three guards and the blonde woman – Krystal. At the end of the room, a bamboo frame hung with a variety of martial arts weapons drew his eye.

McTaggart walked over to the weapons and stood to one side. Clyde was okay with the prospect of being the main event in a contest, a spectacle put on for the boss-man. It would get his hands free and get him close enough to do what he came for.

'If you manage to defeat Krystal, I will consider you entering my employ. Then, you will tell me who sent you. If she defeats you, well, I will just have to wonder who sent you and prepare for the next assassin.'

Clyde took a deep breath and at last, nodded.

'Go ahead, choose,' said McTaggart.

Clyde raised his hands, showing that the handcuffs were still on.

'Oh yes, remove the manacles,' ordered McTaggart.

The three guards looked at each other and then one of them

removed the cuffs. Clyde looked at the weapons. There was a katana, a staff, a pair of Sai, a hand-axe, a long knife, some nunchucks and a bunch of weapons that Clyde didn't recognise. He liked the look of the hand-axe. It looked sharp, and on the opposite side, it had a long, wicked spike.

Krystal handed her pistol to one of the guards and stood with her hands on her hips, proudly surveying the weapons.

*

The ground floor was shrouded in darkness. An occasional lamp provided dim light. Seb observed a dining area between the living room and a kitchen. The table was recently used. Trays of food, plates with scraps and some half-drunk bottles of wine and beer sat in a way that suggested that whoever had been there had recently hurried away. He could see other rooms, down the far end of the house, glimpsed through darkened doorways. Those rooms were quiet and still.

Seb chose to go upstairs, looking above in case a guard was stationed at the top. His feet squeaked on each tread as he slowly advanced. He listened, straining to hear any movement. At the top of the stairs, he crouched, waiting and listening. Then he crept slowly down a long hallway, spying rooms on either side, some open and others closed.

There was a sitting room with a large window facing the sea, overlooking the balcony below. No one occupied the room though a lamp was on. He had the sensation that he was being monitored, but he hadn't identified any more wall-mounted cameras.

At the end of the hall, another door faced him. It was different, for it was a modern addition. There was no lock. Instead, on the wall beside it, a keypad, barely illuminated with little blue lights. This was interesting. Was this a cell? It seemed unlikely. But perhaps Angel was in there. He edged up to the door, noting that it was much heavier than it at first appeared. Without the PIN code for the door, he wasn't getting in. He considered backing off and searching elsewhere. How much time did he have? Was Miller still alive? He paused, listening to the house, feeling the subtle vibrations of pounding waves against the cliff below. The weight of silence pressed in on him.

After a moment of indecision, he stepped up to the door, quietly, and put his ear to it. There were voices. He pressed his ear hard against the door, the muffled voices became clearer.

Did you see where they went? This came from a woman, though it wasn't Angel.

Nah, but I think they were going to the gymnasium. This was a young guy.

Another voice, louder and closer than the first two. *It's not a gymnasium, it's a dojo.*

The girl spoke. *Are there any cameras in there? I think the boss is going to make Krystal fight that guy.*

How do you know?

Why else would they take him in there? Anyway, my money would be on Krystal, she's a badass.

The guy with the louder voice spoke, but it sounded like he was talking to someone else. *Check in, people. I repeat, call in. Hey, I'm looking at you. That's it, wave at the camera. Stop smoking, asshole.*

Seb didn't hear any response. He pictured a guy on the radio, maybe talking to the guards outside, the responses coming back to him through headphones.

Okay. Next check in will be ten minutes. I repeat – mark – ten minutes. Stay alert. Out.

Seb took a step back. They had a control room? It made a certain sense. If he could get in there, maybe he could get some quick answers and narrow his search. He looked at his watch and noted the time. He had ten minutes before they would make further contact with the outside security team. Seb hurried back the way he came, descended the stairs, fast, not caring if he made some noise. The living room was still empty. He went to the centre, pivoting, covering his angles. There was a kitchen to one side, through another short hall. He advanced, entered fast. On one side, a door, and above it, a sign – *Basement*. Beside the door, there was another keypad. He stared at the door, then again at the keypad. Some areas were really secured. The ones that mattered most, he figured.

He looked around. The kitchen was old. There were dishes piled up everywhere. He put his gun in his belt and used both hands to start looking through the cupboards, high and low. Within thirty seconds he found what he needed.

*

'Are you sure you want to do this?' asked Clyde.

McTaggart just stared at him.

'Okay then.' Clyde reached out and selected the little axe, roughly the size of a tomahawk.

Krystal walked past him and grabbed the short, curved katana. Clyde hoped she didn't really know how to use it.

McTaggart backed away, looking excited, motioning the three security guards back. The guards watched, odd expressions on their faces.

Krystal had a wild look in her eye, though Clyde could tell she was scared. He had seen enough scared people in his life to know. He walked a few feet away, forcing her to follow him. She circled him and moved quickly in and back, fast on her feet. The katana had flashed out at him, a discovering strike that was well short of his face.

'You're going to have to get closer than that, Krystal.'

Krystal snarled. McTaggart clapped just once in delight, a short laugh escaping him.

She came again, the sword swiping up and across, and then

back again, in a flurry of fast strikes aimed at disembowelling him. Clyde stepped in close, his big frame grappling her, taking her into his embrace, but not before he took one angry cut across his side, which opened his flesh in a long, inch-deep gash. He swung her around and flung her down. She rolled, but he followed in close, knowing he had to finish Krystal quickly or be worn down. As Krystal righted herself, he kneed her in the head. The thud was loud, and she groaned in pain and stumbled back, swaying.

Clyde glanced at McTaggart and seeing no response, walked in close, and as Krystal lifted the blade, he caught her wrist, keeping her on her knees, applying more pressure, feeling it snap. She screamed.

Clyde took the sword away and kicked it across the floor. Krystal was now looking at McTaggart, big eyes pleading. McTaggart was unmoved. Clyde lifted the axe high, stretching up to his full height, paused for heartbeat, then pounded the spiked side of the axe into the top of her head.

*

Seb returned to what he believed was a 'control' room. He knelt outside the door and placed the towel on the floor outside the room. He pressed it in firmly against the crack under the door and then took the lighter and zipped it. A flame appeared. The towel, unwashed and covered in grease, immediately caught fire. Seb took a couple of steps back, his Beretta up and aimed at the door.

It suddenly opened. An unarmed security guard stood there in front of him. Behind him, in the room, three young people, each wearing headsets, dressed like civilians were gawking. Instantly, Seb stepped up and lashed the security guard across the nose with the pistol. The guy fell back into the room, clutching his shattered nose. Seb hustled inside, pressing the gun into the side of the guard's throat. He kicked the door closed behind him with his heel. They were all together now in a tight space, just a small room jammed with computers, monitors, microphones and bits of kit.

Seb stood the guard up and pressed the Beretta hard into his neck. The techs had their hands in the air.

The woman spoke. 'Please... please...'

'Shut it,' said Seb.

'Man, what are you doing in here?' began the tech with the glasses. Seb turned ten degrees and aimed the gun at his face, finger tightening on the trigger.

'Who the fuck are you, man? Get outta here!' said the bearded tech.

The Beretta wasn't that loud, but it might bring trouble. About six minutes had passed since the last control room 'check in' and Seb calculated that left him just four more minutes before he might expect someone to come looking. He pressed the gun back against the guard's neck.

'You have someone here in a cell. I need to know where she is.'

The girl was working her mouth, trying to form words.

'Speak,' Seb urged.

'Don't you say a fuckin' word,' said the bearded guy, looking at his colleague.

She closed her mouth, her eyes darting.

Seb looked at the bearded tech. The guy said, 'What the fuck are you looking–'

Bang. The bearded tech's brains sprayed against the female tech's cheek.

Her mouth gaped. Through short rapid breaths, she managed to say, 'She's... in... cell three.'

'How *many* cells do you have? Tell me where that is.'

'Basement level two.' Her eyes were pinned to her dead colleague.

'How do I get there?'

'There's a door down past the kitchen, which goes to the wine cellar. One level under that is cell three.'

Seb was looking at the bank of monitors. One of them showed a dark room where two women sat unmoving huddled on a stone floor. The room looked strange because there seemed to be a large, gaping black hole in the middle of it, like a wide well.

The female tech noticed where he was looking. 'That's cell three.'

Seb was staring at the monitor, amazed at the sight of his sister, sitting with someone who looked vaguely familiar to him. Then he realised – it was the girl from the cabin, Codi.

'You can't do this,' said the guard, his nose streaming blood.

Seb raised the gun and cracked it down with a sickening thump on the back of the guy's head. He was out cold as he slid to the floor.

He trained his Beretta back on the two remaining techs. 'Which one of you do I have to kill now?'

'Who's going to do the check-in now?' said the guy with the glasses.

'You are,' said Seb, glancing at his watch.

'What do I say? They'll know something's wrong.'

'You'll have to get creative because you have one minute.'

'Okay, but please don't shoot,' said the guy. He reached out toward his keyboard, his fingers trembling. Seb leant in and aimed the gun at his face. 'Easy, man, I'm just switching the channel.'

Seb watched them, unblinking.

'Hey, ahhh, yeah… he had to go to the John. Yeah, he said to do his check-in. Okay, thanks.' The guy took off his glasses with shaking hands and rubbed his eyes where sweat had formed. 'I think they bought it.'

'You better hope so.'

'One of you is going to take me down to my sister.'

'We don't know the door codes,' said the guy.

'Don't bullshit me.'

'They don't tell us everything. We just do our job in here. It's just a job.'

Seb raised the gun, pointing at the remaining male tech, his face unreadable.

'Wait. I know something that could help,' said the woman. 'There's an override code. It opens every door in the place.'

The guy looked horrified. He said, 'What are you doing?'

'Keeping us alive, dumb-ass,' she barked back at him.

Seb put his finger to his lips, the Beretta twitching toward the male tech. The guy shut his mouth and closed his eyes. 'You don't want to open every door.'

The female tech continued, 'I'm not supposed to know, but... I can do this, and you can leave here, leave us...'

'Enter the code.'

She brought up a menu. Her hands trembled. She managed to rapidly jump through a bunch of menus, until arriving at a screen that demanded a password. She entered a string of letters and numbers. Her face was flushed. She hit enter and another screen opened. This one had a list of items, one of which said 'master security door override'. She opened the menu item and hit 'enable override'.

'That's it?' asked Seb.

She tried to smile. 'Yes.'

'Okay, maybe you get to live,' said Seb.

At that moment Seb heard the PIN code of the door being entered. Seb had just enough time to haul the female tech to her feet and pull her in front of him before the door flew open.

'Put the gun down!' yelled one of the guards.

Their HK sub-machine guns were up, aimed at Seb, but he was almost entirely obscured by the woman. She began screaming, twisting, kicking, but Seb held her tight, the gun to her head. Feeling the barrel pressed hard, she stopped squirming, staring at three guards. No one had anywhere to go. It was only a moment before they opened fire.

Almost instantaneously Seb returned fire, squeezing the trigger, emptying fourteen rounds through the doorway, where the trio were gathered in tight. He couldn't miss. And neither could they. The opening spray had cut the woman down, her torso taking most of the shots. The male tech, cowering behind was also shot, where he sat in his chair. Seb had collapsed back, falling onto his back, the female tech already a deadweight on top of him. She had shielded him. Somehow, they had missed him. Cordite drifted in the air, mixed with burnt wiring from shattered computers.

One of them was still up, though wounded. He stumbled through the doorway, peering down. Seb was pinned. He scrambled to reload the Beretta, shoving in the next clip. The guard saw him, went to fire, realised he was spent, reached for the pistol on his belt, but was shot through the face. Seb pushed the lifeless corpse off, slowly got up, and peered down the hall.

It was then that the siren went off.

CHAPTER 42

Angel thought she heard something – a faint click. She turned, expecting the door to the cell to be flung open, but nothing happened. She sat still. Her body suddenly tense.

'What is it?' asked Codi sleepily.

'I don't know. Wait here.'

Angel moved to the cell door and listened. Nothing. If there had been a handle, she would have pulled on the door – just to test it. She backed away. A few moments passed and she thought she heard gunshots, though the sounds were muffled.

A siren began. It was loud. Something was happening.

*

Clyde Miller levered the axe from her skull and watched as Krystal slumped to the floor. Blood was pumping from the large hole in her head. Some of his own blood joined hers. She had cut him pretty deep. He flipped her away with his boot and she rolled several times, a bleached-blonde, blood-spattered ragdoll. She came to rest, eyes staring back at him, surprise on her features.

McTaggart was watching, a small smile touching his lips. His hand had tightened on the handle of the long katana. Clyde wondered if the guy was going to suddenly attack him. He decided to hold onto the axe, though he allowed it to dangle at his side.

A siren sounded.

It was not loud but it instantly had everyone's attention. The guards looked to McTaggart. McTaggart looked at Clyde, and his eyes narrowed with the realisation that the intruder had not come alone. Clyde hoped he had bought Seb enough time.

The hitman moved fast, straight at McTaggart. A guard stepped in front, bringing up the HK machine gun – too slow. As it fired, Clyde knocked it aside, slashed the guy's throat with the return sweep and grabbed him as he fell. He swivelled as the second guard fired, the burst ripping into the first guard's back, Clyde already tucked in behind him.

Dropping the dead guard, he hurled the hand-axe. It flipped once, hit the next guard in the chest, buried deep. Clyde advanced on McTaggart. The final guard, though only a few yards away, didn't want to hit McTaggart. He brought up the weapon and fired, slightly off-target, except a couple of rounds that caught Clyde's shoulder. It slowed him down as he reached McTaggart's throat. His hands stretched out, intent to crush his windpipe. McTaggart stepped away, out of reach, Miller falling forward off-balance. Then McTaggart's katana was suddenly out, flashing down across Clyde's neck.

*

Seb took a submachine gun from a dead guard, loaded it and pocketed a spare mag. He left the control room, darting along the corridor to the top of the stairs. Glancing down, he tracked two guards coming up from the bottom, moving fast, though careless.

He crouched and waited, and as they reached the first landing, he fired a long burst, sweeping across them. They fell, sprawling. Seb paused over them, fired another burst into each guy's head, removed the spent clip and shoved in another.

At the kitchen, there was a door with a keypad. Holding his breath, he reached out and pulled. *Click.* It opened up, and he was through and heading down some steep stairs toward the basement. The siren continued, loud, masking his footfalls.

*

McTaggart was hurrying, though not running, never running as he crossed the lawn toward the cliff house. There were three siren tones programmed for the complex. The first was for a fire, the second was a general alert and the third was for the sub-basement laboratory door being breached. The siren that was blaring at the cliff house was the third type. Of the three, this was the worst kind.

Katana in hand, he strode, imagining himself to be the true embodiment of a shogun warlord.

The security guard kept pace at his shoulder. 'No response from the control room,' he said.

They entered the house. McTaggart suddenly wished the two night crews were here. He needed both Gunther's and Leo's assistance now. He would get to the control room and get them on the radio. Yes – he would call them back. Then, he would have to go to the laboratory... and that was a truly worrying thought. On the stairs, he stepped over two dead security guards, their bodies riddled with bullets.

At the control room, he stepped across the bodies of the guards and found all the technicians dead. He stared down at them, blood draining from his face. The radio was broken, smashed by a projectile. The computers had also been damaged. Two monitor screens were shattered where bullets had penetrated them. But one screen was left and he sat before it, entering a special passcode for a surveillance camera that only he could access. He brought up an image on the screen, which initially crackled. It showed the laboratory. At this time of night, only one of the scientists would be there and McTaggart recognised him, backing up, face pale, slowly edging backwards, away from something not within the camera's view.

'We have a big problem,' he said.

*

Seb found that the first basement level had a few cells, but each was empty. When he looked inside, none of them had the large round well-like hole in the midst of the floor. Angel's cell must be further below. He returned to the stairs and went another level down, pushed through another door with a keypad that had been bypassed.

Down a corridor, he found a couple more cells and in the last, when he pushed the door inward, two shadowy forms turned in surprise.

'Don't come any closer, you bastard. I'll kill you,' said a familiar voice.

'It's me, dummy.'

'Seb? Holy… shit!' Angel came toward him, throwing herself into his arms.

'Yeah, I know.'

'Hey, I know you,' said Codi. 'You're *that guy*.'

'We need to go,' he said, holding Angel at arm's length and staring at her. 'You took some finding, sis. Damn, but it's good to see you!' She looked pale and gaunt. Dark, haunted eyes regarded him.

After a moment, as tears spilled down her cheeks, she smiled. 'You came… I can't believe you're here.'

Just then, echoing up from below, from the gaping hole in the floor there issued a long scream of pure terror and pain.

Seb shivered. 'I know what's down there. We need to get out.'

Angel nodded once and gripped Codi's hand, pulling her with them toward the open door.

'We go up – two flights, through the house and out the front gate. We kill anyone that gets in our way, okay?' Seb handed Angel his Beretta. 'Stay very close.'

'Was there anyone else in the house?' asked Angel.

'No. They're not here,' he said.

CHAPTER 43

The Jeep bounced along. When they made it down out of the hills, onto flat land, the road simply ended. One minute it was there and the next, it was gone. They were now forced to cross a barren plain, swerving around stunted trees, bouncing across rocks, driving over low shrubs.

'Is that the interstate?' asked Jaz.

'Yeah, but it's a long way off. When we cross the train track, we will be roughly halfway there,' said Benson, looking at Jaz in the rear-view mirror.

Jaz positioned herself in the back seat, looking back through the rear window and then off to each side. She had been certain that they were being tailed. Benson thought otherwise. She had reasoned that if they were being followed, they would at least see their pursuer's headlights in the hills behind them.

'Be good to find a road,' said Jaz.

'If you see one, call it out,' snapped Benson, 'because I can't see Jack.'

'This reminds me of something,' said Jaz, frowning.

'Yeah?'

'Yeah. You know, I've seen this place.' Jaz frowned, thinking. 'Is this where they found that kid – Eric Winters?'

Benson shook her head. 'Winters?'

Jaz gazed out the window, looking at the starry night. She recalled the newspaper article that she had finally got to read and her discussion with Joshua. 'Yeah, he made it all the way out here somewhere, on a bicycle – that's a long way from the Cove.'

Benson nodded. 'Oh, you mean that kid from the video?'

Jaz nodded. 'Yeah. They found him out here near the train tracks.'

Something zipped past them, fast, motor shrieking, kicking up small stones onto the windscreen. Jaz jumped and Benson swore. They hadn't heard them approach. The sudden roar and whine of engines filled the night.

'Oh my God,' said Jaz.

Benson yanked the vehicle hard to the left and jumped on the gas pedal.

'I count five bikes,' said Jaz.

'In the back, there's another gun,' said Benson. 'Get it!'

'I have a gun.'

'Not like this one,' said Benson, yanking the Jeep to the right as the riders made a second pass. Two rode behind them, tracking them from around thirty yards. Three more hovered, two on their right and one to their left. Benson was swerving at the riders on their right, hoping to hit them.

Jaz flopped into the back of the Jeep and found the M4 carbine under the blanket.

'I'm gonna make for the interstate!' said Benson. 'If they get close, shoot them!'

'What are they doing?' shouted Jaz, climbing into the backseat.

'Playing with us.'

There was a sudden flash of bright flames as something glass smashed over the side of the hood and left passenger window.

'Molotovs!' said Jaz.

'On your left!' cried Benson.

Jaz could see a rider and the pillion passenger keeping pace with the Jeep. Jaz thought it looked like a kid sitting on the back, lighting a rag for the next projectile to be hurled at them.

'Shoot him!' yelled Benson.

Jaz opened the window and tried to aim the M4's long barrel through the opening. With the foregrip, she found that she could aim the weapon without too much trouble. The bike with the kid on the back swooped in, the second Molotov lit and ready. Jaz fired a short burst but the Jeep hit a bump and her shots went into the Molotov, exploding it across the riders. They heard a scream and could see the rider and the passenger in flames, swerving away from them , a fiery beacon against the darkled landscape.

'Do you think that will do it?' said Benson.

'I hope so,' said Jaz.

But the other bikes zipped in close and as Jaz prepared to open fire, one of the riders leapt across from the motorcycle onto the hood of the Jeep. It was an amazing feat, thought Benson, her mouth hanging open. He had jumped through the air, maybe eight metres from the seat of his bike, which went tumbling away. Grinning psychotically at them through the windscreen, the wind tugged at his dark hair. He looked like he was having a ball. In that moment, Jaz recognised the face. It was one of her missing persons – the seventeen-year-old Judd Filmore – presumed dead. It was a face she had seen on her laptop a hundred times, a face imprinted in her brain. To his crew, he was Screamer.

Benson swerved, hit a hole and the Jeep dipped, but Screamer held on without any trouble. Screamer pulled back his hand, made a fist.

'What's this clown doing?' said Benson.

Bang. It was like a large rock had hit the windscreen. It cracked, a small, jagged scar forming in the glass.

'What the hell?' choked Benson.

He drew back his hand once more, grinning. *Bang.* The fist nearly broke through, a patina of glass, shaped like a spiderweb formed from where he hit the screen. Benson pulled a pistol, aimed it through the glass and began shooting – *pop, pop, pop.* But Screamer had jumped onto the roof with a thump. She'd missed him.

Benson started swerving from side to side, as Jaz drew her snub-nose revolver and fired up through the roof. Screamer held on and every now and then he peeped down, hanging over the edge of the roof.

'Kill him! Keep firing!' shouted Benson.

Jaz was shaking her head, in disbelief and amazement. Benson was swerving, trying to shake him loose. The Jeep leapt from side to side, bumping hard over rough ground. They approached the rail line, joggling up a steep embankment, hitting the rails, bouncing hard, dislodging their unwanted passenger, who went tumbling away with a wild shout of joy.

'Interstate is a couple of miles,' said Benson, wiping sweat from her eyes. 'We got this.'

They looked up. There was a guy standing in front of them, suddenly appearing in the headlights, leaning against his Harley, arms crossed. Benson swerved late, base instincts to preserve life, and rolled the Jeep.

It flipped and rolled three or four times, a cloud of dust billowing into the air. When it at last came to rest, it was on its roof, the wheels still spinning.

Benson swore. 'Are you okay?'

Jaz didn't reply. Benson looked into the rear compartment. The FBI agent was unconscious, lying in a crooked tangle.

Benson crawled out on her belly and then on her knees. A moan escaped her. Her left arm was broken. She began crawling across the dirt, dragging her useless arm, hoping she was invisible to the gang, feeling sickening guilt at leaving Jaz behind. But her instinct was to live, to get away.

They found her, all six of them. Those on bikes rolled to a stop, grinning and laughing. Even the guys that had been burnt with their own Molotov were smiling. Benson could see some burnt flesh on their arms and faces, but somehow they seemed unaware of it.

'Didn't need to fire a shot,' said one proudly.

'We got 'em, Leo,' said Little Bear, his voice that of a child.

'Yes, we did, Little Bear. You all did well,' he said.

'Where's the other one?' Screamer asked.

'Oh, she's back there, in the Jeep. She could be dead. She isn't moving,' said another.

Benson collapsed on her back, looking up at the stars, knowing her gun was probably somewhere in the Jeep's interior. Their smiles had disappeared. They were looking down at her, hungrily now, their heads tilting from side to side, just watching her. Benson thought they might not even be aware of how odd they looked, or that they were doing it.

She began to back away but was suddenly kicked in the gut. Air whooshed from her lungs with a grunt, as she lifted off the ground, ribs smashed. She rolled several times across the dusty earth before finally coming to a stop, coughing blood.

'Easy, kid,' said Leo. 'We haven't decided yet.'

'What's the vote?' asked Little Bear.

'Kill,' said one.

'Kill,' said another.

'I want to play,' said Screamer. 'She's cute. I vote *capture*.'

'Capture,' said another. 'I want some of her too.'

'Kill,' said another.

'That leaves me,' said Leo. 'Three for *kill*, and two for *capture*.' He looked down at Benson, watching her face. At last, he said, 'I vote *kill*.' He smiled, and it was cold.

'Don't I get a vote?' said Jaz. She had emerged quietly, unseen, a cut over her eye, the M4 carbine at her shoulder. They looked up, and she flipped the switch to fully automatic, the gun erupting into them, from left to right, in an arc of fire, the muzzle flash leaping tongues of flame. It was a long magazine and she had enough for them all.

When she finished the magazine, she ejected it and swapped in another. Two of the gang were crawling on their bellies, bullet-riddled and bloody. They should have been dead. They weren't. She fired into them at point-blank. The sound echoed for miles and slowly died.

Jaz examined them each closely. 'Looks like they're all dead... they aren't breathing. Hey Benson, you okay?'

Jaz took out her phone and snapped a few photos of the scene: the rolled Jeep, the motorbikes and the bodies, including a close-up of each face. It was all evidence.

She wandered back to Benson. She could see that her arm was broken in more than one place, with bone just protruding.

'Can you walk?' she asked.

Benson tried to say something but sputtered blood down her chin.

Jaz knelt beside Benson. The cop's face, white beneath the starlight, gazed up at her.

Grasping Benson's hand, Jaz said, 'I'll be back soon. You hold on.'

Benson made eye contact with Jaz, then looked to the sky. Her ragged breathing becoming shallow. After a minute, her eyes were fixed on the stars and the blood flow from her mouth ceased.

Jaz left let go of Benson's limp hand and strode away, blinking tears, heading in the direction of the interstate.

After a half hour, as Jaz neared the road, she saw an occasional truck, headlights shining as they sped along the interstate. Jaz opened her phone. Finally, there was a signal. She brought up the contacts and hit 'Harvey'.

At around three a.m., after four rings, he answered.

CHAPTER 44

Seb, Angel and Codi crept up the steep staircase, the wailing siren masking their footfalls.

He cracked the door to the kitchen and peered out. Nothing. They pushed through, went into the living room and skidded to a halt as McTaggart turned on a lamp. The old man was seated in a comfortable chair, his silken robes spattered with blood.

'Do you know what you've done?' McTaggart stood, stretched his neck and loosened his shoulder. He drew the katana from its sheath. The blade glittered gold, reflected off lamplight.

Seb brought up the submachine gun and aimed it at McTaggart. At the same moment, Angel raised the Beretta, pushing Codi behind her.

But then a quiet voice said, 'He is mine. Do not kill him.'

At first, the figure was hard to see. Standing across the room, in the darkest corner, it seemed to blend into the background of the antique wallpaper. Its eyes shone dimly – green and luminous. Seeming to absorb darkness, Seb was certain he would not have noticed the creature unless it had spoken.

McTaggart stiffened, then he slowly turned to the new adversary, raising his katana above his head.

The figure's head tilted to one side, as if listening. Its tongue darted out and it hissed, displaying venomous hooked teeth. Seb circled around the room, away from the creature, moving slowly, Angel and Codi staying close behind him.

McTaggart swallowed hard. 'Come then.'

Seb, Angel and Codi ran the last few yards out onto the balcony overlooking the sea. The moon was gone, hidden behind thick clouds. They angled toward the front gate at a run. Seb hoped the gates were open and the car Clyde had stolen was still there. There was a long mournful scream that shattered the night, going out above the pitch of the siren.

Knowing no one else was back there, it had to have come from McTaggart.

As they approached the gate, they found it open. The car remained parked where Clyde had left it, the driver-side door open. Seb looked in, discovering the keys still in the ignition.

Headlights suddenly illuminated the whole area around them. Five riders sat quietly – their forms lost behind bright headlights. Seb raised a hand, trying to shield his face. They were blocking the exit. Seb had not heard them approach above the wailing of the siren at the house. The night crew climbed off their motorcycles. A tall man approached. Angel recognised Gunther's silhouette.

The motorcycle lights doused, plunging them back into darkness. Gunther's crew spread out in a ragged line. Seb held the sub-machine gun pointed at the ground, though ready should he need it.

'Let me go, Gunther,' pleaded Angel.

Gunther's wild eyes regarded them. He looked as unhinged as Angel had ever seen him. The night crew stalked closer, blood spatter covering their faces. Now on either side and very close, Seb quickly discarded any notion that killing them all was an option.

Gunther halted. Seb marvelled at his height. The giant's face was a blank mask, though Angel noticed his left eye spasm and twitch. She had ridden with Leo's crew for long enough to know that Gunther's crew were hanging by a thread. Something big had shaken them up… something that sent them running home to their master.

Seb swallowed, forcing calm, his instincts screaming that he needed to remain absolutely still. Gunther peered down at him with a predator's eyes for a long time. Then, the crew simply walked around Seb, Angel, and Codi, past the wrought iron gates. They continued on slowly cross the lawn, toward the cliff house, heads tilted as if listening to something beyond the wail of the siren.

Turning back to the car, Seb let out an explosive breath. 'Get in, hurry up.'

The glow of the headlamps revealed a pool of mist around them, shrouding the twisted trees, and the dirt track, forcing Seb to drive slower than he would have liked. In the back seat, Codi leant against the window, weeping softly.

'Hey, kid.'

Wiping away tears, Codi met Seb's eyes in the rear vision mirror. 'It's over. You'll be okay.'

EPILOGUE

The afternoon of the next day, Jaz came back to Crabtree Cove. She brought a convoy of around twenty black SUVs, each containing field agents and agents from their specialised weapons and tactics teams. Their first stop had been the place where Benson had rolled the Jeep. The bodies of six crew members lay there, just as she had left them.

They went on to the cliff house, Harvey and Jaz in an advance helicopter. As they swooped in along the coast, before they had even landed in the grounds, they could see plumes of black smoke rising into the air and the charred timbers of the old mansion. They would spend days sifting through what was left of the house. Evidence would be collected, of cells where people had been imprisoned, as well as the remains of two women's bodies in another cell. The women appeared to have been gnawed on by something, though the bite marks were not ones that any of the investigators or the crime scene technicians recognised.

In this strange chamber, accessible through a small hatch from a basement laboratory and also from a cell above through a wide round hole, they also located McTaggart's body. He had been bitten on the face by something. Around the wound, the skin had blackened. A post-mortem would later identify that he had been injected with a toxin of unknown origin. From the positioning of his corpse and the frozen scream on his face, McTaggart appeared to have died in extreme agony.

A week later, they arrested the local police chief and all the local police. They held them in custody as evidence was quickly pulled together from Special Agent Jaz Freeman and a long line of local residents that came forward at the urging of Father John O'Malley.

Money trails would be uncovered, linking the local police to McTaggart. Other money trails, funds provided to McTaggart, could not be so easily traced. The FBI began a further investigation, this time to uncover McTaggart's associates.

Two weeks later, the body of Sheriff Joe Donnelly was pulled from a shallow grave no more than a hundred yards from his burnt-out Mustang. This came after an anonymous phone call from a woman, who said she witnessed him killed by the local police and State Troopers at a nearby roadblock.

The investigation broadened to the State Police. There would be more arrests. Sebastian Straeker and his sister Angel would eventually be interviewed, though much of the interviews would be kept in secret files. Seb would be evasive about the people he killed in 'self-defence'. He escaped facing charges on the basis he would cooperate with an investigation and give a full account of what he had seen at McTaggart's mansion.

Gunther and his night crew had been placed at the scene of the massacre and subsequent arson that destroyed the Underground nightclub where the charred bodies of twenty-eight people were found. He and his crew were now on the FBI's 'most wanted' list.

When they came for Seb, he was sitting, enjoying the sun on his face, not too far from the jetty. Angel joined him on the park bench, smiling as they took turns tossing a stick into the water for Ripley. The dog leapt in joyously, swimming to retrieve it for maybe the twentieth time.

A car pulled up behind them in the parking lot, and a police officer in a Crabtree Cove uniform wandered over to them. She lifted her mirrored aviators and for a moment, Seb thought it was Benson. But it wasn't, and it never would be.

'Hey, Straeker, I have some people here to see you.'

The Cove's new police chief escorted two military police over to Seb, who sighed and lost his smile.

'You'll need to come back with us, Captain,' said a fresh-faced young guy, his MP ranger uniform impeccably pressed. He saluted, produced some handcuffs and stood to the side, waiting, almost at attention.

Seb stood. He looked down at Angel, who forced a fake smile back up at him. He said, 'I'll be back soon.'

New Found Books Australia Pty Ltd

www.newfoundbooks.au

Printed in the USA
CPSIA information can be obtained
at www.ICGtesting.com
LVHW031337140924
791002LV00018B/309